Vampire

The Curse of Sekhmet

By

K. M. Ashman

Copyright K M Ashman 2013

All rights are reserved. No part of this publication may be
reproduced, stored, or transmitted in any form or by any means,
without prior written permission of the copyright owner.

All characters depicted within this publication are fictitious and
any resemblance to any real persons living or dead is entirely
coincidental.

More Books by K. M. Ashman

The India Sommers Mysteries
The Dead Virgins
The Treasures of Suleiman
The Mummies of the Reich
The Tomb Builders

The Roman Chronicles
The Fall of Britannia
The Rise of Caratacus
The Wrath of Boudicca

The Medieval Sagas
Blood of the Cross
In Shadows of Kings
Sword of Liberty
Ring of Steel

Novels
Savage Eden
The Last Citadel
Vampire

The Blood of Kings
A Land Divided
A Wounded Realm

Audio books
Blood of the Cross
The Last Citadel
A Land Divided
A Wounded Realm

KMAshman.com

Prologue

The Kadesh Plains
Lands of the Hittites
1458 BC

Abasi walked slowly, picking his way amongst the dead and the dying, his leather sandals seemingly reluctant to break the tacky grip of the endless sea of human blood. All around the calls of the wounded echoed through the canyon. Some were begging for help, some were begging for death. Most were silently awaiting the arrival of Anubis to carry their soul to the afterlife.

The main battle had ended earlier in the day but this final skirmish had taken place in the hills high above Kadesh where Abasi's chariots had pursued the last of the Hittite infantry. It should have been a foregone conclusion with hundreds of Hittite soldiers being despatched to meet whatever heathen gods they worshipped but it hadn't turned out that way. It was not Hittite blood cloying at his feet, but Egyptian.

The Hittite ambush had been perfect. The entrance of the canyon was broad, but narrowed quickly until it was only wide enough for a few soldiers abreast to pass at any one time. The rocky cliffs on either side were high enough to prevent anyone from climbing up, yet well within the range of the hidden archers who awaited the doomed Egyptians. It had been a slaughter and hundreds of Abasi's infantry had fallen beneath the hail of arrows before the lucky few realised they had been tricked and managed to escape the carnage.

Eventually Abasi's scouts had reported the Hittites had withdrawn, and he had ridden up to the canyon to see the massacre for himself. It was worse than he had feared. Over seven hundred men had entered the canyons. However, less than two hundred had escaped with their lives, and many of them were wounded. This was a disaster for Abasi, not only in a military sense but on a personal level as well. Back on the Kadesh plain, the main battle had been won already. Ramesses himself had sent messengers to all junior officers to break off any engagements and rendezvous back at the river Orontes.

However, Abasi had ignored the orders and continued to lead his men in pursuit of the retreating army, caught up in the bloodlust that closely followed the day of triumph. If he had been successful, he would have returned a hero. No doubt, his Pharaoh would have rewarded him handsomely. Gold, wives, slaves, all such rewards awaited successful commanders on the field of war, whilst only shame, demotion and even death could be expected for those who failed.

4

Abasi knew that Ramesses would already be aware of his failure, and indeed of his insubordination. The best he could hope for was demotion to the ranks. If that was the case, at least he would have a chance to redeem himself in battle, and, perhaps in time, he would earn the Pharaoh's trust once more.

But that was for later. First, he had to look after his men. All through the canyon, dozens of Nubian slaves carried water skins between the wounded, making them as comfortable as they possibly could. It would be at least morning before the Pharaoh could send any help to rescue the men and Abasi was determined to make their night as comfortable as possible.

'Well, Ishaq,' said Abasi, addressing the man at his side, 'it seems that the gods have forsaken me today. If I had only taken the time to pay tribute at the Temple of Horus, then I would not be punished so.'

'We cannot presume to know the will of the gods, Sire,' answered Ishaq, a faithful servant who had carried Abasi's shield into many battles over the years. 'It just might be that they have a different path for you. Perhaps it is a greater one.'

'I doubt it, Ishaq,' said Abasi, 'I have seen the wrath of Ramesses, and it does not bear countenance. No, I fear I have ridden at the head of my division for the last time, but that worry is for tomorrow. Tonight we will comfort our men. Discard your burdens and give the wounded your attention.'

'Yes, Sire,' said Ishaq and joined the others in administering what help he could. The survivors of the conflict lit fires and using the light of the full moon above, carried the wounded to glean what heat they could from the flames. The dead were left where they lay, and though Abasi knew that many would attract the attention of the jackals through the night, there was no other option. The burning of the corpses would have to wait until the morning when reinforcements would surely arrive.

Several hours later, the wounded were wrapped in the capes of the healthy and lay around the fires, staring into the dancing glow of the flames. Ishaq had made his own fire off to one side and shared the warmth alongside his master. Abasi was fast asleep, wrapped in a horsehair blanket supplied by one of his slaves. The night was half spent and the moon had long gone on her way, yet the canyon was surprisingly light as the reflections of the many fires bounced off the rocky walls. Ishaq dozed fitfully, as although there were guards all around the canyon; he knew that if the Hittites returned in any numbers, then they were doomed.

He sat up suddenly, unsure of what had awakened him, but aware that something was wrong. He looked around, trying to make out anything different above the groans of the wounded, before reaching over to shake Abasi by the shoulder.

'What is it?' asked the commander, sitting up instantly.

'One of the guards is approaching, Sire,' said Ishaq.

A soldier appeared out of the darkness and saluted Abasi.

'Report,' ordered Abasi, standing up.

'Sire, there are sounds of chariots outside the canyon,' he said.

Abasi turned to Ishaq.

'Hittite?' he suggested.

'Has to be,' said Ishaq. 'Ramesses would not risk the rest of our chariots in the dark in this strange place.'

'Then awaken the men,' said Abasi. 'Tell them to make ready and issue spears to any wounded who are able to bear arms. If the Hittite filth think we are done, then they are sadly mistaken. Our lifespan may be counted in hours, Ishaq, but by the gods, I swear we will take many with us to the lands of the two fields.'

'Yes, Sire,' said Ishaq, and ran into the darkness accompanied by the guard.

Abasi picked up his leather armour and fastened it around his chest. As a charioteer, his lower body would ordinarily have been protected by the walls of the two-man chariot, so he wore no protection on his legs, but the bands of leather around his chest offered cursory protection from all but the strongest thrust of an enemy spear or an arrow fired from a close range bow. His sandals followed along with his leather headdress and despite the night's coolness, he felt a bead of sweat running down his bald head.

He picked up his spear but as he started to kick the sand over the embers of the fire, Ishaq appeared once more, running up the slope of the canyon.

'Sire,' he gasped, 'good news, they are Egyptian.'

'Surely not,' said Abasi. 'Why would Ramesses send men out in the middle of the night?'

'I don't know,' said Ishaq, 'but they are definitely Egyptian, unless the Hittites have suddenly started to use two-man chariots, instead of three.'

'I wouldn't put anything past those heathen,' said Abasi, 'so if you don't mind, I will withhold my celebration until I see the banner of Ramesses with my own eyes.'

A noise echoed through the valley and both men looked up to see lines of soldiers running along the tops of the canyon walls a few cubits above them.

Abasi's eyes narrowed in thought. The silhouettes did indeed look Egyptian, yet the way they deployed concerned him. Within minutes the entire canyon was surrounded by the shapes of many soldiers, their silhouettes dark against the lighter night sky. Once again the only sounds breaking the silence of the night were the groans of the wounded. In the centre of the canyon, the remainder of Abasi's command had gathered near the larger central fire, all looking up in confusion.

'Hello,' called Abasi to the men above, 'who is in command?'

When there was no answer, Abasi turned to Ishaq.

'There's something wrong,' he said. 'Go down to the men, and tell them to take defensive positions in the rocks.'

'Yes, Sire,' answered Ishaq and turned to run back down to the main body of men.

'Slowly,' hissed Abasi, 'do not arouse their suspicion.' He watched Ishaq walk away, but before he had gone a few steps, the familiar sound of an arrow's flight cut through the night sky, closely followed by the thud of impact. Ishaq fell forward in the dust, his hands clawing uselessly at the arrow through his throat.

'What do you think you are doing?' screamed Abasi. 'Who is in command there? I demand to know!'

'Silence,' roared a voice from the darkness above, just as threatening as it was imperial.

'It can't be,' thought Abasi, in confusion. 'It sounded like Ramesses, but surely the Pharaoh would not come in person. He wouldn't have made an appearance in the daylight, let alone the dark of the night in enemy territory.'

'Sire, is that you?' asked Abasi.

'Do you not know the voice of your Pharaoh?' answered Ramesses.

Abasi fell to his knees.

'Sire, forgive me,' he said. 'I did not expect you, we are honoured.' He prostrated himself face down in the dust.

'Stand up, Abasi,' ordered Ramesses, 'and face me.'

Abasi stood and looked up at the silhouette of a man he had known as a living god for most of his life.

'This has been a very bloody day, Abasi, and a triumphant one, the results of which will be carved on Stelae through my kingdom. Granite pillars will exceed the height of all others that have gone before. Stelae that will extol my triumphs and proclaiming how I, Ramesses II, defeated the Hittites in the greatest battle these lands have ever seen.'

'May you be blessed by the gods, Sire,' answered Abasi.

'At one point I stood alone against a thousand chariots, Abasi. Yet the gods were with me and I smote my enemies as I would a fly. It was a sight to behold, Abasi, and minstrels will sing about my greatness for the rest of time.'

Abasi sighed inwardly at the boastfulness of the Pharaoh. He had known Ramesses for many years and whilst there was no doubting the king's bravery, Abasi knew that any feats of courage on the ruler's part would be exaggerated beyond all imagination. Such was the way of kings.

'Lord, I would expect no less from a living god,' answered Abasi.

'Yet, if you had been there, Abasi,' continued Ramesses, 'you would have seen my majesty with your own eyes. If you had been there, Abasi, then my sword arm would not have been needed to save our armies from certain slaughter.' He paused before adding, 'If you had been there, Abasi, then

7

there would not be the need for me to carry out the retribution that I now find forced upon me.'

Abasi's heart sank. Ramesses had come to see him killed for his insubordination; that much was clear. However, he still wondered why the Pharaoh had come in person. It would have been just as easy to order one of the other officers to kill him. Indeed, if his Pharaoh had ordered it, he would have taken his own life gladly. At least there was some honour in that, but for the king to come in person meant he had something more in mind. Something special.

'Sire, I thought I could secure another great victory in your glorious name.'

'You defied me,' said Ramesses.

'I made a military decision, Sire.'

'Which cost the lives of hundreds of men.'

'Admittedly, and I take full responsibility. I accept your judgement and do not deserve to live, but it was my decision alone. My men are guilty of nothing more than obeying orders. At least, allow them to live.'

'They are not your men, Abasi, they are my men and mine to do with how I see fit.'

'Of course, Sire, I meant no insult. I am only concerned for their welfare. I have wounded here, and those who are fit have not eaten since dawn.'

'It is a shame you did not have that sentiment when you sent them to their death.'

'As I said, Sire, I made a mistake.' Up above, a messenger approached the Pharaoh and whispered in his ear before bowing and retreating into the darkness.

'Enough discourse,' said Ramesses, 'it seems our visitors have arrived.'

'Visitors, Sire?'

'Do not excite yourself, Abasi,' said Ramesses, 'I fear you will not extend them a welcome.'

'And my men?' asked Abasi.

'Ah yes, your men;' answered Ramesses, 'thank you for reminding me.' He raised an arm and dropped it sharply. Instantly, the night sky was filled with hundreds of arrows and the remainder of Abasi's men fell screaming in a hail of death from their own countrymen high on the canyon walls.'

'Nooo,' screamed Abasi, watching helplessly as the last of his command died. When it was over, he turned back to face the Pharaoh.

'Why, Sire?' he shouted. 'Yes, take my life. I deserve to die, but why my men?'

'You dare to question my whim, Abasi!' snarled the Pharaoh. 'They were nothing to me. Their lives were mine to grant or deny as I decree, and

8

today I decreed that they would die. I have done them a favour, for now their families and descendants will know they have died during a great victory led by a living god, and not as the victims of one man's stupidity.'

Abasi fell silent as the reasons became clear. Apart from the king's personal guard above, there were now no witnesses to this defeat, and Ramesses could bask in his embellished tales of victory with no possibility of any other version being made public.

'And what of me, Sire?' he asked eventually. 'Am I to expect an arrow from an unseen assassin?'

'No, Abasi, your indiscretion has actually provided me with an ideal opportunity.'

'An opportunity, Sire?'

'Yes, an opportunity to repay a pact made between gods.'

'I don't understand.'

'You don't have to understand, Abasi, just be thankful that today you are to witness something that is denied to most men. Today, you will be in the presence of not one, but two gods.'

Abasi withheld a gasp. Like all his countrymen, he was deeply religious and prayed to many gods on a daily basis. The revelation that he was to stand before another took his breath away.

'Lord, I am truly blessed,' he said.

'Withhold your gratitude, Abasi, for you know not whom I invoke. Look to your rear and witness the approach of a deity.'

Abasi turned and looked down the canyon to where he could see movement. Though still quite dark, he could make out a column of figures, all dressed in white robes, making their way toward the dead and the dying. Behind them, a column of infantry stopped a hundred yards short of the wounded, and lined up side by side across the canyon, blocking any escape. Abasi stared uncomprehendingly, not sure what he was witnessing. The white clothed people seemed to be priestesses, and in amongst them he could see a litter being carried by four naked slaves, their jet black skin a sharp contrast amongst the swathes of white linen. An order rang out through the valley and all the soldiers, both in the canyon and up on the canyon rim, turned as one to face away from the scene unfolding in front of them.

The occupant of the litter stepped out, and with the help of the slaves, slowly made her way toward him. Abasi was transfixed. The woman was obviously extremely old and she struggled to walk the last few yards of the rocky path.

Finally, she stood before him, and Abasi felt sick at the stench of death she exuded. She was dressed in a wrap of pure white linen and her face was covered by a veil. The hands were the only flesh visible and Abasi could see they were virtual claws; such was the age of the woman. The very sight of her was enough to strike fear into any man's heart and he knew that a terrible fate lay before him.

She looked up at the ridge and a barely audible voice seemed to drift from beneath the veil.

'Is this the one?' she asked.

'It is;' answered Ramesses, 'and with his soul I repay my debt to you.'

'And has he a fighting spirit?' asked the woman.

'He has the heart of a lion,' said Ramesses.

'And the rest;' asked the woman, 'do they still breathe?'

'Many are dead, holy one, though enough hearts still beat to satisfy even your follower's extreme tastes.'

'Then I am satisfied,' said the woman. She turned to the soldier at last and looked up at him through her veil.

'Do you know who I am, soldier?'

Abasi shook his head, unable to speak.

'Then let me ask this;' said the woman, 'do you know your gods?'

'Yes, Mother,' said Abasi, the terror evident in his voice.

'Then face me and invoke my name,' she said and lifted the veil from her face.

Abasi's eyes opened wide in terror and an involuntary groan escaped his lips. The unveiled face was extremely old and barely more than a skull covered with a yellowed parchment of wrinkled skin. The few wispy strands of hair left on the baldhead fell about her neck like a tangle of snakes, and her sunken eyes were bottomless pools of midnight black.

The soldier mumbled incoherently and took a step backwards.

'Say my name, soldier,' said the woman.

'No,' he moaned, 'it cannot be.'

'What's the matter, soldier?' said the woman. 'Do you not find my countenance fair?'

Abasi didn't answer.

'I am waiting, soldier. Is not the face of a god good enough for you? What did you expect, youth, beauty?'

'I know not,' stuttered Abasi.

'Oh, I was beautiful once, soldier. In my youth I was considered the fairest of them all. Men travelled from countries afar to fall at my feet and embrace the fate that awaits you now. But that was a long time ago. It was long before Khufu laid the first block of the great pyramid: a time before the sphinx, when these lands were covered with trees and alive with game; a time when even the Nile itself wound a different course. Can you imagine that, soldier? Can your puny mortal mind embrace a time so long ago that our ancestors still inhabited lands far away and no human foot had ever stepped in the lands of Kemet?'

'You can't be that old,' mumbled Abasi. 'No one can be that old.'

'Really, soldier? What if I was to tell you that every king that has ever ruled this land has bent their knee before me, from the very first to Ramesses himself?'

'It can't be true,' moaned Abasi, 'why would a god live in a man's world?'

'A man's world?' cackled the old woman. 'Oh, that's good, soldier. This world does not belong to men, but to me and others like me. Men are but cattle to us, to be bred and farmed as we see fit. We are all powerful, soldier. We always have been and we always will be. Now, say my name.'

'No,' said Abasi taking a step backward.

'Say my name, soldier,' said the woman again.

'No, I will not.'

The woman raised a finger and, without warning, the four slaves fell on Abasi, pinning him to the ground. The warrior struggled for a moment, but then screamed in pain as a stone hammer smashed one knee into pieces. No sooner had the scream finished, when a second scream rang out around the canyon, as the second knee went the way of the first. The slaves fell upon him again, and wrenched his arms backwards beyond their natural limit, dislocating them from the sockets.

Abasi was barely conscious as the woman leaned over his helpless body, her pure black eyes reflecting the dancing flames of the fire.

'You are about to die at the hands of a God, soldier,' whispered the old woman, 'Keep your council and the pain will last for hours. Say my name and it will soon be over.'

'I will not,' groaned Abasi, 'it is forbidden.'

The woman pulled away to allow the approach of one of her slaves and watched without emotion as he cut away the leather armour to reveal Abasi's chest. Without hesitation the slave's sharp knife sliced through skin and flesh, until the whites of the ribs could be glimpsed through the flowing blood.

'Say my name, soldier,' said the woman quietly.

'Nooo,' groaned Abasi.

Again the slave set to work, this time plunging his hands into the wound and forcing the ribs apart to expose the cavity beneath. Abasi passed out in pain, but a pungent substance waved under his nose, immediately brought him around.

'I can make it stop, soldier,' she said soothingly as she gazed down into the pulsating pool of blood within his chest, 'All you have to do is say my name and all this pain will go away.'

Abasi looked up through tear filled eyes. He knew his life was over, but he couldn't stand the pain any longer. The never-ending depths of black from the old woman's eyes met his gaze and Abasi's rambling mind could swear he could see the souls of thousands of men, floundering in their depths.

'Say my name, soldier,' she said.

'Sekhmet.' he whispered, 'You are Sekhmet.'

A look of contentment filled her face, as her scrawny hand reached out to wipe his brow, much as his mother had done when he was an ill child.

'That's right,' she said, 'your people do indeed call me by that name. Sekhmet, goddess of war, bringer of destruction, mother of death, but that is just one name amongst many that I bear. I am known by thousands of names to thousands of cultures, Soldier, for I am Sekhmet, nightwalker of Kemet.

Her lips peeled back in a grotesque smile and Abasi's eyes widened one last time in horror as they focussed on the row of pointed yellow fangs that filled her mouth.

'Nooo,' he moaned, 'please don't.'

'Remember my name, soldier,' she hissed, the stink of death on her breath, 'and take it to hell.'

The screams that went before were nothing compared to the last scream of the commander as it echoed around the canyon. As he died Abasi's last conscious thought was of those terrible pointed teeth, tearing at the still beating heart within his chest.

Above, on the canyon walls, the one person who had witnessed the ritual raised his gaze to look further back into the canyon. The dying scream of Abasi was the signal the rest of the priestesses had been waiting for and all of them fell on the wounded with equal savagery. All around him the mountains echoed with the screams of the dying as their throats were torn open by the sisters of Sekhmet. Ramesses turned away and descended the hills to his chariot, closely followed by his bodyguards. Waiting for him was Atmar, his closest advisor and lifelong companion.

'Is it done?' asked Atmar.

'It is,' said Ramesses, 'but it brings me no great pleasure.'

'It is a necessary evil,' said Atmar.

'Why?' asked Ramesses. 'Why do these creatures continue to hold such influence over me, the greatest king this land has ever seen? They should be bending a knee to me, not the other way around.'

'She is the oldest god of them all,' said Atmar, 'and her blessing caused us to win this battle. Surely, that demands our respect!'

'Am I not also a god, Atmar? Do they not owe me homage?'

'Be careful not to incur their wrath, lord,' said Atmar as they climbed aboard the royal chariot. 'They have eyes and ears everywhere.'

'As do I, Atmar,' said Ramesses, 'and my spies tell me a very different story to what Sekhmet would have us believe.'

'What tales are those?' asked Atmar.

'All in good time, Atmar, but suffice it to say, when the Hittite itch is scratched, my attention will turn to Sekhmet. There is room for only one living god in these lands.' With that he snapped the reins and caused the horses to gallop down the slope at breakneck speed, closely followed by a hundred chariots of his royal household.

Chapter One

London 2012
The British Antiquities Museum

'Amy, will you get the phone, please?' shouted Becky Ryan from the store cupboard.

Though Amy didn't answer, the cessation of the ringing told Becky her assistant had heard the request. She continued the task at hand, rummaging through the box of archived files to find the reference material she needed to finish her report.

'Got it,' she said with a self-satisfied flourish and left the cupboard to return to her desk.

Rebecca Ryan was a historian based in the British Antiquities Museum. Standing six feet tall in her bare feet, she was a striking figure with long blonde hair tied up into an untidy bun, held in place with an ornamental clasp she had bought in Rome. The dark, horn-rimmed glasses were only worn for work purposes, but on the rare occasion when she did go out socially, she suffered the fuss of contact lenses. Her jeans and baggy sweat top hid a shapely figure, and her face lacked any makeup, except for the tiniest amount of eye liner. In different circumstances she could be described as naturally beautiful, and indeed, despite her apparent disregard for anything fashionable, her presence always drew second glances from the male wardens around the museum.

Nevertheless, despite her appearance, it was Rebecca Ryan's mind that was making her a formidable reputation. She had an encyclopaedic knowledge of Egyptian history, and as a teenager, had spent many years accompanying her parents on archaeological digs throughout the country. She had no qualifications of which to boast, but as a young woman, she had applied for the job as a researcher, and had won over the interview panel with her understanding of hieroglyphics, command of the Egyptian language, and knowledge of the country's history. Those three things alone were enough to win her a place, but the fact that she had done her homework as well, and wore the shortest mini skirt she dared had certainly made the decision easier for the all-male interview panel.

The role included shared workspace in the large air-conditioned office of the records department, but despite that, she preferred to work in a converted cleaner's cupboard, deep in the depths of the Museum's vaults. It was hot, stuffy and lacked a mobile phone signal, but it had a computer terminal and a small sink where she could get water for her kettle. The main benefit was the proximity to the vast store of exhibits which were stored either permanently or on a visiting basis from other Museums. The very atmosphere, reeking of ghosts, and secrets yet unknown, helped her concentrate on whatever task she had been given. Although most of the other staff would not have worked down there for love nor money, luckily her assistant, Amy, didn't share their views.

'Who was it, Amy?' asked Becky, as she re-entered the tiny office.

'I think it was your father,' she said, 'but the line was awful and he said to ring him back.'

'Oh right,' said Becky,' I'll ring him in a while.'

Becky's dad was an eminent Egyptologist who rang Becky most days, usually to discuss his findings or those of their peers. Though he was an excellent Egyptologist, his one fault, at least in Becky's eyes, was his obsession with finding the location of Itjawi, the lost royal city built by twelfth dynasty king, Amenemhat. For two years at a time he would work for the British Antiquities Museum on sponsored digs, but for as long as she could remember every third year he took time out and researched every document, record or Stelae he could, with the aim of finding the famed city. It had cost a lot of time and a fortune in cash, all to no avail. Still, since her mother had died, it gave him a focus in life.

'Be a gem and put the kettle on, will you?' she said eventually. 'I'm parched.'

With an exaggerated huff, Amy pulled herself from her chair and stomped toward the sink. Becky hid a smile, because despite the theatrics, Amy was actually very helpful and extremely good as an assistant. Her computer skills were exceptional, and Becky even turned a blind eye to Amy's regular forays onto the social networking sites during working hours.

The teenager's appearance was very striking. Her clothing was the same every day; a long flowing black dress, black army boots and fingerless black gloves, complimented by dyed black hair, black eye shadow and the occasional application of black lipstick. Occasionally she spiced the whole ensemble with a blood red rose, but usually her style was black and plenty of it. The whole effect was homage to the so called 'Goth movement,' but, despite her outward indifference to the snide remarks and derision from some of her colleagues, when Becky offered her a part time post as her assistant, she jumped at the chance. To Amy it was perfect. She got to spend the hours away from the boring people in the other offices and was surrounded every day by the dead and the ancient. It was a situation that suited her persona down to the ground.

'Becky,' she said, while spinning around and around in her computer chair. 'Can I ask you for a favour?'

'Ask away,' said Becky, turning on her laptop.

'One weekend,' said Amy, 'can I sleep down here?'

Becky looked over her glasses at the teenager.

'And why would you want to do that?' she asked.

'Oh, I don't know. To be closer to the dead, I suppose. You know, immerse myself in the unknown and see if I can communicate with the other side.'

'The other side,' said Becky.

'Yeah, ghosts, lost souls, that sort of thing.'

The researcher decided to play along, because despite the teenager's appearance, Becky knew that underneath all the morbidity and bravado there was a pretty girl with feelings. All this Goth business was a passing fad and she was sure that Amy had a promising career in front of her.

'You wouldn't be afraid, Amy?'

'Nah,' answered the girl. 'I understand the spirit world. I have an affinity with the afterlife that nobody understands, not even you.'

'Really?' said Becky.

'Yup, I'm not scared of the dead. It's the living who worry me.'

'I know what you mean,' answered Becky, 'but still, spending a whole night down here on your own is quite scary. Are you sure you would last through the night?'

'No problem,' answered Amy. 'Wouldn't bother me one bit.'

'Are you sure?'

'Positive.'

'Okay,' said Becky and turned back to her screen, waiting for the next comment that she knew would surely come.

'Sorry?' said Amy. 'Did you say yes?'

'I did,' said Becky. 'You can stay the night. I'll have to put some safety things in place with the security guards, but I am sure it will be fine.'

'Oh,' said Amy staring over at her.

'Is that a problem?' asked Becky, enjoying the game.

'No, not at all,' said Amy, 'I'll look forward to it.'

'Why not do it tonight?' suggested Becky. 'No time like the present. Anyway, if you get bored, you could make a start on those Roman gravestones that came in. Clean them up a bit if you like.'

'I, um, I can't tonight,' said Amy. 'I've made plans, but in a few weeks, I'll do it, no problem.'

'Sure,' said Becky with a smile. 'You just let me know when you're free and I'll make the arrangements.'

'Yeah, I will,' said Amy and turned back to her screen.

Becky smiled inwardly. The brazen Goth exterior hid a gentle soul and Becky was sure it would come out eventually, all she needed was time.

'You okay to work Saturday?' asked Becky eventually.

'Yeah, should be,' said Amy. 'Why, what do we have going on?'

'The curator wants us to start on that latest shipment from Egypt,' she said, 'and to be honest, I have a personal interest in it. My father was part of the team that sent it over.'

'Really?'

'Yup.'

'Cool, what's in it, a mummy?'

16

'No, nothing so exciting, I'm afraid. The paperwork says it's a shipment of twelve Ushabti.'

Amy's face betrayed her disappointment.

'More dolls?' she said, referring to the small figurines which were common funerary ornaments in Egyptian tombs. 'We have some of them already.'

'They are still artefacts,' said Becky, 'and as such need to be checked for detail, documented and catalogued. Apparently these are a bit different and form part of a collection spanning two thousand years, showing the marked difference in production techniques. If they are good enough, they may even make it out into the displays.'

'Still boring,' said Amy. 'When are we ever going to get a mummy to investigate?'

'Those days are long gone, I'm afraid,' said Becky. 'Any discoveries of interest are kept for examination by the Cairo museum these days, and to be honest, I think that's how it should be. These Ushabti are on loan for the next three years.'

'Still boring,' said Amy again under her breath, but just loud enough for Becky to hear.

The afternoon continued with the normal paperwork that dogged their Fridays, until eventually, Becky sat back and stretched her arms above her head.

'That's it,' she said, 'I'm done. Let's call it a day.'

'Sounds good to me,' said Amy, going through the shutdown process on her computer, 'I'm off to the cinema later.'

'Really, what are you going to see?'

'The new vampire film,' said Amy.

'Haven't you seen that before?'

'Three times,' said Amy, 'but Dean Patrick is gorgeous.'

'Dean Patrick?'

'The lead actor. Surely you have heard of him?' laughed Amy.

'Can't say I have,' said Becky.

'You don't know what you are missing,' said Amy. 'Why don't you come along? There's a group of us going together.'

'Nah, don't think so, thanks anyway. Look, you take off, and I'll finish up here.'

'Okay, see you tomorrow,' said Amy and left the room to make her way up to the staff area to clock out.

Becky switched everything off and also left the office, but on the way through the vault, she paused briefly to take a look at the Ushabti which needed their attention the following day. All were lined up on the Formica workbench and each lay snugly in a bubble wrap shroud, inside its own cardboard box, ironically looking like miniature mummies in miniature coffins. Becky couldn't help herself and she picked up one of them to unwrap it. Using her nails she picked the packing tape loose and carefully took the bubble wrap from around the doll. As soon as it was free she donned a pair of white cotton gloves and examined the clay ornament in detail.

The doll was about eight inches tall and formed the typical mummy shape so familiar to millions of people throughout the world. It was formed from fired clay, and though the once vibrant colours had faded, the detail was still clear.

'If only you could speak,' said Becky quietly as she held the doll up to the light, 'what tales you could tell.' Carefully, she placed the doll back in the box and picked up the cardboard lid to read the inscription.

'Ushabti from tomb, X3-163/1. Unknown minor royal of Ptolemaic period, circa 127 BC. Discovered 13/June/2009.'

'Oooh, Cleopatra's era,' said Becky to herself. 'How fascinating.' She replaced the lid and placed the box back in line with the rest. Despite wanting to unwrap and examine them all, she resisted the temptation and forced herself to leave the vault, locking the doors behind her. The rest could wait until morning.

Becky closed her apartment door behind her and picked up the mail from the floor, sorting it into order of importance as she walked into the kitchen.

'Bill, bill, bill,' she muttered as she read the windows of the envelopes, 'junk mail and another bill. Nothing special,' she said to Smokey, the grey Persian cat waiting patiently on the worktop for her daily treat. 'How did your day go?'

The cat replied with a silent meow, staring at the woman as if understanding every word.

'That good, huh?' said Becky, opening the fridge to get the milk.

Ten minutes later she was sitting on her settee with a microwave lasagne on a tray and the TV remote control at her side. A glass of wine stood on the side table and through the door she could see Smokey getting stuck into a bowl of tinned Tuna in the kitchen.

'Same old, same old,' Becky sighed. She was about to turn on the TV when a knock came on the door.

'Perfect timing,' said Becky and putting the unappetizing meal to one side, she walked out into the hall, peering through the spy hole and was surprised to see two police officers outside.

'Can I help you?' she asked opening the door.

'Hello there,' said a policewoman. 'We are looking for Rebecca Ryan.'

'That's me.'

'Miss Ryan. I am Sergeant Wentlock and this is police constable Varnier. Could we come in for a moment please?'

'Is something wrong?' asked Becky.

'We have some bad news, Miss Ryan; it would be better to do this inside.'

'Oh,' said Becky. 'Yes, of course, please come in.'

'Perhaps you would like to sit down, Miss Ryan,' said Sergeant Wentlock.

'Look,' said Becky, 'I don't mean to be rude, but whatever you have come to tell me, please just spit it out.'

The police woman glanced at her colleague, before clearing her throat.

'Okay,' she said, 'there's no easy way to say this, Miss Ryan. I am afraid I have bad news about your father.'

'What about him? Is he okay?'

'No, I'm afraid he's not, Miss Ryan. I am awfully sorry, but your father is dead.'

Becky stared at each of the police officers several times before speaking.

'Are you sure?' she asked, simply.

'We are. His body was identified a few hours ago. We were contacted by the British Embassy in Cairo.'

Becky sat down on one of the two chairs at her tiny dining table.

'I don't understand.' she said. 'Just this afternoon, he called me. Surely he couldn't just die in that short time?'

'Miss Ryan,' said the officer, 'there is more. I have to tell you that it wasn't due to natural causes. At least, we don't think so. The fact is your father was found hanging from a tree in the hotel grounds where he was staying. At this time, there doesn't seem to be any suspicious circumstances.'

'Suicide,' gasped Becky, 'that's ridiculous. Why would he do that? He had everything to live for.'

'We don't know at this time,' said the police officer. 'Obviously there will be an investigation by the Egyptian police and a post mortem, but I have to be honest, it does look like he took his own life.'

'I don't believe it,' said Becky quietly, 'he would never do something like that.'

An awkward silence followed before PC Varnier spoke up.

'Can I get you a cup of tea or something?' he said. 'Or maybe call someone for you?'

'No, I'll be fine,' said Becky, wiping the unwelcome tears from her eyes. 'Do you have the details?'

'Details?' asked Sergeant Wentlock.

'Yes; location of the body, circumstances, that sort of thing…'

'Of course,' said the officer, 'do you have a pen?'

The next few minutes were taken up with Becky scribbling down the information before she finally stood up.

'Thank you for coming,' she said, 'but if you don't mind, I have to make arrangements.'

'What sort of arrangements,' asked the police woman.

'Flights, hotel room, taxis, et cetera.' answered Becky.

'Are you going over there?'

'Of course,' said Becky, 'I'm not letting anyone else bring him home.'

'Miss Ryan, are you sure there's nobody that we can call? You really shouldn't be on your own at a time like this.'

'I will be fine, honestly. I just need to keep busy.'

'Well, if you're sure, we will be on our way.'

'Thank you,' said Becky and showed them to the door.

'You know where we are if you need us,' said Sergeant Wentlock. 'I'm sorry for your loss.'

'Goodbye,' said Becky and closed the door behind them.

The two police officers got back into their car and fastened their seatbelts.

'Wow, she took that well,' said PC Varnier.

'Yeah, she did,' said Sergeant Wentlock. 'Seemed like a cold hearted bitch to me.'

'Takes all sorts,' her colleague sighed and released the handbrake to drive off down the street.

Back in the flat Smokey was sitting on the rug in front of the artificial fire, studiously cleaning one paw. For a second the cat paused and looked at the human across the room. Becky was sitting on the settee, clutching a cushion tightly to her chest as she rocked back and forth, her shoulders shaking violently in time with her uncontrollable sobs.

'Oh, Dad,' she cried out emotionally at the ceiling, 'what have you done?'

Ten days later Becky Ryan stood at the side of her father's grave in a small church on the outskirts of London. The funeral had been the previous day, attended by all their family and friends. As was the way of most funerals, it had been a very emotional day, and Becky found herself taking more time caring for her elderly relatives than spending time grieving. The wake was held at her brother's home and the guests had included many of her father's colleagues from the world of Egyptology. To redress the feeling of unfinished business, Becky had returned to the cemetery on her own with a single white rose that she had picked up from the florist on the way. She was alone with her thoughts and shed a few tears as she recalled many of the good times spent with her father as a girl.

The times shared in the vaults of Cairo Museum were particularly memorable. He would studiously write up his reports, while she explored the fascinating artefacts that were not on show to the public. He was very meticulous in his work, but she could always tear him away to explain some fact or another, and when he was in instruction mode, there was no stopping him. Within months she had a fantastic grounding in the history of the country, and within two years, had gained a basic understanding of hieroglyphics. Her mind had been like a sponge, soaking up the information, and she had known immediately this was how she wanted to spend her life. For years she had spent every holiday she could with her father, and had only come home when her mother had fallen ill.

When her mother finally passed away, Becky took the temporary job at the museum, thinking it would only be for a few months, but she had loved it so much, when a permanent role came up, she had accepted immediately and hadn't returned to Egypt since.

A few more tears fell before she said goodbye to her father for the last time, and after kissing the rose, she laid it on the raw earth before standing up to leave. As she turned her heart missed a beat as she saw a tall man dressed in a long black coat, standing silently a few yards away.

'Oh,' she said, 'you made me jump.'

'I'm sorry,' said the man. 'I didn't want to interrupt your privacy. It is a very sad time.'

Becky's eyes narrowed as she stared at the man beneath the floppy black hat. His face sported a full beard and he had deep, walnut brown eyes. He looked strangely familiar.

'Do I know you?' asked Becky.

The man stepped forward and removed a glove.

'We have met before, albeit very briefly. My name is John Deacon. I worked with your father for a few years. We met at your mother's funeral.'

'Mr Deacon,' said Becky, 'nice to meet you properly at last. My father spoke very highly of you. I seem to recall you didn't have the, um…' Her hand subconsciously touched her own chin.

'Oh, yes, the beard,' he said. 'I've been back in the UK for twelve months and it is a luxury I allow myself now and again.'

'I suspect it would be a bit uncomfortable in Egypt's heat,' she said. There was a silence before Becky continued. 'I didn't see you at the funeral, Mr Deacon.'

'No, I only found out yesterday. By the time I found out, it was too late to make the service.'

'So you came down today,' smiled Becky, 'that's very kind of you.'

'Well, I wanted to pay my respects, because he was a great friend, but there is also another reason I am here, Miss Ryan.'

'Really?'

'Yes, I need to speak with you in private. Is there somewhere we could go?'

'I suppose so,' said Becky, 'I think there's a café not far from here, fancy a coffee?'

'Coffee would be great,' said the man. 'Perhaps we could meet in ten minutes or so. I'd like to say my goodbyes to your father.'

'Of course,' said Becky, I'll go and get the coffees.'

Half an hour later they both sat at a table in the cafe. Finally, an awkward silence was broken by the bearded man.

'Miss Ryan,' he started…'

'Please, call me Becky,' she said.

'Thank you,' said the man, 'and you must call me John. I will come straight to the point. There's something you should know about your father.'

'Go on,' said Becky.

'The thing is, for the past year he didn't work for the Cairo Museum. In fact, he didn't work for anyone.'

'I don't understand,' said Becky. 'I have talked to him dozens of times over the past twelve months, he would have said something.'

'Not necessarily,' said John, 'he didn't want you to be concerned.'

'Why would I be concerned? He took sabbaticals quite often. I suspect he was working for some smaller organisation on some obscure project, knowing him.'

'Becky,' interrupted John, 'he wasn't working for anyone, because nobody would employ him. He was sacked.'

'Sacked,' gasped Becky. 'Why on earth would he be sacked? He was one of the most respected men in his field.'

'I know,' said John, 'but something happened that stripped him of any respectability that he had.'

'What could he have possibly done that could cause him to be sacked?' asked Becky. 'You are making no sense.'

'Sorry,' said John, 'let me start again.' He took a sip of his coffee and took a deep sigh before sitting back in his seat and looking into her eyes.

'Becky,' he said, 'your father and I worked closely for over two years. We met in a seminar in Cairo and over a conversation during a coffee break, we found out we shared a very special interest.'

'Don't tell me,' groaned Becky, 'Itjawi.'

'Itjawi,' confirmed John, 'We found out that not only did we have the same passion for finding the city, we also had similar theories. Over a period of a few weeks, we shared our knowledge and agreed to combine our resources.'

'What a waste of time that must have turned out to be,' sighed Becky with a grim smile, 'gone to his grave with a lifetime's ambition unrealised.'

'Well, that's where you are wrong,' said John. 'Your father and I did find Itjawi. In fact, we found it three years ago.'

'What?' gasped Becky in astonishment. 'How can that be? He never said anything. There's nothing in any of the journals or on any website. If

Itjawi had been found, surely it would have been on the front page of every paper from here to Cairo.'

'You are right,' said John. 'If the news had become common knowledge, then it would have been one of the greatest stories since Tutankhamen. Nothing excites the imagination like a lost city of an ancient Pharaoh.'

'But why not tell anyone? Surely, on a find like that, you would want the whole world to know.'

'Ordinarily, yes,' said John, 'but we had to be sure. If we were right, and our findings could be verified, this find would be of such historical importance, that it would have the potential to alter the pages of history.'

'Why?' asked Becky. 'Archaeologists find cities all of the time beneath the sands. It takes years, if not decades to get permission to excavate and even if you are right and it is Itjawi, nobody would accept it as proved until the Cairo museum verified any artefacts.'

'I know, but that wasn't the issue here, as it needed hardly any verification.'

'Why not?'

'Becky, what I am about to tell you has to be kept between us. You can't tell anyone, at least, not yet.'

'Why not?'

'Because there are organisations that would do anything to ensure our findings are kept secret.'

'Oh for heaven's sake,' said Becky, 'now you are being ridiculous. Any new find is worth a fortune to the Egyptian government. Just the dollar income would add up to millions in tourism alone.'

John took a sip of his coffee before taking a deep breath and telling the young girl the most astonishing thing she had ever heard.

'Becky, what your father and I found was what we thought was a series of catacombs. As you know, there are many catacombs throughout Egypt and, like those; they had suffered the attentions of tomb robbers. Anything of inherent value had obviously been stripped from the bodies and at first glance, we thought there was little left. However, as you know, the rubbish from millennia ago now has a different value and the number of pottery fragments and hieroglyphics alone had the potential to keep the experts busy for many years to come.'

'So, what happened?'

'Well, at first we did what you would expect and started to catalogue everything in the many different passageways.'

'You didn't report the find to the authorities?'

'No, not at first. We wanted to make sure our suspicions were correct. So many false claims had been presented over the years; we didn't want to be tarred with the same brush. That went on for a few months, but soon the dig season approached and the Cairo museum contacted us to take up attachments in the east.'

'Wait a minute; you were working out of season?'

'We were. It may not be ethical, but it was necessary. Anyway, so not to arouse suspicion, we closed the dig, intending to come back the following year, but not before we found something extraordinary.'

'What did you find?' asked Becky.

'At the farthest end of the catacombs, your father found a shrine piled up with the remains of ancient offerings.'

'Whose was it?'

'Well, that was the strange thing,' said John. 'There were no markings or idols whatsoever. Just a plain stone table set against a blank wall. It had obviously been used as recently as a few hundred years ago, but it had no indication as to who it was for. For days we searched for clues until eventually, we removed the shrine and looked behind.'

'What did you find?'

'A false wall,' said John. 'We took it down and behind it found an original stone wall, covered with the most extraordinary hieroglyphics.'

'It must have been wonderful,' said Becky, absolutely entranced at the images he invoked.

'I suppose it must have,' said John, 'but we hardly noticed them, because in the centre of the wall was something far, far more exciting; an unopened doorway.'

'Unopened?'

'Yes, the seal was still intact and the door untouched.'

'I don't understand,' said Becky. 'Why would grave robbers leave a door unopened? They must have known it was there, those people found their way into the greatest pyramids. I'm sure a simple false wall wouldn't have kept them out for long.'

'Well, that is what was so intriguing. Even though it was hidden, the doorway was obviously well known and had lain untouched since the time it was sealed.'

'Was the inscription intact?' asked Becky.

'Some of it was; the usual threats and curses aimed at any tomb robbers, but the main name had been chiselled out, as if somebody wanted to hide the identity of the occupant.'

'Possibly,' said Becky, engrossed in the tale. 'Goes someway to deter the curious, I suppose.'

'Could be,' said John, 'But if that's the case, they didn't do a very good job.'

'You could see the name?' asked Becky.

'No. But the dedication remained at the bottom and I almost had a heart attack when your father read it out aloud.'

'What did it say?' asked Becky, hardly able to contain herself.

"Belonging to the justice of Re,' said John, and Becky's mouth fell open in astonishment.

'I assume by your reaction that you are aware of that dedication?' asked John.

'Of course, I am,' stuttered Becky, 'it was the throne name of Amenemhat the third, a twelfth dynasty Pharaoh, thought to be the greatest king of the middle kingdom. He reigned for over forty years and gained vast amounts of wealth from dominating Nubia, leading several expeditions himself.'

'That's right,' said John, 'also famous for building the black pyramid at Dashwar, as well as the pyramid at Hawara.'

'Hang on,' said Becky, 'if what you are saying is true, not only did you and my father find a complex of catacombs as yet un-catalogued, which in itself is quite astonishing, but you also claim to have found the sealed door to another tomb, bearing the mark of one of the greatest Egyptian kings to have lived throughout the twelfth dynasty.'

'Yes, quite exciting isn't it?'

'I don't believe you,' said Becky. 'If all this was true, I would know about it. Shit, the whole damned world would know about it.'

'Look, I know it's hard to take in,' said John, 'but I promise you it is all true. Imagine how we felt when we found it. We were in a daze for weeks. The shattered pottery and broken statues left behind in the catacombs are astonishing enough, but imagine what lies behind that locked door.'

'You didn't open it?'

'No, credit us with some ethics,' John said. 'First we set about cataloguing everything in the outer chambers, before we could even think about opening the door. To be honest, we got a bit carried away and your father even saw himself as a modern day Howard Carter.'

'That's silly,' said Becky, 'Howard Carter found Tutankhamen's intact burial chamber complete with all the funerary ornaments. Despite what it says on that door you found, it can't be Amenemhat's tomb, because his burial chamber has already been found.'

'Has it?' asked John with a slight smirk on his lips.

'You know it has,' said Becky. 'He was buried in the Hawara pyramid.'

'Remember your training as an Egyptologist, Becky,' said John, 'then re-examine your last statement.'

Becky paused, with a thoughtful look on her face, before making the statement again, with a slight change.

'His burial chamber was found in the Hawara pyramid,' she said.

'Exactly,' said John. 'No mummy was ever found, at least, nothing that could be identified as Amenemhat.'

'But there were remains of a burnt wooden coffin in the chamber, left by the tomb robbers.'

'Exactly, as usual for the time, the tomb robbers burnt whatever mummy was there as a quick way to access any jewellery wrapped within the wraps or the body itself, but there is no scientific evidence that it was actually the man himself.'

'But why?' asked Becky. 'It doesn't make any sense.'

'Actually, it makes every sense,' said John. 'Amenemhat was a wily old dog. Not only did he last forty five years as king of Egypt, which is a huge feat in itself, but don't forget the steps he took to protect the burial chamber in the Hawara pyramid.'

'The trap doors and blind passages,' said Becky.

'Exactly,' said John. 'He built in secret passages, sliding doors and pitfalls, all designed to prevent grave robbers from accessing his final resting place, but even back then, grave robbers had a formidable reputation and he knew that his body would be at risk of plunder. It was entirely possible that even as they were building the pyramid, some of the builders were working out how to rob the bloody thing. I think Amenemhat knew that, and planned accordingly.'

'Then why build the pyramid in the first place?'

'Think about it. Whilst to all intents and purposes, he was preparing a massive monument as his last resting place; behind the scenes he was making other plans. Preparing somewhere that would not be so obvious, where his body would be safe for eternity.'

'So where do you think he is?' asked Becky. 'In the tomb behind the door?'

'Not exactly;' said John, 'first of all, I don't believe it is a tomb.'

'You don't?'

'No, Amenemhat was also famous for building something else; in fact, he had a bit of a fixation for the type of structure I am thinking about.'

'Labyrinths,' said Becky.

'Exactly, he built bloody dozens of them, and was quite famous for it. He even built the most famous of them all, the labyrinth referred to by Herodotus in the 5th century BC. Herodotus described it as a feature that not only exceeded the pyramids in grandeur and achievement, but equated them to exceeding the sum of all Greek constructions in the ancient world in achievement, scale and beauty. Some statement for a Greek, don't you think?'

'I have to admit I'm not too familiar with them,' said Becky.

'Amenemhat built an enormous labyrinth at the base of the Hawara pyramid. It was built over several stories and consisted of over three thousand rooms with countless corridors, each made from solid stone with marble facings. Hell, even the roof was made of giant stone slabs supported on tens of thousands of columns, each ornately carved from solid granite.

26

Throughout the labyrinth, there were countless artefacts, statues, paintings, all collected from across many countries throughout the known world at that time. Tombs of minor royals and crocodile gods were tucked away throughout the system, each holding unknown treasures of their own. It must have been spectacular.'

'I don't see your point,' said Becky. 'If the Labyrinth was located just outside the Hawara pyramid, then why would he go to all that trouble only to be buried somewhere else?'

'Don't forget, Becky, all the earthly goods in the world meant nothing compared to the ultimate prize, a safe passage into the afterlife. To achieve that, his body had to rest in peace. If the grave robbers thought they had found his last resting place in the labyrinth or the pyramid, they would be unlikely to look too hard elsewhere.'

'The ultimate bluff,' said Becky.

'Exactly, and that's what I think he did. Provided a great big pyramid, surrounded by the greatest labyrinth the world has ever seen, all filled with wealth untold, and designed to attract any tomb robbers away from his final resting place.'

'So you think he is in a tomb behind the door?' suggested Becky.

'Possibly, though I suspect it won't be that straightforward. Knowing the man's obsession, I suspect there may be another labyrinth, perhaps greater than the other one.'

'There's one unanswered question,' said Becky. 'If the entrance to this new labyrinth was found over a thousand years ago, and has been visited often since then by someone leaving offerings, why was the door left intact? It doesn't make sense. Tomb robbers had no time for curses or other such mumbo jumbo. Why wouldn't they just smash it down and plunder whatever is inside?'

'That I don't know,' said John, 'but I think your father did.'

'What makes you think that?' asked Becky

'Because he opened the door, Becky. Your father went inside.'

Chapter Two

Itjawi 1245   BC
The Caverns of Sekhmet

Sekhmet sat on her ornate throne of human skulls, gazing down at the scene before her in contempt. The walls all around the audience chamber were painted with graphic images of the dead and the dying, and pools of blood red fluid were sunk into the black marble floor. Swathes of semi-transparent fabric hung from the ceilings and the smell of death permeated everything. She sat quietly, letting the whole atmosphere of the room sink in, gazing down at the man sprawled face down on the audience chamber floor before her, his arms spread wide in acknowledgement of her supreme dominance. In the background a constant murmur of forbidden verses from unseen voices whispered through the audience chamber, sending their own tendrils of fear into the man's heart, whilst offering familiar chords of comfort to the undead god.

Sekhmet knew it was dramatic and it sent lightning bolts of fear into everyone unfortunate enough to enter her presence, but that was exactly what it was designed for. If those who feared her knew the extent of her own weakness, then it could cause the consequence that she feared most.

The temple was relatively small and situated deep in the rocky cliffs above Itjawi. The opening was a natural cleft in the rock, but once inside, it opened up into a series of passages and side chambers, ultimately leading to the audience chamber.

With a flick of her hand, she dismissed the attending acolytes, knowing full well that they would be disappointed at the feeding being denied them. When the room was finally empty, she spoke, her words ethereal and soft amongst the swaying fabrics.

'Stand, Ramesses,' she said, 'and gaze upon a true living god.'

Ramesses II got to his feet and dared to raise his head to peer through to Sekhmet. As usual, she was indistinct, as not only did the fabrics obscure her form, but the few burning torches and complete lack of windows in the temple, combined to ensure the light was only enough to see around him.

'Sekhmet, mother of gods, bringer of death, I bring you salutations and reverence,' he said and bowed his head once again.

The old woman allowed herself an inner smile. The usual venerations uttered by most men who dared to enter her domain were irrelevant and irritable. She had heard it so often before that it ground on her patience, but to hear it uttered by a Pharaoh was always satisfying. Especially in this instance, where Ramesses II, probably the strongest monarch this country of Kemet had ever seen, acknowledged her superiority without any hesitation.

'Ramesses,' she said. 'It is not six moons since we last spoke on the dying fields of Kadesh. I hear you won no great victory, yet suffered no great defeat. An unsatisfactory outcome for you, I would imagine.'

Ramesses lifted his head once more and stared toward her ghostly image, his eyes slightly narrowed in anger.

'My victory was great, Sekhmet,' he said, 'and the Hittites were vanquished. Your spies tell you untruths.'

'Perhaps,' Sekhmet sighed. 'But I care not either way. Hittites, Hyksos, Nubians, I have seen them all come and I have seen them all go. When your body rots in whatever puny temple you eventually build for yourself, there will, no doubt, be a different race calling themselves master. Yet I will still be here, and they too will prostate themselves before me or suffer the consequences.'

'That won't happen, Sekhmet,' said Ramesses. 'I am building an empire such as this country has never seen and my legacy will be eternal.'

'Eternal,' laughed Sekhmet and the sound of the cackle sent shivers down the king's spine. 'Do you even understand the meaning of eternal? Can your puny mortal mind even imagine the concept?'

'Heaven is eternal,' said Ramesses, 'the gods are eternal and my name will rank amongst them in the two fields of the afterlife.'

'Oh, Ramesses,' sighed Sekhmet, 'I expected so much more of you, yet you are no different to all the rest. When will you learn? The two fields that you speak of are nothing more than childish dreams, encouraged and propagated by those who have gone before you. There is no afterlife, Ramesses; there is only death, dust and nothingness. Despite your constant declarations of being a living god, and claims to immortality, you are a mortal being with a defined lifespan. When you die, Ramesses, there will be pain, fear and an end of life. That is all there is. You may build the highest pyramid, or dig the deepest tombs filled with all the riches in the world, but you will not change that fact. All you can hope for, Ramesses is as little suffering as possible before Anubis drags your soul to hell.'

Ramesses bit his tongue. He knew Sekhmet was goading him into reaction and though he wanted to rush forward and take the filth's head from her shoulders, her very aura sent rivers of fear through his veins.

'What's the matter, Ramesses?' she continued. 'Do my words offend you?'

'They do, Sekhmet, for though I have heard them before, I know them to be untrue. Every priest in every temple across this land tells me so. It is written on papyrus and into stones from times so far back, my ancestors walked across plains where pyramids now stand. They can't all be wrong, yet you alone say that everything my whole people believe in is a falsehood.'

'Ramesses, I have no reason to lie, but I care not whether you believe me. I have had this conversation with many kings, across many lands, yet all are too insecure in their own little worlds to accept the truth. I thought you were better, Ramesses. When you ascended the throne, I thought that at last, this man's mind may be great enough to embrace the truth, but alas, you are just one more cow in a herd of unseeing cattle.'

Once again, Ramesses held back his temper. Sacrilege against his gods was one thing, but personal insults against his own person ripped at his vanity.

'You always speak of such things,' said Ramesses, 'yet, without pause for breath, claim immortality for yourself. How can these two views be balanced in equal argument? Either immortality exists and can be achieved or it does not. Which side of the chariot do you ride, Sekhmet? Your argument makes no sense. I demand clarity.'

Through the folds of the transparent cloth, Ramesses could make out the figure of Sekhmet rising from her throne and walking slowly down the steps toward him. At first, his heart raced in fear as she approached the sheets, but she stopped short, less than ten paces from him.

'Ramesses,' she said, 'I may have been hasty in my dismissal of you. Nobody has ever stepped within these walls and demanded anything, let alone an explanation from a god. Either they accept the way and follow as lambs, or nod meaningless understanding and then carry on in their own little worlds, irrespective of my truths. Only you, amongst thousands have demanded explanation and this is new to me. I wonder whether it merits consideration or your execution.'

'You will not kill me, Sekhmet.'

The woman's head tilted back and that ancient cackle rang out once more.

'Oh, Ramesses,' she said eventually, 'your self-belief is amusing. You are nothing more than a rich man with an army.'

'An army that could tear down this temple within weeks,' said Ramesses, knowing full well that he was now risking everything.

The woman stared at him through the veils and Ramesses could see the faintest of smiles on her shrivelled face.

'Are you threatening me, Ramesses?' she asked softly.

All around, the room seemed to echo with the whispers of the unseen, and though he kept catching movement at the perimeter of his vision, no matter how quickly he turned his head, there was never anyone there. Even the drapes seemed to waft of their own accord, as if disturbed by the implied violence. Ramesses gulped as he realised he had probably overstepped the mark.

'I offer no threat, Sekhmet,' he said, 'but only a thirst for knowledge. I am torn between the teachings of my ancestors and the strange truth of your words. How can I decide which way to travel when my knowledge is so limited, and an alternate path beckons?'

'An alternate path,' said Sekhmet, 'I think you misunderstand. There is only the one path available to you, Ramesses, and that is the one which you are already upon. The path of life, pain and death.'

'But if your words are true, Sekhmet, then immortality is possible. You proclaim to be immortal, yet you are flesh and bone, like me. The veils before me cannot conceal the fact that you age as we do, and if it was not for the fact that my father's father referred to you as being old when he was yet a boy, then I would dismiss your claims forthwith and level this place to the ground. Surely, in support of your own stance, then you must believe that immortality is possible, for you are the proof. Either that or your words are false. My dilemma is evident and I cannot reconcile both facts.'

Sekhmet walked slowly forward, the veils parting before her until she was half an arm's length before the king. The stench was overwhelming and it was all Ramesses could do to keep from vomiting.

'You seek the truth, Ramesses?' she asked.

'I do.'

'And what will you do with the truth?'

'I will change the minds of my people,' said Ramesses. 'Enlighten them to the true path, whatever that may be.'

'Even, if that path involves embracing me and others like me as the true gods?'

'If that is the truth, then that is what I will proclaim,' said Ramesses.

The old woman retreated back through the fabrics and walked toward a side door in the wall alongside her throne. As she reached the doorway, she half turned and spoke over her shoulder.

'You have given me much to consider, Ramesses, but now is not the time to make such decisions. Be gone from this place and I will give your representation thought.'

'When should I return?' asked Ramesses.

'I will let you know,' said Sekhmet and disappeared through the doorway.

From behind him two acolytes approached and accompanied him back to the entrance, stopping short of where the sunlight crept a few paces into the cleft. Ramesses paused and looked back into the temple, knowing full well that he could have this place torn from the face of the earth within days, but though he doubted the old hag's words, a tiny part of him was afraid, very afraid.

Inside the temple Sekhmet entered her room, weary and hungry. The room itself was extremely basic and was carved out of the rock itself. It contained no furniture, except the one extravagance that she allowed herself; the one thing that was a nod toward the culture of the country in which she currently existed, a sarcophagus. The granite coffin was lined with silks and she spent most of each day lying within its stone walls. Though she didn't need to stay there, and indeed hadn't slept for longer than she cared to remember, she found the claustrophobic confines of the coffin relaxing and peaceful.

A movement caught her eye in the corner of the room, and she saw a naked baby no more than a few months old, lying contentedly in a basket. At first, there was the slightest twinge of regret, but that was immediately drowned by a more pressing emotion, a primeval need that overwhelmed all her other senses. Hunger!

Followed by his closest advisor, Ramesses walked into the royal palace in Itjawi. Though the capital had been in Avaris since the time of his father, the royal family kept palaces in all the major cities of Kemet. All around, the servants and slaves of the royal household prostrated themselves before him as he passed. Days earlier, many had been sent from Avaris to ensure that everything was up to standard for the Pharaoh's arrival, knowing full well that any major shortfall would result in dismissal from the king's service or worse.

'Was the visit profitable, Sire?' asked Atmar as they walked.

'I would see it as an investment rather than bearing profits,' said Ramesses. 'Her interest is aroused and she has agreed to a further meeting.'

'And you believe she will share the secrets with you?'

'I don't know,' said Ramesses, 'but she is certainly considering something.' He sat on a gold inlaid stool, while Atmar removed the Nemes crown from the Pharaoh's head, and handed it to the jeweller standing close by.

'It is almost dark, Sire,' said Atmar. 'Do you want me to arrange your meal?'

'Yes, do that,' said Ramesses, 'and arrange some entertainment. After being in that place, darkness lays upon my soul. I need something light-hearted to ease my mood.'

'I have already anticipated this, Sire, and arranged for some of Itjawi's famed dancers to be available. All it needs is your command.'

'Good,' said Ramesses, 'I will bathe first and then eat. The dancers can follow the meal. Arrange others to oversee the evening, Atmar. You will eat with me tonight.'

'I am honoured, Sire,' said Atmar and turned to leave the chamber.

'One more thing, Atmar,' said Ramesses, 'double the guard on the Palace tonight. We wouldn't want any unwelcome visitors getting in, would we?'

'No, Sire,' said Atmar, and left Ramesses alone in the room.

Chapter Three

London 2012

John and Becky relocated to a local library to continue their conversation, as the café had turned out to be far too public to continue. They found an empty reading room and made themselves comfortable.

'Becky,' said John when they had settled down, 'before we continue there are other things you should know. I haven't worked with your father since he was sacked. That was over a year ago and I haven't seen him since.'

'Why was he sacked?' asked Becky, 'you haven't said.'

'Well, it wasn't just him who was sacked, it was me as well. The longer we excavated illegally in the catacombs, the harder it became to announce the find publicly. If we had told the authorities, they could have taken away our licenses immediately, and by the time we realised what we had found, it was almost too late. Despite that, your father insisted we do the right thing. Eventually, we approached Dr Samari, the head Egyptologist in the Cairo Museum and told him everything.'

'What did he say?' asked Becky.

'Well, he listened intently and initially was quite excited. Oh, we had our knuckles rapped for not declaring it earlier, but overall, he was very supportive. In fact, he promised he would do everything to obtain funding for an official dig and not only that, promised that the recognition for the find would be equally shared between us both.'

'That's fantastic;' said Becky, 'and did it happen?'

'No, it didn't,' John said. 'In fact, it went very quiet and for a few weeks we couldn't even get Samari on the phone. E-mails went unanswered, messages left on his phone ignored and we were even denied access to his offices.'

'So what did you do?'

'Well, as soon as we could, we went back to Itjawi only to find that the access shaft had been filled in. When we started asking questions, they called the police, and we had to get out from there pretty quickly.'

'They had covered up your find,' said Becky.

'They had,' said John, 'it was so bloody annoying.'

'Out of season, digs are often filled in,' said Becky, 'perhaps it was to wait until resources became available.'

'That's what we thought,' said John, 'and for a while, we took a step back, but something didn't feel right. Samari, ignored every attempt to contact him, so eventually, we managed to corner him after attending a conference.'

'What did he say?'

'Nothing, he just tried to barge past and mumbled something about harassment. Hell, he even threatened going to the police himself if we didn't leave him alone.'

'It doesn't make any sense,' said Becky.

'No, but there was something else in his manner,' said John. 'He seemed very afraid. Anyway, after much lobbying we heard that the Museum was issuing a press release about the discovery of Itjawi. At last, we thought some sense would be made of it all, but when it came out, all it said was that despite rumours to the contrary, the exact location was still a mystery and that two unnamed scientists responsible for circulating unsubstantiated claims had been sacked. Though they weren't named, guess who they were?'

'You and dad,' said Becky.

'Exactly. Obviously we went to the museum immediately to find out what was going on, but our things were waiting at the reception desk along with our severance notice.'

'Did you see anyone?'

'Nope, and when we caused a fuss, we were arrested and kept in jail for two days while our deportation papers were being prepared.'

'But that takes weeks.'

'I know. Luckily, the embassy got us out of there, but not before the authorities made it clear that if we remained in the country, we would spend an awful lot of time behind bars.'

'On what charges?'

'Conspiracy to bring down the government,' said John, 'a charge that carries a life sentence in Egypt.'

'That's preposterous,' Becky said. 'Wasn't there some way you could defend yourself?'

'Possibly, but I for one wasn't hanging around to find out. I was on the next plane out of there.'

'What about dad?'

'Well, that's the thing. He was supposed to meet me at the airport, but he didn't show. At first, I was worried, but he called and told me not to worry and that he had everything in hand. Of course I argued with him, but he had decided to stay and there was no changing his mind.'

'Did you hear from him after that?'

'A few times, but after a few months, all the contact with him stopped, and I got on with my life. That is, until yesterday.'

'Why, what happened yesterday?'

'I received a letter from him. It was posted less than a week ago and it is very disturbing.'

'Do you have it with you?' asked Becky.

'I do,' said John, 'though I have to warn you, it is a bit upsetting.'

'That's okay,' said Becky. 'Can I read it, please?'

34

John reached into an inside jacket pocket, and retrieved a folded envelope before handing it over to the girl. Becky put on her reading glasses and read the letter quietly to herself, gasping out loud at the first line.

Dear John

By the time you read this, I will probably be dead. I know that is not what you would ever expect to hear from someone like me, but to be honest, I can't see any other way out of the predicament in which I have found myself.

John, I have been framed for a crime that I didn't commit. Two weeks ago, Samari's body was found in the Museum. It seems someone had smashed in the back of his skull with an iron bar while he was working late. The thing is apparently, I was the main suspect and spent two days being questioned. Finally, they confiscated my passport and allowed me out pending further investigations.

Last week, I found out from a contact in the police force that they had CCTV coverage of me entering the Museum late that night, and they were on the way to arrest me for murder. For reasons I can't go into here, I did go back to the Museum that night and as I still have the keys for the side entrance, managed to get in with little difficulty. Despite this, John, I swear I had nothing to do with Samari's death. The very thought that I could be involved is preposterous, but it was exactly the evidence they needed. Anyway, I managed to flee the city in time and have been hiding ever since. John, I have no money left, no reputation and nowhere else to run. My face is on posters throughout the country and all over the TV. I did not do it, but the evidence they have managed to contrive against me is convincing. They have even conjured up some DNA evidence and say it is from the murder weapon.

If they find me, I will be arrested, and to be honest, after what I have been through, there is not a cat's chance in hell that I will be found innocent. With that in mind, I have decided I will not spend the rest of my life rotting in an Egyptian jail and will take the coward's way out. Do not worry, for I tire of this life, and look forward to the great adventure that now lies before me.

Thank you for being a friend, John, and I hope that life brings you everything you desire, but there is one more thing before I go. I can't go into too much detail in case this letter is intercepted.

We were right, John, and I now know that our discovery would put Carter's to shame. I know, because I have since been there and seen sights that have blown my mind. I don't expect you to believe me, so I have sent a message to you, via my daughter. I can't bring myself to write to her, but please tell her not to be too upset. I have had a wonderful life and will now get to be with her mother once more. Perhaps this time I won't cock it up.

Anyway, tell her I love her and know that one day she will be one of the best archaeologists in her field.

One last thing, the message I sent contains indisputable evidence of what could be the greatest discovery in the history of archaeology. I'm not sure by sending it if I am doing you a favour or putting you at risk. However, even at this late stage, the scientist in me won't allow me to let it go unexplored. The sensible thing would be to burn the message and move on with your life, but the scientific thing would be to act upon it, because if it is what I think it is, then it will change the way we look at our world forever. That is no longer my choice. The decision is yours.

Have a good life John, and goodbye.

Becky put the letter down on the table and John offered her a clean handkerchief to wipe away the tears in her eyes.

'Sorry you had to read that, Becky, but I think it was important that you did.'

'I'm glad you let me, but to imagine him in such a desperate situation breaks my heart. There's no way he would have killed that man, John. I know my dad and he could no more kill someone than fly to the moon. He just wasn't built that way.'

'I know,' said John, 'and it is so bloody upsetting that someone with such a good heart as his, is made a scapegoat for somebody else's wrongdoing. It stinks.'

'I should go to the police,' said Becky. 'Take the letter with me.'

'Why?' answered John. 'What good would it do your father now?'

'Well it may clear his name,' she said. 'At least that would be something.'

'And how do you see that happening?' asked John. 'All we have is a letter proclaiming his innocence. The Egyptian police have motive, opportunity and DNA. They would simply point to the evidence and claim his suicide was that of a desperate and guilty man. If you go to the police and there is an investigation, all that will happen is that his name will be dragged through the mud, though this time on an international scale.'

'But I can't just let it go,' said Becky, her voice shaking. 'He was innocent. How can I let my father go to his grave with this against his name? After all the good he has done, it is just not fair.'

'I agree,' said John, 'and that is why I intend to do something about it.'

'What are you going to do?' asked Becky.

'I intend to go back to Egypt,' said John 'and trace his steps back into the catacombs. Whatever he found, sounds damned important, especially as the authorities over there have gone to so much trouble to cover it up.'

'Is that wise?' asked Becky.

'No, not at all,' said John, 'but that's why I need your help.'

'Me, how can I help?'

36

'First of all,' said John, 'in the letter, he says he has sent a message to you in the last week or so, with evidence as to what he discovered. We need to get that message and substantiate his theories, whatever they may be.'

'I haven't had any messages,' said Becky, 'unless they were sent to the museum.'

'Does your father write to you there often?'

'Occasionally. Usually personal letters go to my home, while anything to do with work goes to the office.'

'And you haven't seen anything yet?'

'Not unless it went to the main admin office upstairs. My mail often gets backlogged, until Amy decides to go up there and collect it all.'

'Who is Amy?'

'My assistant, she is very helpful.'

'Do you trust her?'

'Of course, I do. She's seventeen and is a little mixed up at the moment, but trustworthy nonetheless.'

'Okay, that's what must have happened. We need to retrieve that letter and see what it says. When are you intending to go back to work?'

'Monday,' said Becky. 'It's pointless sitting at home wallowing in self-pity; my father would have kicked my butt from here to Cairo and back. Anyway, work will take my mind off the situation.'

'Fair point,' said John.

'What is the second thing?' asked Becky, 'You said there were two things you needed help with.'

'Yes, that's right. Obviously, I need to go back to Egypt, but my passport will be flagged up at any airport as banned from entering the country. I have contacts and can get in with no problem, but once there, I will be very limited as to what I can do. Any credit card transactions, hotel bookings, equipment hire; that sort of thing will show up on the government's records and I would be arrested within days. Like your father, I have no desire to spend the rest of my life in some stinking Egyptian prison, so I need your help.'

'Do you want me to go out there?' asked Becky

'No, of course not, it's far too dangerous. What I need is for you to provide support from here. If I need anything, I will call you and you can pay this end using an account we will set up especially for the purpose. I'll deposit some money in the account so you are not out of pocket and that way, there is no electronic record of my whereabouts out in Egypt.'

'Makes sense,' said Becky, 'I suppose most transactions are done online these days.'

'That's right, so as long as the authorities don't get wind of my non-de-plume, I should be fairly safe.'

'Won't you be recognised?'

'No, it's far enough away from Cairo to avoid most of the people who know me.'

'What about the people around the dig site? Won't they know you?'

'If I went in the same way, yes, but I intend to go in by a different route. While we were in the catacombs, we also found the original tunnel used by the tomb robbers all those years ago. It is filled with rubble now, but should be a fairly easy dig. All I need to do is find the entrance and I should get through it in a matter of weeks.'

'How do you intend to find the entrance?' asked Becky.

'I have ways, Miss Ryan, trust me.'

They carried on making plans for another hour or so until Becky looked at her watch.

'Oh dear,' she said, 'look at the time. I have to go.'

'Of course,' said John, 'I have kept you far too long.' He pulled out his wallet and gave her a business card.

'You settle back into work,' he said 'and see if you can find the letter. When you do, give me a ring and I will come back down. Is that okay?'

'Fine,' she said, reading the card as she spoke. 'John Deacon,' she read, 'antiques dealer.' She looked up quizzically.

'Don't be put off, Becky,' he said. 'When I returned from Egypt, I had to make a living somehow. It is all legitimate, I promise you. If you have any doubts, do some research. I am beginning to get a good name for myself.'

Becky smiled.

'If it helps clear my father's name,' she said, 'I don't care if you are Satan himself.' They walked to the car park together, and as they shook hands, John gave her one more reassurance.

'Becky, if this goes well, your father's name will be cleared within months.'

'And if it doesn't?'

'Send me a cake with a file inside,' he said, 'preferably coconut.'

'Why coconut?' she asked, failing to see the significance.

'I like coconut,' he said with a smile. 'Goodbye, Miss Ryan, see you soon.'

'Goodbye, Mr Deacon,' she said, and watched him drive off into the evening gloom.

Becky kept herself busy over the weekend, cleaning up her flat. It had been neglected recently, and despite the occasional unannounced bursts of tears, she managed to make the flat cleaner than she had ever seen it before. Monday morning saw her clock in to the museum and make her way straight down into the archives. It had been two weeks since her father had died, but as she walked through the familiar surroundings, it seemed she had

38

been away just a couple of days. As she approached the office with her keys in hand, she heard an unexpected noise, and unconsciously slowed down. Nobody was ever down here this time in the morning.

'Hello,' she said, 'who's there?' Slowly, she pushed the unlocked door open and almost jumped out of her skin when someone stepped out from behind the door.

'Amy,' she shouted, 'you nearly gave me a heart attack.'

'Sorry, Becky,' grinned her assistant, 'I thought I would give you a surprise.'

'Well, you certainly succeeded there,' said Becky walking into the office.

Amy's early appearance was not the only surprise since the office was completely different. The grubby walls had been painted, the furniture all moved around and there were even some pictures on the wall. As well as all that, the piles of paper on her desk had been tidied up and there was a new filing cabinet in the corner.

'Wow,' said Becky, 'what happened here?'

'Like I said,' said Amy, 'I wanted to surprise you. I had a word with maintenance and they helped me drag everything out so that I could give it a lick of paint. I nicked the filing cabinet from Admin and had a good tidy up.'

'Oh, Amy that's very nice of you,' said Becky.

'Well, it wasn't just me,' said Amy, 'the boys helped as well. We thought it would be nice for you to come back to after…well, you know.'

'And the pictures?' she asked, glancing up at the bare-chested actor peering down from the walls.

'Oh yes, those,' said Amy. 'I did ask the art department for some Rembrandts, but they weren't too keen.'

'I'm not surprised,' said Becky, 'but still, sparkly vampires?'

'Yeah, I know. I brought the posters in from home. They were on my bedroom wall.'

'Thank you,' said Becky. 'Not my cup of tea, but I still really appreciate it. One thing though, you didn't throw my notes away, did you?'

'Nope,' said Amy, 'they are all alphabetically filed in the filing cabinet. If it didn't have a heading, it was filed under miscellaneous. There's quite a lot in miscellaneous.'

'I don't know what to say,' said Becky, 'except thank you.'

'No problem,' said Amy. 'Just don't start blubbering. That would be so un-cool.'

'I promise, no blubbering,' said Becky. 'Now, let's start with a nice cup of coffee, shall we?'

'It's already done,' said Amy, 'and on your desk. Welcome back.'

Amy sat at her clear desk and picked up her coffee. A couple of biscuits were on a side plate, as well as a copy of the weekly museum journal.

'I could get used to this, Amy,' she said between sips.

'Whatever,' said Amy blankly as she stared at her own computer screen, and though Becky couldn't see what she was looking at, she guessed she was networking.

'Some things never change,' she thought to herself, and opened the page of the journal on her own desk. The day went relatively quickly for Becky, and though she knew they were well meaning, she didn't want to run the gauntlet of her colleague's condolences. So, when Amy offered to bring her a sandwich from the canteen, she gratefully accepted.

'Cheese and pickle, please,' she said, 'and an apple. Oh, while you're up there, could you go to admin and pick up any mail?'

'I already have,' said Amy.

'Where is it?' asked Becky, looking at the expanse of clear space on her desk.

'In the filing cabinet, filed under U for unopened mail,' said Amy.

Becky held her breath until Amy had left the room, and for the first time in two weeks, allowed herself to laugh. This new Amy was going to take some getting used to.

She retrieved the pile of mail sitting in the bottom of the drawer and placed it on her desk, discarding the elastic bands that held them together. For the next hour or so, she filtered them out into three piles, junk, work and urgent. The junk mail went into the recycling bin, and the urgent pile was placed on the top of the work pile. By the time home time came, she was up to speed on e-mails, letters and memos, though she had seen nothing from her father.

'Is there anything anywhere else, Amy?' she asked as the girl pulled on her ankle-length black coat.

'I don't think so,' said Amy. 'Why, have you lost something?'

'No, just expecting a personal letter, that's all.'

'Perhaps it will come later in the week,' said Amy. 'The post office is crap, these days.'

'It probably will,' sighed Becky, 'hang on; I'll walk out with you.' Within a few minutes, they were walking arm in arm from the museum.

'See you tomorrow,' said Becky as they reached the tube station.

'Yeah, okay,' said Amy, and carried on to her bus stop.

'Amy,' called Becky as the girl walked away.

Amy turned around.

'Yeah?'

'Can I have chocolate biscuits tomorrow?'

'Now you're pushing your luck,' laughed Amy, and waved goodbye as she got on her bus.

Becky waited until she was on the tube before ringing John Deacon.

'Hello, John,' she said, 'Becky Ryan, here.'

'Hello, Becky,' came the answer,' how are you?'

'I'm fine,' said Becky, 'I'm just ringing to say I haven't seen a letter yet, but it may arrive later in the week.'

'Okay,' said John, 'no problem, I still have some things to organise up here, so there's no rush.'

'I just thought I would let you know,' said Becky.

'That's great,' said John, 'see you soon.'

'Yes, okay. Bye.'

'Bye, Becky,' said John and the phone went dead.

Half an hour later, she was back in her flat, being greeted by a hungry Smokey. All in all, it was as if over the last two weeks, nothing had happened.

Chapter Four

Itjawi Village
1245 BC

Normally Yafeu was fast asleep at this time of night. The hard graft in the quarries of Ramesses saw to that. Yafeu was a chiseller and had the calloused hands to prove it. Every day he would turn up at the quarries and work alongside his friend, Serapis. Each would take a turn holding a the chisel over a marked piece of stone, while the other smote it with a mallet to form a hole in the granite When it was deep enough, and they had a row of similar holes, they would drive in wooden wedges before soaking them with water so they would expand. The wedges would be driven in regularly and kept wet, and as they swelled, the strains in the rock became unbearable until a crack appeared. More wedges were added and ultimately, the rock would split right through, and fall away, providing the architects with one more building block for whatever project was in the king's favour at the time.

Yafeu would toil from dawn to dusk in return for food, beer and a tiny allowance for his family. Though there was no physical money in his world, the worth of his labour would be calculated by the overseer, and he would be issued with a similar worth from the rows of goods provided by the king's merchants. Food, clothing, leather or even tiny statuettes of the gods were available as payment, but despite being a fairly high-grade worker, Yafeu was in financial difficulty due to the debts racked up by his son. One of his neighbours had threatened to report him to the officials if he did not pay the debt, and if that happened, there was a high probability of his son being sold into slavery to pay the man off.

Yafeu knew that if that happened, his son would lead a life of hell, and probably be transported to the desert quarries where all the criminals of the country were sent. His lifespan would be measured in months, not years, and though he was admittedly a rogue, Yafeu would not see his son die alongside murderers, rapists and Hittite filth.

In his world it wasn't in anyone's interest to be walking the streets of Itjawi during the dark hours, but tonight was different. His chisel partner, Serapis, had told him of an opportunity too great to be missed and Yafeu was getting desperate.

'It's simple,' said Serapis in the privacy of Yafeu's hut days earlier, 'every month, the trader passes through the village of Nepum. Rumour has it his pack bags are full of jewels and spices, but he is so disliked, and such an ungodly person that no priest will offer him shelter on his travels. He stays in a peasant's hut on the edge of the desert and thinks that nobody knows of his location. But my cousin knows the farmer, and he said that he lies unguarded once a month. He is due again in three nights.'

'I don't know,' Yafeu had said, 'it sounds too easy.'

'That's because it is,' said Serapis. 'We could get in there, kill him and trade his goods in the next village over the next few months.'

'What if we are caught?'

'How can we be caught? All we have to do is leave his body out for the Jackals. As long as we keep our mouths shut, he will soon be forgotten. There will certainly be no tears shed for him.'

'I am not getting any younger, Serapis,' said Yafeu. 'How do I know I will be able to overcome this man?'

'Leave that to me,' said his friend, and together they had hatched a plan to ease their combined debts as well as set them up for a life far away from the quarries.

The night was particularly dark when the time came, and Yafeu was glad of it. Though there were often gangs of youths abroad in the hours of darkness, Yafeu had grown up in the streets and knew them well enough to remain hidden from prying eyes. He kept close against the walls as he hurried through the town, keeping in the deepest shadows of the darkest alleyways. Within an hour he had reached the outskirts of Nepum and circled around to where Serapis had told him he would find the hut. A break in the clouds allowed enough moonlight to show Yafeu the two donkeys tethered outside the hut; a sure sign that someone was indeed located inside.

Yafeu waited for Serapis. They had agreed to travel separately, so they would not arouse suspicion, and had made a solemn vow that if either was caught, neither would reveal the other's name, even on pain of death. Making the vow was one thing, but should that happen; Yafeu doubted his pain threshold would allow him to keep silent.

An hour later Yafeu was at the point of giving up, when at last a whisper from behind made him jump and he spun around in fright.

'Serapis, in the name of the gods, don't do that,' he snapped, 'you frightened me to death.'

'What's the matter?' laughed his partner quietly. 'Scared of ghosts or something?'

'Look,' said Yafeu, 'I've had time to think and I'm not happy about this. I've changed my mind.'

'Don't be stupid,' said Serapis, 'we are here now, let's get on with it.'

'Serapis, you are not listening to me, I can't do it.'

An awkward silence fell before Serapis grabbed Yafeu's arm.

'Look,' he said, 'I haven't come all this way to give up now. I'll go in and use this,' he pulled an axe from beneath his robe. 'You stay here and keep watch. If anyone comes, just shout and I'll get out of there.'

'I'm not sure…' started Yafeu.

'Think about your son, Yafeu,' hissed Serapis. Before his friend could argue any more, Serapis ran down the slope and toward the hut at the edge of the cornfield.

Yafeu waited for what seemed an age, and he was about to go down to call his friend, when movement from the cornfield on the far side of the hut caught his eye. From his slightly elevated position, he could see a trail appearing, as if someone was walking through the crops. However, as the corn was so high, he couldn't see who or what was leaving it.

He looked across the cornfield in confusion. The clouds had now cleared away and the moon lit up the scene as if illuminated by hundreds of torches. He could see more trails now and counted more than a dozen, each coming from a different direction and converging on the hut.

Yafeu's first instinct was to call out, but he knew it was too late and nothing he could do would save his friend. He wanted to run, but curiosity kept him transfixed, so he awaited the outcome of the strange phenomenon with bated breath. He wasn't sure what he expected to emerge from the corn, perhaps robbers or even cattle but the last thing he expected to see, were women.

His heart missed a beat, as one by one, several white robed women seemed to glide from the corn, forming a semi-circle around the front of the hut. Some approached the two donkeys and calmed them down, while others peered through the slats of the shuttered windows. Finally, one individual entered the hut and a dread silence seemed to fall over the entire scene.

Yafeu refocused on the ones comforting the donkeys. They seemed to be very tactile, smoothing their heads and running their fingers through their manes as they caressed the necks of the animals. Yafeu looked again; the soothing nature of the women's attention seemed very unnatural. In fact, if he wasn't mistaken, they seemed to be kissing their necks.

Yafeu felt a rush of revulsion and barely contained a gasp of disgust. He didn't know what was happening here but whatever it was, it wasn't natural. Just as he contemplated leaving, a sickening scream of unparalleled terror echoed from the hut and across the fields of corn, chilling his heart to the core. It was as if the remaining women had been waiting for this spine-chilling signal and without a sound, those attending the donkeys, sliced the animals' throats wide open and stepped back as the donkeys struggled to escape their tethers. Within seconds, the animals collapsed and the rest of the women fell upon the dying animals in a frenzy of aggression, tearing at the wounds with their bare hands and immersing their faces in the fountains of blood, fighting amongst each other for the prime positions.

Despite his revulsion, Yafeu was transfixed and watched the frenzied women tearing at the poor animals with blades and teeth, causing fresh streams of blood on every free area of flesh they could find. Even when the blood had stopped flowing, they ripped chunks of raw meat from the bodies and chewed ferociously at their bloody prizes, with raw animal juices running down their faces.

Yafeu came to his senses and rose from his hiding place. He had to get out of there and realised that now was the best time, while their attention was diverted. Just as he was about to turn, his eyes were drawn to the doorway of the hut and his eyes opened wide in fright when he realised the woman who had initially entered the building, had now emerged and stood in the doorway, staring right up at him. For a second, he paused, staring in horror at the blood that surrounded her mouth and fell from her chin, staining the white gown she was wearing. Yafeu realised with a sinking heart that the blood about her face had to be human, and more than likely, belonged to Serapis.

For what seemed an age they stared at each other, each with different intentions, but as she started to walk toward him, Yafeu came to his senses and fled in terror back the way he had come.

Ramesses moaned in his sleep, the subject of nightmares fuelled by his life of violence. The harem girls had been dismissed and had left him fast asleep beneath the silken covers of his sleeping dais. Outside his chambers two of his trusted soldiers stood on guard, willing to lay down their lives to protect their beloved king. Throughout the palace soldiers talked quietly amongst themselves, disappointed that the extra duty meant they had to forego the brothels that every city boasted.

Officers strolled around the luxurious corridors, making sure that everyone was where they were supposed to be, and despite not knowing why the extra guards had been requested, each knew that their own fates relied on the safety of the king. If anything should happen to him on their watch, then every officer, soldier and household servant would be put to death, irrespective of the severity of assault. It was a blunt consequence, but one that ensured every member of the king's staff went out of their way to ensure his safety.

Midnight had long passed and the time crept toward the deepest part of the night. The time when the land fell into silence and even animals held their breath in anticipation of the coming dawn.

Ramesses opened his eyes, momentarily confused as to his whereabouts. His confusion was quickly overtaken by revulsion as the smell of death assaulted his senses. He sat up quickly and pushed himself back against the wall in fear as his eyes became accustomed to the dark. That smell could only mean one thing, the presence of Sekhmet.

He looked around the room frightened. Despite her age, Ramesses had seen Sekhmet kill men larger than him, before they could even draw sword. Her speed of movement at close range was astonishing, and no matter how strong the victim, without a throat, they were usually unconscious before they could retaliate. Ramesses did not intend to underestimate her and though he held a knife beneath his sheets, he spoke calmly and clearly.

'I know you are here, Sekhmet,' he said, 'show yourself.'

'Is that a tremble of fear I hear in your voice, great King?' asked a gentle voice from the darkness.

'I have no fear, Sekhmet. It is caution you hear.'

'You are right to show caution, Ramesses, but it is a mistake not to fear me. You of all people should know this.'

'How did you get in here, Sekhmet?' he asked.

'I have my ways,' the answer came.

The king's eyes followed the hint of something moving across the dark room and his hand closed on the grip of the knife. Except for his death, he could imagine no other purpose for the woman's visit.

'If you dare try to take my life,' said the king, 'you and your kind will be wiped from the face of this world forever.'

'Ramesses,' said the voice, 'I tire of your empty threats. If I wanted to take your meaningless life, then you would already be dead.'

'You dare to threaten Pharaoh?'

'I have killed many men in my time, Ramesses, and amongst them were many kings. Do not presume favour from me. I allow your grandiose ramblings for no other reason, than you amuse me.'

'Then why are you here?' he asked.

Gradually the woman appeared from the darkest corner of the room, seemingly gliding over the luxurious carpet that covered the marble floor.

'I have spoken to many kings, Ramesses, and you alone stand out. All have cowered in fear before me, overwhelmed in the presence of an immortal, yet you alone dare to question me. Nobody has even dared hold such discourse, but simply accept my majesty without thought. You, however, question my very existence, my claim to immortality and even veil threats beneath clever words. I have often thought about snuffing out that tiny light you call a soul and move on to the next. Yet there is an arrogance about you that draws me like a moth to a candle. Why is this, Ramesses? What is this magic you possess that has spared you from my wrath on more than one occasion?'

Ramesses swallowed hard. The fact that she had considered killing him brought him to a cold sweat, for the reach of her retribution knew no limits.

'I don't know such things, Sekhmet,' he said, 'but I was born of a long line of kings. Majesty is in my bloodline and it is incumbent on me to ensure my people serve the gods to the best of their ability. Those who ruled before me were but tributaries to the Nile of my ambition. My name will be remembered until the stars fade in the sky, for I am the greatest Pharaoh that this land has ever seen, or will ever see. My name will be eternal and I am truly a living god to my people. Yet in the darkest hours, at times such as this, devils of doubt pierce my soul and I question my mortality.'

'Then you are condemned by your own words, Ramesses,' said Sekhmet. 'No god doubts their mortality. I would not see this as a weakness, but an acceptance of reality. I watch from the side-lines as your people spend time and wealth in preparing tombs, only for their bodies to rot, as does the poorest slave. Gold or prayers to meaningless gods will not buy your immortality, Ramesses. You are man born of man, and that burden alone will carry you to your death in a blink of an eye.'

'Then answer the question I posed in your temple, Sekhmet. If you alone can see life to the end of time, then provide substance to your claim, if only to open my eyes to the futility of my quest. What is your story, Sekhmet? Share your tale with one who seeks the truth.'

'And if I do, Ramesses, what can me and my kind expect in return?'

'Whatever you desire,' said Ramesses, 'land, gold, jewels. You name your price and it will be supplied tenfold with joy in my heart. I will give you my kingdom, if that is what you require. All I ask in return is the truth.'

'I seek no gold, Ramesses. I have enjoyed riches you can't imagine and had loves that women only dream of. I have walked this world from ocean to ocean and I have seen things that are beyond imagination. Yet, your offer stirs a desire within me. There is something I require, Ramesses, something simple that it is within your power to deliver.'

'Name it and it will be yours,' said Ramesses.

'All in good time, Ramesses, the dawn approaches and I need to leave this place to return to my sisters. This night, they have fed well and are restless to return to the place where they feel safe.'

'Where are they now?' asked Ramesses.

'Everywhere,' said Sekhmet and walked to the door.

'When will you return?' asked Ramesses.

'I will not,' said Sekhmet. 'Present yourself to me at the next full moon. Come alone and all will be revealed.'

'Wait,' said Ramesses, 'I will have to arrange your safe exit. If you are seen leaving my chambers, you will be killed without question.'

'There is no need,' said Sekhmet, 'it has already been arranged.' With that she left the room and walked slowly down the corridor to the far doors.

When she had gone, Ramesses got of his bed and called to his bedroom servant in the next room.

'Garai,' come quickly.

When there was no response, he stormed into the servant's chambers, furious that he had not been attended to immediately.

'Garai,' he shouted, 'I want to know who commanded the guard tonight and how that woman got into my palace.' He stopped short in disbelief.

47

Garai's naked body was dangling backwards from the bed, his blood still dripping from the huge tear where his throat should have been. All around the room, blood splattered the white marble walls and Ramesses stared in horror at all the other bodies scattered around the quarters, each mutilated in a similar fashion. The king walked into the other rooms, in search of anyone still alive, but found only similar scenes, with each servant revealing equally grotesque fates.

'By the gods, Sekhmet,' whispered Ramesses to himself, 'I swear you will pay for this.'

The following morning saw the entire king's entourage lined up in the grounds of the temple. Lines of chariots and infantry stood ready to escort the royal wagons east to the Nile where the royal party would board the boats to take them back to the capital. Rows of palace servants crouched in terror along one wall, tied together with ropes that wrapped around their wrists and fed between their legs to be repeated on the man, woman or child behind them. A murmur of fear rippled amongst them, and many already bore bleeding welts across their backs, evidence of the priests' whips as retribution for failing the king.

Across the other side of the courtyard, over fifty soldiers knelt on the stone courtyard. Each was stripped naked and had their hands tied behind their backs. All had their heads bowed in shame and fear, knowing exactly what fate awaited them.

Up above, in the king's chambers, Atmar was adjusting Ramesses' headdress, ensuring he looked every part the king before leaving the building.

'You are clear about my instructions?' Asked Ramesses when his aide had finished.

'Yes, Sire,' said Atmar. 'All will be ready before we see the Nile's next inundation.'

'Good, let nothing prevent you from completing this task. If the gods are willing, there will be a reckoning across this land that, will not only release my people from that monster's fearful grip, but will show once and for all who really holds the power.'

'We will be ready, Sire,' said Atmar. 'At the time, all you will have to do is raise an eyebrow and a wall of manpower will descend upon this place like the sands of a storm.'

'Good. Now, before I go, have you made the arrangements for today?'

'I have, Sire. The people will feel the wrath of your justice and everyone will know what fate awaits those who fail you.'

'Then let it be done,' said Ramesses, and walked out onto the balcony accompanied by Atmar.

Below them, the gathered crowd fell to their knees in subjugation. The two men waited for the noise to die down before Atmar took a deep breath and addressed the gathering.

'Citizens of Itjawi,' he said, 'last night, those whom you see tethered before you allowed assassins into this palace. Their incompetence placed the life of your Pharaoh at risk, and only the power of his sword saw him defeat the hordes single handedly. Despite this, those who were entrusted with his safety do not deserve to live.' He turned to face the condemned guards. 'You men are from the king's most trusted ranks. You have enjoyed privilege and reward, second to no other man, yet you failed in your duty. Your sentence is this. You will be taken from this place to the black river and there you will be tethered until Sobek has feasted on your souls.'

The crowd murmured in awe as they realised the men were being fed to the crocodiles. Atmar turned to the servants cowering against the wall.

'You people are citizens of this city and it was your duty to provide comfort and safety to our king. Again, you failed in your task. Your fate is to dig a pit in the desert to a depth of three men, and when it is done, you will stand in this pit, whilst your own families fill it in with the king's sands.' A terrified groan rippled along the servants, before the crack of whips beat them into silence once more.

'Finally, there is one more punishment to bestow,' said Atmar, turning to one man being held separately from the rest. 'You are captain of the guard and you alone hold ultimate responsibility. But due to your previous loyalty and courage on the field of battle, the king, in his infinite mercy will not cast sentence of death upon you. Instead, he sets you a task. In order to secure your life, you will be taken to the hills above Itjawi unto the temple of Sekhmet. There you will enter the lair as the sun sets, to be fed upon as the night walkers see fit.'

At the last statement, the priests and overseers herded the condemned out of the palace grounds and through the town to meet their fates. Ramesses, who had remained silent throughout the ceremony, finally spoke up.

'Make sure my will is carried out,' he said. 'In thirty days I will return and will expect service befitting a god.'

'I will oversee it myself, Sire,' said Atmar. 'Travel well.'

Within the hour, the royal entourage were travelling along the stone paved roadway toward the Nile where the luxurious royal barges awaited their arrival.

Chapter Five

The City of Faiyum
Egypt 2012

John Deacon paid the taxi driver and walked into the hotel in
Faiyum, passing the usual assortment of clichéd tourists. Most of the men
sported cream knee length shorts, crisp white polo shirts and had Ray-Ban
sunglasses perched precariously on receding hairlines. The women, on the
other hand, wore floral patterned dresses reaching down to the floor with
Armani sunglasses carefully threaded through bleached blonde hair. The
group were obviously a coach party on a trip from one of the many cruise
ships on the Nile and had stopped off for a pre-arranged lunch at the hotel.

John wore creased trousers and sweat-stained shirt with the rolled up
sleeves bunched above his elbow, so when he navigated his way through the
crowd, he received more than one look of disdain from disapproving tourists.

'Excuse me,' he said to the receptionist, 'I am meeting someone
here.'

'Hey, get to the back of the queue,' said a clipped English accent,
and John glanced briefly at the man waiting to be seen.

'I'm sorry,' said John, addressing the receptionist, this time in
Egyptian, 'could you tell me where your restaurant is please?'

Surprised at being spoken to in his own language, the male
receptionist answered immediately and pointed the way.

'Thank you,' said John and leaving the crowd behind him, walked
into the spacious restaurant overlooking a winding river that threaded its way
through the city. A few moments later, he spotted his target and made his
way over to join her at the window table.

The woman wore a large floppy hat and had the largest sunglasses he
had ever seen. Combined with the cold drink she was sipping, it had the
effect of covering most of her face and he was not sure if she was actually
who he thought she was.

'Becky?' he asked hesitantly.

'John,' she said with a smile, 'nice to see you again.'

'I wasn't sure for a moment there,' said John, 'you look so different.'

'You can talk,' said Becky, 'where's the beard?'

'Oh that,' said John rubbing his chin. 'Beards are not very practical
in Egypt. What's with the glasses?'

'Thought they may help me to merge into the crowd,' said Becky.
'Too much?'

'Just a little,' said John with a smile. 'A bit too much Elton John for
my liking.'

'Let me get you a drink,' said Becky and poured him a glass of iced
lemon water from the jug on the table.

After emptying half of his glass, John sat back, removed his hat and placed it on the table.

'Well,' he said, looking around nervously, 'This wasn't something I was expecting to be doing today.'

'I know,' said Becky, 'but after I had your phone call last week, I had to come.'

'But why?' asked John. 'You know how dangerous it is. If I am caught, you will be guilty by association. At least, back in London you were safe. Out here, who knows what can happen? I want you to get the next flight back home.'

'I can't do that, John,' said Becky. 'Now that I know you are so close to the tomb, there was no way I could stay in that pokey little office waiting for news. Don't forget, I am also an Egyptologist and quite apart from the opportunity this holds to clear my father's name, the chance to be part of a ground breaking discovery is a chance I couldn't pass up.'

'That may be the case, Becky, but we don't know what we are dealing with here. For all we know, there is nothing in that tomb and all this could be a waste of time. Don't forget, I walked across the border from Libya, and if I am caught, I don't think my false papers will hold up to examination.'

'You haven't been caught yet,' said Becky.

'That's because I keep a low profile. I am staying in one room in the house of one of my workers from years ago. I hardly go out in the day and spend the nights clearing the tomb robber's tunnel. I've had to pay the local thugs a minor fortune to keep my activities quiet and then only after promising them a share of anything I find.'

'You did what?' gasped Becky, 'You can't do that.'

'I had to,' said John. 'Look, tomb robbers are a fundamental part of Egypt's culture. They are part of the underbelly of every city in the country, a bit like the mafia in Sicily, but love them or hate them, they are a fact of life. Many families base their entire lives around dealing with unrecorded artefacts and many antiquities come onto the market from sources unknown. They have contacts and communication networks that stretch across the country and many have ancestors that were robbing tombs thousands of years ago. I couldn't go to the government, so I had no option and turned to the next best thing.'

'What did you do?'

'Look, we can't talk here,' said John, 'There are too many prying eyes. Is there somewhere we can go?'

'I have a room booked,' said Becky. 'We can talk there.'

Five minutes later, they sat at either side of a tiny dressing table in a hotel bedroom.

'So,' said Becky, 'bring me up to speed.'

'Six weeks ago,' said John, 'I arrived in Faiyum and made my way straight to the dig site. I had made arrangements with one of my contacts and he set me up a meeting with the biggest antiquities dealer in Faiyum.'

'Is he legitimate?' asked Becky.

'Of course he's not,' said John, 'it's all a thin cover for his illicit dealings. Anyway, the fact is, they know of every tomb ever discovered in this part of the world and the probable location of many that are still to be found.'

'Did they know of the one you and my father found?'

'They did, but were very wary of getting involved.'

'I suppose that was because the government.'

'That was part of it,' said John, 'but there was something else, reluctance on religious grounds.'

'That's absurd,' said Becky. 'Since when did those sort of people care about religion?'

'I know, but that's how it is.'

'A curse of some sort?' asked Becky.

'I suppose so,' said John. 'Anyway, at first they treated me with deep suspicion and I got nowhere, but after being passed from contact to contact, they eventually introduced me to another guy. Someone who had no such principles, but even though he would help me find the way in, he made it clear that he would only go so far. I was taken by car to a suburb where I was shown into a surprisingly modern house and in the cellar; there was an amateur excavation where the owners had found an old grave. Many Egyptian families know that due to the copious amounts of history beneath their feet, the chances are there may be a grave or two. Anyway, this family struck it lucky and found a couple of ornaments. Not much, but enough to pay the bills for a couple of months. The thing is that during the excavation they found what was obviously a filled in tunnel of some sort and as soon as I saw it, I knew that it led down in the right direction to intercept the catacombs.'

'So you started to excavate?'

'We did, though not before passing bundles of dollars to dozens of people. Anyway, the dig was relatively easy and consisted mainly of loose rubble. The hardest part was finding somewhere to put it all so that we didn't alert the neighbours. They now have rubble in almost every room of the house, but three days ago, we made a break through.'

'You got into the catacombs?'

'Not quite. Just before we were about to break through, I heard voices the other side.'

'There was someone in there?'

'Yup, and not just anyone either. I managed to clear a tiny hole in the last of the rubble, just enough to see through, and there were two people talking, One I didn't know, but the other one I would recognise anywhere.'

'Who was it?'

''I don't know how to tell you this, Becky, but it was Dr Samari.'

'Dr Samari,' said Becky. 'But that's impossible, he's dead.'

'It was him, Becky; he was almost in touching distance. Despite what we thought, it would seem that he didn't die in that assault. Either that, or the assault didn't take place at all and it was all an elaborate ploy to frame your father.'

'But that means...' began Becky.

'He died in vain, Becky,' said John. 'Your father killed himself for no reason.'

'But a friend of his in the police warned him that he was to be charged with murder. Why would he say Samari was dead if he wasn't?'

'He was probably on the payroll of whoever is behind this, but if you think about it, it is a perfect outcome for them. Your father was found hanged and even if he had told anyone about the Samari accusation before he died, they could produce the healthy doctor and claim your dad had lost his mind. No body, no murder, just a foreign archaeologist with a grudge for being sacked for operating an illegal dig.'

'It doesn't make any sense,' said Becky, 'why go to all that trouble, just to claim a new find for themselves? Even if it is the biggest discovery ever found, the days of artefacts being carted halfway around the world are over. Egypt would keep the treasures, and my father would simply profit from having his name associated with the find.'

'Well, that depends,' said John.

'On what?'

'On what they found behind that door. Don't forget your father's letter. He said that, whatever it was that he found, had the potential to be the greatest discovery in the history of archaeology. I suspect that whatever the credentials of the people involved, the control of such a discovery was too great to be attributed to one man, and a foreign one at that.'

'So you think they reopened the dig?'

'I think so. As soon as your father and I were off the scene, they came back and carried on where we left off.'

'Where is the entrance?' asked Becky.

'It's in the side of a banking, hidden behind the reed beds of the river, not far from here,' said John, 'Most of the year it's under water, but the shaft leads upward above the water line then drops sharply into the catacombs.'

'Wait a minute,' said Becky, 'something doesn't add up here. You said you found the tomb in Itjawi, not Faiyum.'

'We did,' said John, 'for years everyone has been scrambling around in the deserts around Faiyum when all the time it was right here.'

'Faiyum is Itjawi?' asked Becky.

53

'Not exactly,' said John. 'If your father was correct, Faiyum is built on top of Itjawi.'

'No, that can't be right,' said Becky. 'The authorities discarded that theory years ago. All the excavations uncovered throughout the city have turned out to be from Crocodilopolis, which came far later than Itjawi. Beneath those are metres of virgin ground.'

'So we have been led to believe,' said John, 'but those catacombs are far lower than the ruins of Crocodilopolis.'

'They may just be dug into the bedrock,' said Becky.

'I don't think so,' said John. 'The walls of the catacombs have been built with granite blocks similar to the pyramids. They were placed one on top of the other and are capped with stone slabs for a roof. If they were just dug into the substrata, there would be no need for walls or roofs, the natural rock would furnish both.'

'If that's the case,' said Becky, 'how are they so deep beneath Crocodilopolis. Surely the covering soils couldn't be just the residue over the years, we are talking almost twenty metres of overfill.'

'Who knows?' said John. 'Perhaps there was a prolonged period of sandstorms that covered the city completely. The thing is, we believed that Itjawi lies beneath our feet and quite apart from what lies behind that door, just confirmation of that fact will be ground breaking in itself.'

'No wonder it had remained hidden for so long,' said Becky. 'I suppose there is no chance of using the same entrance that you and dad found?'

'I don't think so,' said John. 'A couple of nights ago, I went up to the entrance to see if it was still accessible, well, as close as I was able anyway. They have put a great big steel door over the shaft and two armed soldiers now guard it. Whatever it is down there, it is pretty damned important.'

'I'm still gutted that the message he sent me didn't turn up,' said Becky. 'Perhaps if we had that, then at least we would know what's down there. Do you think they found out about the letter and intercepted it?'

'Possibly,' said John, 'but we'll never know. The thing is, I am very close to finding out anyway.'

'John, I don't think it's worth it,' said Becky. 'If they've gone to all this trouble to hide it from the world, then they'll probably not think twice about making you or me disappear. Don't forget that officially you are not even in the country?'

'I know, but what worries me is that your name is obviously the same as your father. All it would take is one overzealous official to make the link and they could have someone watching you within hours.'

'Then surely that is all the more reason to leave?'

'I can't, Becky, I am so close. After everything we have been through, I'm not going to turn away now.'

'And how do you intend to find out anything?' asked Becky. 'If there are already people down there, how will you get past them?'

'I have watched them from the outside,' said John, 'every night they lock the steel door and go back to their hotels. If I can break through the last few feet of the tomb robber's tunnel just after they leave, I will have almost eight hours before they come back. That should be plenty of time.'

Becky looked at him for a long time, thoughts racing around her head.

'When are you going to do it?' she asked.

'Tonight,' said John. 'If I wait too long, word is going to get out and they'll discover the tunnel.'

'Okay,' said Becky, 'you go downstairs and wait for me there, I'll get changed and meet you in ten minutes.'

'What are you on about?' asked John.

'You don't think I'm going to stay here, while you go down there on your own, do you?' asked Becky.

'Yes, actually, I do,' said John,

'Well think again,' said Becky. 'You said yourself that there may be another labyrinth behind that door. If there is, there is no way you will search even part of it in eight hours. If I am with you, we cut the time in half.'

'But Becky…' started John.

'But nothing,' said Becky. 'Don't forget, my father died because of this and I intend to find out once and for all what it was that cost him his life.'

John sighed in resignation.

'You do know we will probably be caught,' said John, 'and if we are, there is no way we will be supported by the British embassy.'

'Then we had better not get caught,' said Becky. 'Come on, we are wasting time, I'll get changed, you call us a taxi.'

Two hours later, they were walking down a dark alleyway, heading for the outskirts of the town. John had insisted on being dropped off more than half a mile away to leave no trace at all of the location of the second tunnel. Finally, he knocked on a door of the second house in a row of four, and with a quick look around to make sure they weren't being followed, entered the house containing the tunnel entrance.

A young boy carrying a lamp showed them down to the cellar and John passed him a twenty-dollar note for his services. As soon as he had received the money, the boy put down the lamp and ran back up the stairs.

'Right,' said John, putting down the bag he was carrying, 'we won't be disturbed until dawn, so we had better get on with it.' He pulled two large torches from the bag, handing one over to Becky along with two spare batteries and a bottle of water.

'We could be down there for some time,' he explained.

She put the batteries and water in the small rucksack brought along especially for the job before shining her torch around the cellar.

'Well, where is it?'

'Behind here,' said John, and pulled a dirty tapestry to one side, revealing a jagged hole at the base of the wall.

'After you,' she said and watched nervously as John crawled, headfirst into the hole. She followed close behind and found the passage sloping steeply downward. Within five minutes, they came to a halt.

'What's the matter?' asked Becky.

'This is it,' said John. 'We are at the end of the tunnel. The catacombs are just the other side of this mound of rubble.'

'Then what are we waiting for?' asked Becky. 'Start digging.'

For the next fifteen minutes, John lay on his stomach, prying rocks from the compacted pile to his front. Slowly, he passed them back and Becky pushed them to the sides of the tunnel wherever there was room. Finally, Becky heard a crash and she knew he had broken through.

'Got it,' said John, 'come on, we're in.'

Becky crawled through the dust to the end of the tunnel and out into the catacombs. Both torch beams swept around the room like world war two searchlights, and both of them fell silent with awe at the vibrant colours bouncing back at them. Covering every available flat surface were richly decorated scenes of life in the city, from thousands of years earlier. Scenes of hunting, eating and god worship were contrasted by depictions of executions, wars and burial rituals. Becky was awestruck and stood staring at the fabulous pictures that had probably never seen the light of day.

'This is amazing,' she said quietly.

'Come on,' said John, 'this is just a side chamber. The room we want is along here.'

Becky followed behind, her eyes hardly able to take in all the fabulous artistry as she went. Within minutes, they entered the main chamber and Becky stepped forward to stand alongside John. Her eyes focussed on the wall at the end of John's torch beam, or rather, the open doorway in the solid wall.

'Is that it?' she whispered.

'It is,' said John, 'though last time I was down here, that doorway was blocked and sealed.'

'Well, pointless standing around here,' said Becky, 'what are we waiting for?'

John reached into his pocket to reveal two pieces of chalk, one blue, one white.

'Let's stick together for the first hour or so until we know how big this place is,' said John. 'If it is as big as the one at Hawara was supposed to have been, then we could be down here for days.'

'Why the different coloured chalks?' asked Becky.

'Blue to mark the confirmed route back,' said John, 'and white to mark side passages as we check them. We'll start with one turn only off the main corridor, that way we won't get lost. Once we have checked that out, we can come back here and start exploring the side corridors in detail. Here, I have some for you as well.'

Becky took the chalk and after taking a deep breath of the warm and musty air, ducked down to follow John into the labyrinth.

Across the country, in an office of the Cairo museum, two men sat opposite each other across a table. One man fidgeted nervously, obviously uncomfortable in the other's presence, while the second oozed confidence as he retrieved a cigarette from an ornate silver case. The smoker struck a match and inhaled deeply to ignite the cigarette before speaking again.

'Dr Samari,' said the gaunt faced man, squinting his eyes because of the smoke, 'I don't think you quite understand your position here. I don't care what superstitious claptrap your diggers are telling you, this is potentially the greatest find in the history of mankind. If the initial findings from the lab are correct, then no force on this planet will stop my sponsors from obtaining this information.'

'Mr Leatherman,' said the nervous Egyptologist, 'please, you have to understand. This is far bigger than you or I, ever imagined. If this is not handled very, very carefully, then it could be disastrous. Heaven knows what contamination lies in that tomb. We have been in there only a few weeks and already have enough information to rip up almost every book from the Bible, to Darwin's theory of evolution. I need more resources before I dare move anything and it has to be done properly. If you would just allow me to declare our find, even within the confines of our own circles, or at least to the museum sponsors, then I could move everything here and we could continue our studies in a scientific environment.'

'No,' snapped Leatherman, 'don't forget where your first loyalties lie, Samari. When you first approached me for funding on that other little unauthorised project of yours, we made a deal.'

'And you were repaid handsomely for that investment,' said Samari. 'That death mask was worth millions and it rivals the mask of Tutankhamen himself. If the museum was to find out that one of the most important artefacts ever found hangs on the wall of a private collector, I would spend the rest of my life in jail.'

'You would,' said Leatherman, 'and don't you forget it. But with regards to this situation, you obviously thought there was another little get-rich quick project for you to get your grubby little fingers on, but when it went belly up, and you found what you did, who did you come running to?'

'I know,' said Samari, 'but this is different. This is bigger than all of us, and deserves the resources of science to find out the meaning. Please, Mr Leatherman, You have to see sense here. Let me get the experts involved and we can move forward together. I will even make sure you get a share of the recognition, whatever you want, but we can't do this by ourselves.'

'No,' snapped Leatherman, 'it is not negotiable, and this is what is going to happen. First, you are going to ring your people in Faiyum and tell them to get the artefact ready for removal. As we speak, there is a convoy of vehicles on the way there, and when it arrives, we will remove it to a safe place.'

'Where?'

'You don't need to know. Just make sure that it is ready. Secondly, you will pay your labourers to destroy the tomb completely and collapse the entrance.'

'But why? The site alone contains history unlike anything we have ever found. Surely there is no need to destroy it completely?'

'Dr Samari,' said Leatherman, 'if what you have found turns out to be what we think it is; we want exclusivity. What we don't want is someone checking out that tomb after us and drawing conclusions that may affect our work.'

'But what about the workers?' asked Samari. 'People talk. I can't guarantee they will remain silent.'

'How much are you paying them?' asked Leatherman.

'The equivalent of a thousand dollars,' said Samari.

'Then pay them five thousand to keep silent,' said Leatherman, 'and tell them there is another five thousand in two years' time, as long as the whereabouts of the tomb remains unknown. By then, we will have our own arrangements in place and anyone blabbing will be thought mad. Nobody in their right mind will believe them.'

'And what about me?' asked Samari, 'Where do I feature in all this?'

'Oh, that is simple,' said Leatherman, 'we are not unreasonable men, Samari, so I offer you a deal I think you will find irresistible. In my pocket, I have two items. You can choose either, but in return, you will remain silent.'

'This,' continued Leatherman, unwrapping a folded piece of paper, 'is a cheque for two hundred thousand dollars. It can be in any bank you specify within two hours. There are also another four checks like this with your name on them, and each will be deposited on the first day of January for the next four years. If you accept them, you will be rich beyond your wildest dreams and will never hear from us again.'

'And the second item?' asked Samari.

'Oh, yes,' said Leatherman and placed a small metallic object next to the cheque. 'I am sure you can guess what this is, but just to make it clear, I will spell it out. This is a 9mm bullet from a semi-automatic pistol. If you decide to refuse my sponsor's generous offer, or run to the authorities, this too can be in its destination within two hours.'

'And where is that?' gulped Samari.

'Your brain,' said Leatherman. 'The choice is yours, Dr Samari, take your pick.'

Sweat ran down Samari's astonished face as the implications sunk in.

'You wouldn't dare,' he said.

'Wouldn't we?' asked Leatherman. 'One way or the other you will know in two hours. Now, are you going to make that telephone call or not?'

After a few moments' pause, Samari reached out and picked up the phone.

'Right decision,' said Leatherman and returned the bullet to his pocket. 'Now, where can a man get a whiskey around here?'

Back in the labyrinth, Becky and John had spent several hours searching blind tunnels and side rooms, but despite the richness of the artefacts they contained, remained focussed on finding whatever Becky's father had found.

'This place is amazing,' said Becky, when they stopped for a drink. 'There's more down here than in the entire vaults of the British Antiquities museum.'

'I know,' said John. 'There's a lifetime's study in the hieroglyphs alone, and I've lost count of the unopened sarcophagi we've seen so far.'

'Perhaps that was what my father was referring to,' said Becky, 'just the wealth of riches throughout these tunnels.'

'No, I don't think so,' said John. 'He was convinced that Amenemhat is buried down here somewhere and he wanted the grand prize

'You're right,' said Becky, 'come on, let's keep going.' A few minutes later, Becky grabbed John's arm and pulled him to a stop.

'What's the matter?' asked Jon.

'Shhh,' said Becky, 'listen, I can hear something.'

John screwed up his face and listened intently.

'I hear it too,' he said. 'What is it?'

'I'm not sure,' said Becky. 'A sort of humming.'

'Come on,' said John, 'we'll carry on, but keep quiet.' They crept forward until once again they stopped.

'Look,' he said and pointed his torch beam to something hanging from the ceiling.

'What is it?' asked Becky.

'It looks like armoured cable,' said John, reaching out to touch it, 'and it's vibrating.' He pointed his torch upward again, illuminating where the cable disappeared through a jagged hole in the stone slab. 'This is the source of the noise,' he said, 'I think somewhere up on the surface there must be a generator and they have drilled down through the ground to provide an electrical supply.'

'Wow, that's some serious commitment,' said Becky.

'It also makes our job much easier,' said John.

'How?'

'All we have to do is follow the cable,' said John. 'Come on, I think we are getting close.

A few minutes later, they came to a modern door that had obviously been installed in the last few weeks.

'Why on earth would they put a door in here?' asked Becky in astonishment.

'I have no idea,' said John, 'but I aim to find out.' He gently tried the door handle and pushed forward. 'It's locked,' he said.

Becky knelt down and peered through the keyhole.

'Wow,' she said, 'it's lit up like Blackpool tower in there. There are lights everywhere.'

'What else can you see?' whispered John.

'Nothing really, it seems the floor has been swept and there is something hanging from the ceiling in the centre. It looks like…polythene.'

John was about to ask if he could take a look, when suddenly Becky jumped back from the door.

'Shit,' she whispered, 'there's someone in there.'

'What do you mean someone in there?' asked John.

'Exactly what I said,' said Becky, 'someone just walked past the door.'

'Who?'

'How on earth would I know?' hissed Becky.

'Out of my way,' said John, 'let me see.' He replaced her at the door and peered through the keyhole.

'Oh, no,' he said, standing up quickly.

'What's the matter?' asked Becky, the fright now evident in her voice.

'You're right,' said John, 'there is someone in there and they are coming out. Quick, we need to hide somewhere.' They turned quickly and ran back down the passage before ducking into a side room.

'Behind here,' said Becky and they ducked behind a sarcophagus. They heard a bunch of keys rattling and peered over the sealed coffin as two men in white overalls walked past the entrance to the room.

'You said there would be no one down here,' whispered Becky.

'How did I know they would be locked in?' said John. 'Whatever it is they are working on must be damned interesting. Come on.'

'Where are you going?' asked Becky.

'I heard them unlock the door when they came out,' said John, 'but I didn't hear them lock it again. I'm going in there.'

'But they could be back any minute,' said Becky.

'This could be our only chance,' said John. 'Are you coming or what?'

Becky hesitated a few seconds before following him to the doorway. John tried the handle again and this time it eased silently inward. They both stepped into the well-lit room and stood in silence before Becky finally spoke.

'Bloody hell, John,' she said, 'just what is going on here?'

Chapter Six

Itjawi - 1245 BC
The Caverns of Sekhmet

Ramesses stood before the opening in the cliff above Itjawi.

'Are you ready, Sire?' asked Atmar.

'As ready as I'll ever be,' said Ramesses, 'you know what to do?'

'I do,' said Atmar.

'By the time the sun rises, Atmar, I will be truly immortal. If I do not emerge alive, then use the full force of my armies to wipe these parasites from this world.'

'Everything is ready, Lord,' said Atmar.

'Good, then it is time to meet my destiny.' Without another word, he entered the natural entrance and walked through the rocky passages into the temple of Sekhmet. The path led downward into the heart of the hill and within minutes, two of Sekhmet's acolytes joined him. He had expected to be taken to the audience chamber, but before he reached the familiar room, he was led in a different direction. Finally, he entered a small cavern and his ethereal companions left him alone in the room.

The glow from the few rush lights placed around the room was hardly enough for him to see, and his eyes stung from the fumes of the burning tallow. Finally, he became accustomed to the poor light and he could see someone sitting amongst a pile of luxurious cushions at the centre of the room. With a deep breath, Ramesses stepped forward until he stood behind the hooded woman.

'Well, Sekhmet,' he said, 'I am here.' He waited patiently for an answer, but when there was no response, he walked around the seated figure to stand before her.

'Sekhmet,' he said, 'what is this game you play? I am a king and it is not becoming of a king to be ignored.'

The sitting figure lifted her hands and slowly pulled back the hood from her face before looking up at the king. Ramesses' eyes widened in shock and he took a step backwards in confusion. Before him a beautiful young woman looked up at him with deep green eyes, as yet untainted by the black tinge that came from a diet of blood and raw meat.

'Who are you?' he asked, 'Where is Sekhmet?'

'I am known as Nephthys,' said the girl.

'Nephthys,' said Ramesses, 'the goddess of darkness, afterlife and immortality. Are you such a goddess?'

'I am no goddess,' said Nephthys, 'but one day soon, I will join the immortals.'

'And, how will you achieve that?' asked Ramesses.

'My mother will bestow me with that gift.'

'Your mother?'

'The goddess Sekhmet,' said Nephthys.

'Sekhmet is your mother?'

'She is the only mother I have ever known.'

'Then you are truly a lost soul,' said Ramesses.

A stench of death swept through the room and Nephthys stood to await the arrival of the old woman. Ramesses spun around to find Sekhmet standing a few paces away in the shadows.

'Your method of arrival surprises me still,' said Ramesses.

'A skill long in the learning,' said Sekhmet and nodded toward Nephthys who promptly left the room.

'The child is not as you,' said Ramesses.

'She has not yet been initiated into our ways,' said Sekhmet.

'And will she be?'

'That remains to be seen.'

'Then why is she here?'

'She was brought here as a gift from a worshipper when she was a child.'

'You mean as a sacrifice.'

'Yes. Many such gifts arrive at my temple from the enlightened.'

'Yet she still lives?'

'She does, for unlike the others, there is a spark of life about her. Her eyes are the pathways to her soul and even when she was an infant, her soul challenged mine.'

'So you spared her?'

'I did, though there is an ultimate price to be paid. But we get ahead of ourselves, Ramesses; first there is a bargain to be struck.'

'There is,' said Ramesses. 'So let us begin.'

A movement caught Ramesses' eye and he turned to see a shuffling figure approach him carrying a stool. The figure was male and his naked body was covered with both healed and open wounds. His feet were tethered close together and his head hung low in abject despair. The desperate figure placed the stool near Ramesses, and returned the way he had come, without even acknowledging his presence.

'Who is he?' asked the king.

'He is nothing,' said Sekhmet. 'He does not exist and does not deserve acknowledgement.'

'Yet, he is a man,' said Ramesses.

'He was a man,' said Sekhmet, 'now, he just is.'

'Those wounds bear the similarity of men attacked by beasts,' said Ramesses.

'My sisters need to feed, Ramesses.'

'You keep him alive to drink from him as we do cattle?' asked Ramesses in astonishment.

'There have always been such souls, Ramesses. Many offer themselves of their own free will, desperate to be close to a god.'

'There are more?'

'There are many, but it leaves a sour taste in my mouth to discuss them so. They are but dogs to be treated as we see fit. Be seated, Ramesses,' said Sekhmet, 'it will be a long night.'

Ramesses sat on the stool in the centre of the room while Sekhmet seemed to glide in amongst the shadows of the room.

'State your requirements, Ramesses,' she said eventually.

'I want to know the secrets of immortality, Sekhmet;' said Ramesses, 'to know how you came to enjoy its embrace and how you maintain the blessing of everlasting life.'

'Questions asked by many such as you,' said Sekhmet. 'Yet, answers I have denied them all. Tell me why you deserve this knowledge.'

'For I am the greatest king this country has ever seen,' said Ramesses, 'and my feats to come will be like mountains compared to the termite mounds of those who went before me.'

'A bold statement, but why would that affect me?'

'Because you can be part of it, Sekhmet,' he said. 'Grant me what I seek and you can be part of this new era. Once your name was known across all lands, feared and revered by all, yet since the time of Amenemhat, your kind has hidden themselves away from the gaze of our people.'

'You dare speak his name in my presence,' snarled Sekhmet.

'I know of your hatred of him,' said Ramesses, 'and tales of how he persecuted your kind have been passed from generation to generation. It is also said that he almost succeeded in wiping your species from this world.'

'Oh, Ramesses,' she said, 'don't believe the exaggerations of descendants living on past glories. Yes, there was persecution and yes, he sought out my sisters before slaughtering them and scattering their ashes to the four winds. But as for eliminating me and those like me, then no, he wasn't even close. It is true we were forced to hide like common criminals and I watched in fury as he ripped down my temples across the land and struck my name from the walls. But I have endured such ignominy before and no doubt will do so again. My kind is eternal, Ramesses and we will rise and fall like the tides of the sea. Over time, we will once more dominate and that is one thing that we have, an abundance of time.'

'But why wait, Sekhmet?' asked Ramesses. 'Provide me with what I desire, and those days can be here within the space of a few seasons. I will re-enter the name of Sekhmet into our culture and encourage worship in your name. Temples will be raised once more to your glory and you will enjoy the trappings as befits a true goddess. Grant me this one thing, and your name will be spoken alongside Ra, Isis and Sobek.'

'You promise much, Ramesses. Yet, it will take years to build the temples you speak of. My name may be spoken, yet I will still hide away in this place, feeding on the wretched and watching my sisters rot in their frustration.

'Then let it be so, Sekhmet,' said Ramesses. 'Instruct me in your secrets and I can change this immediately. I have already given instruction to prepare a temporary temple for your reverence, a place where you can see the commitment of my promise.'

'And where is this place?' asked Sekhmet.

'The tomb of Amenemhat himself,' said Ramesses.

Sekhmet stayed silent for a minute and then Ramesses' flesh crawled as he heard her laugh.

'Oh, that is good, Ramesses,' said Sekhmet, 'you are indeed a force to be reckoned with. Of all the places in Kemet, you have chosen the one place that you knew would appeal to me.'

'Think about it,' said Ramesses, 'the last resting place of the king who caused you and your kind so much frustration. A lasting violation of his memory.'

'You would do this?' asked Sekhmet.

'I will break the seal with my own hands,' said Ramesses.

'And his remains?'

'Yours to do with as you wish.'

For a while, Sekhmet remained silent, before speaking again.

'I care not for such things,' she said eventually, 'but there are others who deserve to know the freedom of my youth. Those of us who have known nothing but the walls of these caverns should regain their place as gods amongst the people. So I will grant you your wish and tell you everything there is to know, but be warned, it may not be what you expect. Ask your questions, Ramesses, hell awaits.'

Ramesses took a deep breath and started to ask the questions he had pondered all his life.

'First of all,' he asked, 'are you truly immortal?'

'If immortality is judged by a human lifespan, then yes, I am.'

'How old are you?' asked Ramesses.

'I know not, but I was here before Amenemhat, before the pyramids and before your ancestors first walked these lands.'

'How do I know you speak the truth?'

'You don't.'

'Are you truly a god?' asked Ramesses.

'Yes, in human eyes, but there are no heavenly bodies that your kind revere,' said Sekhmet, 'they are all versions of me and others like me.'

'There are others?'

'There were, I know not if any still survive.'

'So you can die?'

'We cannot die, but we can cease to exist.'

'I cannot see the difference,' said Ramesses.

'Give me your blade,' said Sekhmet.

'I have no blade,' said Ramesses nervously.

'Do not lie, Great king. It is beneath you. Give me your blade.'

Ramesses retrieved the knife from beneath his robes and slid it across the floor to where he could see her shape in the gloom. Sekhmet stepped forward to pick up the blade and Ramesses watched in amazement as she pushed it through the palm of her hand without as much as a flinch.

'Damage to flesh and bone kills humans,' said Sekhmet. 'I do not suffer such limitation. This blade gives no pain and causes limited injury. In a matter of days, it will heal. I don't know how and I don't know why.' She withdrew the knife and threw it back across the room. 'It is a blessing and it is a curse.'

'How can this be a curse?' asked Ramesses. 'To not suffer death through injury, surely it is a gift.'

'In the beginning it was,' said Sekhmet, 'but when you have lived as long as I, then sometimes you yearn for the peace of death. There is nowhere that I have not been, and nothing that I have not seen. Death is a journey desired, yet denied me.'

'Surely that cannot be true,' said Ramesses. 'A wound that heals is one thing, but what if your head was removed from your shoulders?'

'My body would be incapacitated, yet my mind would still be aware.'

'And burning?'

'I suspect that would end my physical existence, Ramesses, but as to my awareness, who knows? I have an awareness of those who went before me. Their spirits haunt me every day, they cry out for release from whatever hell awaits our souls, yet even though the pain of their souls torment me, I still envy their state. How I wish that I could die.'

'Then why do you not do it?' said Ramesses. 'Why not cast yourself into the flames and end your existence?'

'I have contemplated it, Ramesses,' said Sekhmet. 'Contemplated it so many times that there are no numbers to count them, but always there is the one thing that holds me back, the thirst for blood.'

'Is this an addiction that all your kind shares?'

'All are cursed so, and though we can live on the blood of animals, it is human blood that drives our needs.'

'Is this the secret to immortality?'

'Perhaps, but there is so much more. Look at me, Ramesses, I am an old hag with a thirst for human blood. I do not sleep and have not walked in daylight for thousands of years. Yet it was not always so. Once I was like others of your kind. I was born of woman and fathered by man. My early years were spent in a village far south of here on the edge of a great lake. It was so long ago, I barely remember them, but some things remain in my memory. I remember how I used to love gathering the fruit and seeds from the bushes with my mother, and how we would stop when the sun was at its hottest and she allowed me to swim in the lake. I also remember sitting with my family and eating the food that the women prepared when the men's hunt was successful. Of course, the flavours and textures escape me, but I know that I relished them.'

'And yet, here you are,' said Ramesses. 'Something must have happened to make you this way. Were you touched by the hand of a god?'

'Oh, no, Ramesses,' said Sekhmet, 'nothing quite as mystical. I don't know how, but I do recall the exact day my life changed. Whether it will help you in your quest, I do not know.'

Ramesses maintained a calm exterior for at last, he was about to learn the secret of eternal life.

Chapter Seven

Itjawi 2012
The Labyrinth of Amenemhat

Becky and John looked around the subterranean chamber in confusion. The room was approximately fifty feet square with a vaulted ceiling more than twenty feet above their heads. There was only one exit; the one they were standing in, and the stone slabbed floor had been meticulously swept from any accumulated dust that had lain there since the tomb was first opened. All around the walls, dozens of fluorescent tubes shone their dazzling light into the room, and tables full of scientific instruments lined the walls.

At the centre of the room, a new, inner space had been formed with aluminium framework, and sheets of hanging polythene from the ceiling above made the whole thing look like a miniature version of a circus tent.

On a row of tables to one side, several monitors flickered blue lights across their screens, recording data of some sort and a further table contained microscopes, laptops and notebooks.

'Look,' whispered Becky and pointed into one corner. A row of plastic bollards connected by red and white chains isolated one small area from the rest of the room and circled what seemed to be a pile of old rags. 'Come on,' she continued, 'let's take a look.'

They walked over and stared at the pile of rubbish before Becky gasped with realisation.

'Oh, my god,' she said, 'it's a mummy.'

'Or what remains of one,' said John, 'it seems to have been ripped into pieces.'

'Tomb robbers?' asked Becky.

'I wouldn't have thought so,' said John. 'They would have simply burned it. Anyway, don't forget, this chamber was still sealed until a few weeks ago.'

'Surely these people wouldn't have done this?' said Becky.

'No, why desecrate a mummy and then put a barrier up around it to make sure it's not interfered with? It doesn't make sense.' John stepped over the chain and knelt down before the butchered corpse.

'What are you doing?' asked Becky.

'Hang on' said John, and pulling a pencil from his pocket, probed gently between the folds of the wrappings. Slowly he hooked it under a chain and lifted up a necklace to the light. Despite its age, the gold still sparkled as the amulet spun and the inlaid precious stones reflected light for the first time in over three thousand years.

'It's an Ankh,' said Becky, recognising the cruciform shape with a looped top, 'the symbol for eternal life.'

'I know,' said John, 'but I have never seen one as ornate as this.'

'These remains obviously haven't been examined yet,' said Becky, 'there must be layers of jewellery between those wraps.'

'I don't understand it,' said John, 'Samari's people have been here for weeks, so why haven't they examined him or at least taken the remains to the museum.'

'Perhaps they found something far more valuable?' said Becky.

'How do you mean?' asked John.

'Look at those,' said Becky and pointed to where the black, snakelike cables wound their way across from the computers to disappear under the walls of the polythene tent.

'What do you think is in there?' he asked.

'Don't know,' sighed Becky, 'but this gets stranger and stranger. Come on, let's take a look.'

Slowly they walked to the polythene tent and unzipped the opening before stepping into the space within. The black cables led to another ring of lights surrounding a stone sarcophagus, as well as feeding a row of multi sockets on a nearby folding table. They both approached the sarcophagus, careful not to trip over the trailing cables and peered into the space within. Becky held her breath, not quite sure what she expected to see, but was slightly disappointed when she saw it was just the dried remains of another human body. This one had not been artificially mummified and did not have the typical wrappings you would expect from a king of Amenemhat's stature. In fact, it seemed that the body within had simply dried naturally in the stale dry air of the tomb over the previous three millennia.

'Strange,' said Becky, and walked slowly around the sarcophagus, examining the body closely.

'What is?' asked John.

'This sarcophagus is made for a king,' said Becky. 'Just look at the hieroglyphics. It screams royalty, yet this person whoever she was, is nothing more than some sort of commoner.'

'Why do you say that?' asked John.

'No mummification or funeral goods and she seemed to have been dressed in some sort of simple linen shroud.'

'Priestess?' asked John.

'Possibly, but even they wore jewellery of some kind. This body is devoid of any ornamentation.'

'Perhaps Samari's men took it?'

'Possibly,' said Becky, before continuing around to the far side and leaning into the coffin. 'Look what happens when I do this.' She gently squeezed the flesh on the back of the corpse's hand between her fingers before releasing it again. The skin slowly returned to the position it had been in originally.

'That's mad,' said John. 'With skin that old, surely that should have crumbled to dust?'

'My thoughts exactly,' said Becky. 'There seems to be some latent moisture in the cadaver. Perhaps they have injected some sort of preservative to maintain the extraordinary detail. I wonder what this is for.' She ran her finger along a cable that looped into the coffin from the table of machines, before it disappeared through a hole formed into the body's chest. John turned and traced the cable back to the connected machine. The laptop screen was dark, with the standby light flashing lazily at the bottom. Alongside the laptop was a bright blue plastic box with a retracting handle along the top. Instantly it reminded him of the type of icebox he had often used to take beers to the beach, but this one was obviously electronic and had a sloping lid containing dials, readouts and switches. Down one side, several coils of clear tubing were connected to tiny valves piercing the plastic, and though it wasn't plugged in, John could see that whatever the purpose was, it was certainly medical. He returned to the laptop and rubbed his finger across the mouse pad. The screen eased into life and showed him a black and white readout of a solid line across the screen, just below a similar red line.

'What is it?' asked Becky.

'Some sort of monitor,' answered John over his shoulder, 'and something that reminds me of an icebox.'

Becky joined him at the table and looked at the two machines.

'I know what that is,' she said, 'at least I think I do, but it makes no sense.'

'What is it?' asked John.

'It can't be,' said Becky, deep in thought as she examined the strange machine.

'Becky, will you explain what you're on about,' said John, 'you are beginning to piss me off.'

'Her hands,' said Becky suddenly, with a worried tone to her voice, 'I need to see her hands.' She walked quickly back to the coffin, closely followed by John who stood on the opposite side. Becky looked in the coffin. Both hands of the dead body were palms up and she reached in to turn one over. It moved surprisingly easily for a corpse, but there was nothing untoward.

'Turn that one over,' she said; pointing at the body's other hand.

'What are we looking for?' he asked.

'Just do it,' said Becky, 'but be careful, you don't break anything.'

'Too late with this one,' said John as he reached inside, 'it seems like she's already lost an index finger at some stage.'

'Just don't do any more damage,' said Becky. 'We are scientists, not bloody vandals.'

John turned it over and stared in confusion at the back of the corpse's hand.

'I don't understand,' he said, 'why would they do that?'

'I'm not sure,' said Becky, 'but I'm getting scared now.'

They both looked down again and though the hand was a virtual claw, one of Samari's men had obviously inserted a needle in the place where a vein would normally have been and secured it in place with a piece of sticky bandage. The end still exposed was connected to a small plastic tube, sealed with a tiny hinged-lid.

'That's the sort of thing they use when a doctor gives you injections,' said John. 'Why would they give a corpse injections?'

'I don't think it's for injections,' said Becky, her eyes staring wildly at John. 'That blue machine on the table; I've seen something similar before. I was visiting a friend in hospital who has renal failure. If I'm correct, then that's a portable dialysis machine. Oh, my god, John, I think they intend trying to pump blood into this body.'

'That's preposterous,' said John. 'Any veins would have collapsed hundreds of years ago.' He retrieved his pencil once more and leaned into the coffin. 'The natural mummification process has kept the body in remarkably good condition for three thousand years, but that is exactly what it is, a dead, and dried out corpse.' As he said the last word, he shoved the point of his pencil deep into the stomach cavity of the body. Behind them, something beeped once and Becky spun around in fright.

'What was that?' she gasped.

'The computer,' said John, 'look at the screen.'

Where there had been a flat red line, there was now a peak where the line had jumped momentarily, forming the shape of a miniature volcano on the screen. They both turned to stare back down at the body in silence, before John finally spoke.

'That's impossible,' he said quietly.

'Do it again,' said Becky slowly.

John leaned over and pressed the pencil against the skin of the mummy. Becky turned and stared at the screen. Nothing happened.

'Press harder,' she said.

'Becky, this is stupid…' said John.

'Just do it,' snapped Becky, 'but this time, harder.'

John leaned over and pressed the pencil in another place. The skin of the mummy bent inwards, until suddenly the pencil broke through into the dried flesh beneath. Again, the computer beeped and another spike appeared on the screen.

'Oh, shit,' moaned Becky, 'that's impossible.'

'Let's not get carried away, here,' said John. 'There has to be a scientific reason for this.'

'I know,' said Becky, 'but whatever it is, it scares the shit out of me.'

A distant sound made them both turn their heads toward the doorway.

'They're coming back,' said John. 'Come on, let's get out of here.'

With John leading the way, they left the polythene tent and ran out of the chamber to hide in the darkened tunnels outside. Within seconds, the two men passed their hiding place and re-entered the burial chamber, locking the door behind them. John turned on his torch and shone it into Becky's face. Her eyes were wide and the fear in them was intense.

'Are you okay, Becky?' he asked.

'No,' she said, 'I'm not. Get me out of here.'

Two hours later, John was sitting at the dressing table in Becky's hotel room. The young woman had been in the bathroom for over half an hour, and for most of that time, John could hear the sound of the shower. Finally she emerged dressed in a hotel robe, with a towel wrapped around her head.

'Do you feel better?' he asked.

'I do,' she said. 'Sorry about that, but for some reason it completely freaked me out. I felt as if I was, I don't know, contaminated I suppose. I know it's stupid, but I just had to clean that room off me. Does that make sense?'

'No, not really,' said John with a smile.

'I don't suppose it does,' said Becky, 'I still can't get my head around it.'

'Neither can I,' said John, 'but there has to be a perfectly good reason for all this. Look, I could really do with a shower myself. I've made a couple of calls and my contact is bringing my things over as we speak. Could you book a room for me? I'd do it myself, but you are the one with the legitimate credit card.'

'Of course,' said Becky. 'Sorry, John, I know I am acting like an idiot, but I'll pull myself together, I promise. There's a second robe in the wardrobe, so you grab your own shower and I'll see if room service can rustle us up a couple of club sandwiches.'

'At four in the morning?'

'It's worth a try,' said Becky, as she threw a clean towel toward him, 'go on, you stink of that tomb.'

Two hundred miles away, a convoy of vehicles made their way through the night, heading toward Faiyum. At its centre, a large container lorry carried a metal and glass chamber, linked to a range of state of the art machinery. A row of security guards sat on either side of the chamber, each not sure what it was they were going to collect, but each happy with the vast bonus they had been paid for the job.

In a car behind, sat a haematologist, along with a nurse, an eminent surgeon and one of the country's most respectable Egyptologists. In the cab of the lorry, a tall unshaven man wearing a leather jacket accompanied the driver. A mobile phone rang and the passenger reached into his pocket to retrieve the device.

'Hi, Leatherman,' he said, reading the name from the display.

'Hello, Mossburgh,' said the voice, 'just checking up. How's everything going?'

'Great,' said Mossburgh, 'we've picked up the equipment as well as the passengers. We are running a bit late but should be there by midday.'

'Good. I suggest you park up outside of town until dark and then move in about midnight. Everything is arranged and the transfer should be quick. Is everyone fully briefed?'

'As much as they need to be at the moment,' said Mossburgh, 'they don't know the final details and won't until the last moment.'

'Good. Make sure the chamber is covered when you move it. As far as the security guards are concerned, it's just a mummy we're taking. They're on the payroll, but the less people know the truth, the better.'

'Will do,' said Mossburgh, 'anything else?'

'Not really, just make sure any of the local workers know the implications if any of them blab.'

'I will. How about our friend, Samari? How did he take it?'

'As well as can be expected, I suppose, but don't worry about him, I can deal with Samari. Is everything ready back in London?'

'Yeah, there's a fully equipped lab waiting back at the lodge. We have a private plane on standby and all the papers we need to send the artefact out of the country.'

'And customs?'

'All taken care of. Enough palms have been greased to fund a small nation. All we have to do is land the plane at the private airfield and present the paperwork. Everything will fly through.'

'Excellent. You carry on but keep me informed.'

'Leave everything to me;' said Mossburgh, 'this time tomorrow, we will be on our way back with the cargo intact. See you then.' He put the phone down and settled back into his seat. There was still a long drive ahead of them.

Becky and John sat at either end of her dressing table, both wrapped in white bathrobes. A tray with two empty plates was sitting on the edge of the bed and they both had a cup of steaming coffee in front of them.

'That's better,' said Becky after taking a few sips.

'You know,' said John thoughtfully as he stirred his coffee, 'we may be jumping the gun here. All we have so far is a jumble of circumstantial evidence without any coherent links to put them all together.'

'I'm not so sure,' said Becky. 'Look; we've been dancing around the issue for the past half hour. I think we are both too scared of looking ridiculous to state what was staring us in the face.'

'Which was?'

'You know what,' said Becky, 'for some reason, Samari and his cronies seem intent on trying to transfuse blood into that corpse. Now, under normal circumstances that would be preposterous and completely futile, but these are not normal circumstances.'

'Go on,' said John.

'Look,' said Becky, 'it may be some sick experiment from a bunch of lunatics, or even some mad ritual by religious fanatics. I don't know and I frankly don't care, but the thing is, whichever way you twist this, there is one fact that we can't ignore.'

'Which is?'

'When you pushed your pencil into the body, it registered pain.'

'Bullshit,' said John.

'Well, it registered something,' snapped Becky. 'Whether it was pain, pressure, nerve reaction, I don't know, but whatever it was, it registered on a monitor over three metres away. No matter how I try to work this out, I can't get away from that simple fact.'

'Becky, think what you are saying here. You saw that body as clearly as I did. No matter which way you look at this, it was at least two thousand years old and probably much older. There is no possible way in any realm of science that body could register feeling of any sort. It is impossible.'

'But you saw it as well,' said Becky.

'I saw something,' said John, 'but I don't know what. For all I know it could have been a motion device fitted beneath the body, or even some type of electrical wave detector picking up my own body's magnetic field. The possibilities are endless.'

'And the dialysis machine?'

'Look, I'm not saying I have all the answers here, but I do think we need time to sift through what we found, and make calculated, well thought out conclusions. With what we have found out so far, I think we may have enough to at least force the Cairo museum to launch an investigation into Samari, and hopefully that may go some way to clear your father's name.'

'And how do we prove that, exactly?' asked Becky. 'As far as they will be concerned, it will just be my word against one of their own. Why would they believe me or you for that matter?'

'They don't have to believe us, Becky. All we need to do is tell them exactly where the entrance is, or even the tomb robber's tunnel, and they can send an investigatory team within days. Once they find the catacombs, our stories will stand up and you can clear your dad's name.'

'You really think they will believe us?' asked Becky.

'They will when I show them this,' said John and pulled out the Ankh pendant from his robe pocket.

'John, that's the pendant from the tomb,' gasped Becky. 'You can't just take something like that without full documentation and permission from the authorities. That's grave robbing.'

'Just call it an insurance policy,' said John. 'I don't intend to keep it, but I will use it to prove to the authorities that we found something. They will be put into a no-win situation. Either they will pronounce it genuine and will have to take us seriously, or they will declare it a fake. If they do that, we will be free to sell it to the highest bidder on the open market.'

'But if it is declared false, who would buy it?' asked Becky, taking it from John's hands and examining it closely.

'Listen, the private collectors are no mugs. They will see this is the real thing and I reckon it is worth fifty grand plus. Either way, whatever the decision by the Cairo museum, we come out of it in front. What do you say?'

'I'm not sure,' said Becky, 'but I want to do some more research. We need to get out of Egypt as soon as possible and gather our thoughts in the safety of our own country. I've only been here three days and I want to get out of here already. For some reason, Egypt doesn't seem the warm welcoming place I have been used to.'

'I agree,' said John. 'Anyway, I'm going to go to my room. Tomorrow after breakfast, I'll make arrangements with my contacts to leave the country the way I came in. You get a flight as soon as you can, and I'll make contact with you back in London.'

'How long will you be?' asked Becky

'If all goes well; about ten days. Don't worry about me, I'll be fine.' He stood up and walked to the door. 'Try to get some sleep, Becky and don't have any nightmares about that mummy. I'm sure there is a perfectly good explanation.'

'I'm sure there is,' said Becky, 'Good night, John.'

'Good night, Becky,' said John and left the room, closing the door behind him.

Chapter Eight

Itjawi - 1245 BC
The Caverns of Sekhmet

Sekhmet had retreated once more into the shadows of the cavern to continue her story.

'I don't remember much of that time, Ramesses,' she said, 'but that night, I remember like it was yesterday. It was just before the wet season and my father had gone hunting with the other men. I remember that it was extremely hot, not just because of the temperature, but because I was ill, seriously ill. I had the sleeping sickness that plagued our people at that time of year. Many of us had it and it was usual to lose many children to the disease. Nobody knew what caused it, but my body was covered with the tiny bites from the flying insects that plagued us during that time. The sickness comes in waves, and if you survive it the first time, then you have a better chance of living. But I was not expected to survive; such was the extent of my illness. I remember my father kissing me goodbye before he left. He knew that I would probably be dead when he came back, but there were others to feed and he had no choice. My mother sang the song of the dead over my sweating body and burnt the bark of the smoke tree, hoping the fumes would chase out the evil spirits, but all knew that I would be dead by morning.'

'In the middle of the night, a hyena's cry broke the darkness and everyone knew that the gods of the dead had come to claim their latest victim. I was taken outside the thorns of our village boundary and despite my illness, I was fully aware of the fate that awaited me. The villagers formed a large half circle and illuminated the scene with burning torches. The drums started and the villagers chanted, summoning the bringer of death to accept their offering so other children may live. For an age, I lay in the dust, waiting for the death to arrive. Finally, through the darkness, I could see the light of the fire reflecting in its eyes. There was only one and he circled for an age, for hyena were wary of men even back then, but hunger has a way of making the weak strong and he soon entered the clearing. I knew I was about to die and closed my eyes to await my fate, but before he dragged me off, another hyena entered the clearing and challenged the first.'

'This had never been seen before, but as soon as it entered the torchlight, my people knew it was different. It was sick with the madness disease that sometimes afflicts the dogs of the village. The fur was hanging and bloody foam fell from its jaws. The eyes were wild and it attacked the other hyena with madness in its soul. The fight was terrible and the mad one killed the smaller one, but still the bloodlust was high, and it turned its attention on me. I still remember the way it half ran and half fell toward me, for it too was grievously wounded. Yet it had strength still to claim its last victim. As it neared, I could smell death upon its breath and stared in horror as the stinking juices from the sores around its gums ran down the huge teeth to drip onto the floor. I was too weak to scream, and as it sank its jaws into my side, I passed out in pain.'

'I know of this disease,' said Ramesses. 'When the dogs of the village suffer from it, they turn mad with rage, and all are killed by the men.'

'What happened next was told to me by my mother,' continued Sekhmet, 'for I had no recollection. The mad Hyena dragged me into the darkness but evidently, he had no strength left to finish his kill, for when the sun rose, the returning hunting party found the dead body of the animal in the bush. Alongside it was my body, and though I was weak from blood loss, I still lived. My father carried me back to the village and the people saw it as a miracle. Nobody had ever returned from the jaws of death and it was a sign. I was still ill from the sleeping illness and my wound from the hyena festered with pus and filth, yet they persevered, and ultimately, I recovered from both to take my place within the village.'

'But something was different. Deep inside I knew I had somehow changed. On the one hand, I felt strong and healthier than I could ever remember, but on the other side, I found that the sun gave me aches that I had never experienced before. I stayed out of the sun, preferring to walk about after it had set, when the nights were cool and the sky was dark. Also, I struggled to keep down my food and always begged my family to share whatever meat they could spare from their bowls. Eventually, I could not eat the berries or the seeds of the gatherings and sought out the bird's eggs and lizards of the undergrowth. Every opportunity I could I foraged for anything that walked, swam, or flew, scorning the cornmeal that was our main food. At first, my mother accepted my strange ways, as she was so happy to have me alive, but eventually, the whispers of the village reached her ears and she started to see me as they did. It was said that I had been infected by the hyena and was taking on its human form. At first, my mother chased away the whisperers with a stick and even when one night she caught me crouched over the body of a village dog, eating its raw flesh, she covered for me. I told her that I had found it dead, but when she saw my knife and the way I had slit its throat, she knew that there was something seriously wrong. Finally, on the night of the fruit festival, I did something so awful that not even a mother's love could protect me from the wrath of the village.'

'What did you do?' asked Ramesses.

'You have to understand, Ramesses, I cannot even begin to describe the hunger this state brings. It envelops every cell of your very being and nothing else exists except the need to drink blood. I was living on frogs, birds and rats. Anything with a beating heart, I targeted, and I killed more than a few dogs to satisfy my needs. Finally, I committed the ultimate crime.' Sekhmet's voice lowered and took on a husky tone. 'I couldn't help it, Ramesses; I was drawn to her like a snake smells out its prey. The whimpers in the darkest hour were enticing me toward where she lay and I knew the villagers were lost in the sleep of the drunk after the festival. It was too easy, and when I entered the hut with no challenge, there was no stopping me. There she was, lying on the bed skins alongside her mother, and I could actually hear her heart beating. Each thump followed by the rush of blood as it poured through her tiny veins.'

'You could hear the blood flowing?' asked Ramesses in astonishment.

'As loud as if it was a river,' said Sekhmet, 'and I knew that nothing would stop me from tasting that young, fresh liquid. I picked up the baby and ran into the night.'

'I won't bore you with the details, Ramesses,' she said after a while, 'but suffice to say, they chased me from the village. In fact they hunted me for days, determined to cast my body from the highest cliffs as a witch, but I was too quick for them. Fleet of foot, I travelled by night and ran unhindered through the darkness. I could see as if it was the brightest day, and for the first time in my life, I felt so alive. By day, I hid in the darkest recesses I could find. I found clefts in the rocks, hollow logs, or even crawled under the rotten leaves on the forest floors. The insects that shared my hiding places no longer held any fear for me. In fact, their scurrying bodies sustained me, when food was scarce. But it was never scarce for long. I learned to avoid the predators and exist alongside the villages throughout the land. It would only be a matter of time before a cow was left alone, or a dog was enticed by my friendly call and both were used as a food source. I learned quickly and where possible, I would just nick the vein of a cow to drink directly without causing harm. That way I could stay in one place for a long time without being found out, but always my need for human blood would let me down. That was my weakness and I lost count of the times I was driven away from villages as a devil.'

'You were still a girl,' said Ramesses, 'How did you survive?'

'I don't know, Ramesses. Perhaps predators recognize other predators and stay away. I fed on everything from insects to humans. I learned how to walk in the shadows without making a noise and to kill ruthlessly and efficiently. For years I wandered the landscape and I became known as a demon. Eventually people stopped reviling me and started to revere me as a vengeful goddess. Sacrifices were left out to appease me, usually animals, but occasionally, humans as well. The condemned, the ill, and the old were often staked out in the dark as an offering. I repaid their homage by leaving their children alone and soon I was an accepted part of their lives. Nobody knew what I looked like, for those unfortunate to see me close up, usually died within seconds.'

'Over time I grew strong and fast. I knew no fear and revelled in my status as goddess to these people. I lost track of time and before I knew it, my body had matured. I had seen civilizations come and go and had travelled across lands from ocean to ocean. It was during this time I found out another gift that I had, and that was the ability to bestow eternal life on other humans.'

Ramesses unconsciously sat up, fascinated by the tale. This was what he had come to find out, how to become immortal.

'How?' he asked, 'what is the process required to bestow this gift.'

'You see it as a gift, Ramesses?' asked Sekhmet with scorn in her voice. 'For I see it as a curse. If indeed you were to become as I, what sort of king would you be? You would have to live in the dark, feeding on nothing but blood, unable to walk your kingdom. How would you achieve the great things you aspire to then, Ramesses? How could you be the greatest king that ever lived, when you would be no more than a prince of darkness?'

'I see the burden, Sekhmet,' said Ramesses, 'and I accept that it may not be the right path. At least; not yet.'

'And when would the time be right, Ramesses?' asked Sekhmet.

'When age creeps upon me like a predator,' said Ramesses. 'During the days of my life, I could build my kingdom with you in the background and when the sleep of eternity is close, you could then bestow your gift upon me, extending my rule by thousands of years.'

'Your ambition knows no bounds, Ramesses,' she said.

'I will be the greatest king this land has ever seen,' said Ramesses. 'That is written. Your gift will enable me to become the greatest of all time, so tell me, Sekhmet, what is this gift?'

'Over the years, I noticed changes in my body,' said Sekhmet. 'When I hunted it was usually to feed, but as I became more powerful, any compassion I once held, fled my body forever. I revelled in my power and often hunted just for the thrill. Many nights I killed indiscriminately, and I often slew dozens in one night. I held no fear and no man would stand against me. I was all-powerful, but there was still a trace of one emotion, floundering in a sea of evil. Since my time as a child I had talked to no person, except to announce their imminent death.'

'You were lonely?' guessed Ramesses.

'I was,' said Sekhmet, 'then one night something happened that changed all that.

'What happened?'

'I had killed early and fed well. The drained corpse was discarded in the river and the crocodiles would ensure that all signs would be gone by morning. Despite this, when a young woman wandered past my resting place near a waterfall, I couldn't help myself. I grabbed her and dragged her to my lair. She pleaded with me for her life and as I sank my teeth into a throat, I paused and stopped myself from tearing the flesh wide open. Instead, I sucked gently at the flow, drinking of her blood, yet allowing my own juices to flow into the wound. I don't know how I had the restraint to do that, as the tearing open of the throat is not just the quickest way of making a kill, but it also gives the greatest pleasure. Yet that is what happened. As that rabid hyena's juices had flowed into my body as a child, mine flowed into that of my victim. She passed out and was unconscious for days. I watched her writhe as the pains wracked her body, and left her only to hunt. Finally she pulled out of her torment and looked up at me with hunger in her eyes and I knew immediately that she had changed.'

'What did you do?'

'I cut the throat of a rat and held it to her mouth. At first she lapped at it like a puppy, but soon grabbed it from me and tore into it as if it was the finest meal she had ever tasted.'

'She was as you?'

'She was. Over the next few nights, I hunted for her as her strength returned and we talked through the night. At first she rebelled and tried to run, but I tied her there, and over time, saw her eyes take on the blackness of the blood she so readily devoured. She begged to be allowed to go back to her people, but soon realized that the sun burned at her eyes. Finally I let her go and she ran into the darkness. Three days she was gone, until one night I heard her approaching. She stood before me, begging me to find her blood to drink. I opened one of my own veins in my arm and she drank as if was the best thing in this life. From that moment I knew she was mine and I taught her the skills needed to survive.'

'What was her name?' asked Ramesses

'She was known as Mukarramma,' said Sekhmet.

'And was she immortal?' asked Ramesses.

'It turned out she was,' said Sekhmet, 'and she hunted alongside me for many years. Together we terrorized the lands and children had nightmares in their beds, dreaming of the spirits that stole them away in the dead of night. We never stayed in one place too long, but moved from country to country, feeling no discomfort from the weather, except of course, the ravages of the sun, for that luxury was denied us.'

'Will you die in the sun's embrace?' asked Ramesses

'No, but the pain it causes is excruciating and we weaken to the point of collapse. Left in its glare, we would be helpless to defend ourselves and be reduced to uselessness. At that point, we are at our weakest. I have no idea why, but it is a burden that comes with the gift.'

'So you live only during the hours of darkness?'

'Usually, yes. We can spend short times in the sun or stay in the shadows, but it is far easier if we make the night our realm.'

'So where is Mukarramma now?' asked Ramesses

'She is dead,' said Sekhmet.

'I thought you said your kind couldn't die.'

'Her body no longer has form and her soul wanders without substance. To the likes of you, that is death.'

'How do you know she is dead?'

'Because I killed her.'

'Why?' asked Ramesses.

'For an age, we were as one. Hunting together by day and laying up at night. We were always on the move, but eventually we found somewhere where we were welcomed. We found a city who embraced our needs and we were feted as gods. That had happened to me before, but the interest soon wanes. I would rather hunt prey that fears the outcome, than feed on tethered humans offered as sacrifice. The chase makes the blood race through my veins and I feel as if I am once more as alive as those who live in the sun. Where is the fun in killing the weak, the old, and the sick?'

'So you moved on?'

'I did, but Mukarramma stayed. She embraced their worship and installed herself as ruler of that place, accepting the sacrifices they offered.'

'What did you do?'

'I left her to it and wandered as I had for generations. But one day I had cause to go past that place again and what I found raised a fury such as I had never known. Over the years, she had made others such as us and the city was overrun by our kind. The surrounding lands were devoid of animal life and every human was either dead or tethered as a food source.'

'And why did this raise your ire?' asked Ramesses.

'For over a thousand years, I was unique, Ramesses. Kings spoke my name in awe, and though I hunted their finest, they knew my wrath would move on and the people were allowed to return to normal until I passed their way again. I was a demon, a spirit of the night that could never be caught. When Mukarramma cheapened our existence, I knew the mystery of our species would be laid open to the world. Kings fearing our expansion would send armies against us and discover the means by which we can die. Even if they were unsuccessful and our numbers became too many to overcome, there could only ever be one outcome, the end of our race.'

'How?'

'Humans provide our sustenance, Ramesses. What shepherd kills all his flock in one season? The way Mukarramma was propagating our kind was unsustainable.'

'So what did you do?'

'I sought them out,' said Sekhmet, 'and killed them all.'

'Every one?'

'Every one. I ripped open their throats and threw the remains into the flames. The screams of their damned souls still echo in my thoughts.'

'And Mukarramma?'

'She fled, but I followed her across three countries, until I cornered her in these lands. She fell to her knees and begged for her life; for us to carry on as we had before, hunting side by side as sisters.'

'So what did you do?'

'I ripped out her heart with my bare hands and fed her body to the crocodiles.'

Ramesses fell quiet for a long time as the information sunk in.

'You are shocked?' asked Sekhmet.

'Confused,' said Ramesses. 'You say you slew those who Mukarramma had made in your image, yet even here in these caverns I see other such as you. What is so different?'

'The difference is, I decide, Ramesses,' said Sekhmet. 'My sisters exist at my whim. If I tire of them, then I destroy them. Not since Mukarramma have I allowed myself to get close to another. My rule is absolute and they exist only as long as I allow them to. Look at my body, Ramesses. Even your untrained eye can see that it approaches the time where it cannot move as it once did. It may be thousands of years, Ramesses, but I am now growing old and I need the sisters to hunt for me. Every night they scour the villages of the poor to bring me the sustenance I need. Yet the time is coming when even they will see my weakness and I have no doubt that one will seize their chance to replace me.'

'So why don't you do to them as you did to Mukarramma's followers?'

'Look at me, Ramesses, my time is done. It is time to step aside to allow a worthy replacement to replace my kind at the top of the food chain.'

'And is there such a one?' asked Ramesses.

Sekhmet remained silent.

Understanding dawned in Ramesses' eyes and he glanced toward the doorway where the young girl had exited the room earlier.

'It's her isn't it?' he said. 'You intend to make Nephthys your successor.'

'She is worthy,' said Sekhmet, quietly, 'and will make a truly great immortal.'

Ramesses sat back and stared at Sekhmet, his mind racing.

'But there is another option, Sekhmet,' he said. 'Make me your successor and I will ensure your name is venerated in every corner of this land.'

'I can't do that, Ramesses,' she said.

'Why not?' asked Ramesses, 'I am already the greatest king this land has ever seen. Who greater to carry on your species?'

'You do not understand, Ramesses,' she said. 'Even if I agree with you, it is impossible.''

'Why, Sekhmet? What stays your arm in this matter?'

Sekhmet motioned with her hand and a row of men similar to the one who had brought the chair shuffled into the room. Each was tethered to the other by the throat and their bodies were covered with suppurating sores. Their heads hung low and they stood in silence, seemingly unaware of anyone else's presence.

'Approach, Ramesses,' said Sekhmet, 'and take a closer look. Lift up their heads and look deep into their eyes.'

Ramesses did as he was bid and yanked back the head of the nearest man. What he saw made him gasp in disgust. The eyes were jet black, similar to those of Sekhmet and a sign of those who lived on the blood of man. He lifted several more heads and saw each bore the same signs. No life or spark of awareness reflected back from those dead pools, just a blank stare of nothingness.

'I don't understand,' said Ramesses. 'They have obviously been taken by you or the sisters, yet they lack life. What is this devilment you show me?'

'The final twist of this curse you call a gift, Ramesses. Throughout my existence, I have many times taken men and bestowed my eternal blood into their veins. I followed the same process each time, keen to enjoy male companionship for my endless journey, but always they turn out so. Yes, they have immortality, but immortality does not necessarily mean life. This is the male version of the gift, Ramesses. If I was to grant you your wish and hold you to my chest as my teeth rake your veins, then this fate awaits you. They are dead, yet they are undead, Ramesses. They do not live, yet they live forever. True immortality is a gift for woman only.'

Ramesses staggered back in shock and fought the anger rising in his chest.

'No, this can't be true,' he said. 'There must be a way. Am I not a living God? I am Ramesses the second, greatest king that ever ruled Kemet. I deserve immortality, it is written. Grant me my destiny Sekhmet, I command you.'

'If this is the immortality you crave, Ramesses, then step into my embrace for this is the only kind I bestow on man.'

'You knew this, Sekhmet,' he snarled eventually, 'all this time you lied to me about being able to grant me immortality.'

'I never lied, Ramesses, you chose to believe what you wanted to believe. I deal only in truth and the destiny of men. Isn't it appropriate that only those who deliver life into the world can enjoy life everlasting? Man is fleeting, Ramesses, woman is immortal.'

Chapter Nine

London 2012

Becky Ryan sat in her office in the depths of the British Antiquities museum and looked at the phone for what seemed like the hundredth time that day. It had been two weeks since she had returned from Egypt, and the last call she had received from John was eight days previously, when he called from the Libyan border. The country was still in a state of turmoil after the recent uprising and Becky worried that he had been caught up in the unrest. Whatever the reason, she should have heard from him by now and she was getting worried.

'You okay, Becky?' asked Amy, bringing her yet another cup of tea.

'Yeah,' she sighed. 'It's just that I was expecting a call days ago and he still hasn't called.'

'Oh,' said Amy, 'man trouble. I should have known.'

'Not that sort of man trouble,' said Becky.

'What's his name?' asked Amy.

'John. I worked with him in Egypt for a while. He said he was going to call when he got back.'

'Holiday romances are never a good idea,' said Amy in a patronizing tone.

'Amy,' said Becky, 'there was no romance, it was all purely work.'

'I don't believe you,' said Amy.

'I don't care what you believe,' said Becky with a smile, 'it is a purely business relationship.'

'Is he married?' asked Amy sipping her own tea.

'I don't know,' laughed Becky, 'now stop this interrogation and get back to work.'

The afternoon dragged on and both women continued with the more boring side to their jobs. Amy was filing documents and typing up notes, while Becky undertook the research her role demanded. Finally, the end of the working day drew closer and Becky allowed Amy to leave early. After her aide left, Becky was deep into a reference book about Roman gravestones, when the shrill ring of the phone almost made her jump out of her seat. She reached for it, hoping it was John, but was disappointed to hear the voice of Andrew Montague, the head curator of the Museum.

'Hello, Becky,' he said, 'glad I caught you, could you pop up to the Egyptian display please.'

'Of course, Andrew,' she said, 'I'm all done here for today anyway, I'll come up straight away.' She turned off all the electrics and made her way up through the various halls to the Egyptian galleries. This part of the museum was closed to the public, due to the display being altered. Becky knew that this often happened throughout the museum as due to the extraordinary amount of artefacts they had in store, they had to rotate them as much as possible. Even then, they had so many artefacts; there were huge amounts that had not been seen by the public for decades. Becky unlocked the door with her pass card and entered the enormous hall.

The exhibit, even in its transient state, had an immediate effect on her as it always did. The staff had gone out of their way to make this exhibition feel as authentic as possible and though it was frowned on by academics, the public loved it. The walls had been decorated with accurate depictions of hieroglyphics and giant blocks of wood, plastic and polystyrene had been cleverly worked to resemble ancient blocks of granite to add to the atmosphere. Cleverly placed images of Egyptian gods, peered down out of subtly lit crevasses, accompanied by suitably spooky music. The overall effect was that you were walking through a corridor in some ancient tomb, with each display covering the history of Egypt over two thousand years. Although the display was fantastic, it was the actual exhibits that always took her breath away. The real statues and the actual coffins of people who lived all that time ago. These were the things that mattered, and though she knew that most of the things had been acquired by less than honest means over the past two centuries, she couldn't help feeling a sense of excitement and pride every time she went there.

This first part of the exhibit was designed to instil a sense of awe in all the visitors and it certainly succeeded in that aspect, but as you exited the other side of the fake tunnel system, people were immediately confronted with something that Becky thought dwarfed the previous exhibit, not only in size, but also in wonder. It was a statue of arguably the greatest king there had ever been throughout the history of Egypt, Ramesses the second. The statue stood over thirty foot tall and weighed over two hundred tones, but Becky knew that despite its enormous size, throughout Egypt there were far greater statues of this king, much grander and much, much bigger. Ramesses had spent much of his life building grand projects dedicated to himself and as he had lived to a ripe old age of ninety years, he had the time to make a massive impact across his country. Becky never failed to be amazed by this statue, and always paused to look up at the king before she proceeded into the more detailed section of the displays.

The statue of Ramesses stared serenely toward the back of the room. The head was covered with the Nemes headdress, the striped folded cloth falling down past the shoulders that was so Iconic of pharaohs throughout history. In turn, this was held in place with a headband in the shape of a rearing cobra with flared hood, itself a symbol of protection to the royal families. Becky knew that the Egyptians believed that the cobra, or Uraeus, as it was known, was also a representation of the goddess Wadjet, thought to guide the spirits of dead pharaohs through the underworld. The statue's arms were crossed and each held a symbol of the king's authority. In one he carried a crook and in the other a flail, emblems of Osiris and represented the virtues of the good shepherd. He exuded authority, age and serenity, and Becky absolutely loved it.

She continued into the back of the halls where it was much brighter and there was a maze of glass cabinets displaying a plethora of smaller artefacts. Toward one side, she could see Andrew Montague with several staff unpacking the exhibits that Becky had arranged to send up earlier.

'Hello, Andrew,' she said.

'Oh, hello, Becky,' he answered. 'Thanks for popping in, what do you think?'

'Looks fantastic, as always,' she said.

'Thanks,' said Andrew. He took her to one side and spoke quietly.

'Look,' he said, 'it's been very busy around here recently and I know it's no excuse, but I've been meaning to try and find a few minutes to offer my condolences about your dad.'

'That's okay,' said Becky, 'I know you've only just come back from a field trip.'

'Nevertheless,' said Andrew, 'I knew your dad well. In fact, we worked together in the Cairo Museum for a couple of weeks a few months ago, collating some loan items for this display, and I don't for one second believe that claptrap that people are whispering.'

'What claptrap?'

'You know; the nonsense about an illegal dig.'

'Oh, that's getting out is it?' she asked, 'Oh well, I suppose it had to emerge one day.'

'We're a small community,' said Andrew. 'Nothing is kept secret for long. Anyway, if there's anything you need, just let me know.'

'Thanks,' said Becky.

'So,' said Andrew with an upturn in his voice, 'now that's done, I thought there was something you could do for me that might cheer you up.'

'What's that?'

'This display cabinet over here,' he said, 'the top shelf looks a little empty and I want something to represent Egypt through the ages. I thought it may be nice if we displayed the Ushabti your father organized for me.'

'Really?' asked Becky.

'Yes,' said Andrew, 'I thought it may be a nice gesture.'

'He would have liked that,' said Becky. 'Thank you.'

'No problem,' said Andrew, 'you bring them up sometime tomorrow and I'll arrange to have them displayed.'

'Thanks, Andrew,' she said. 'Good night.'

'Good night,' Becky, 'See you tomorrow.'

Across London, Amy shut the front door of her house a little too hard and walked out into the kitchen.

'Is that you, Amy?' called a voice.

'Yes, mum,' she answered with an air of resignation. She walked to the fridge and grabbed some sliced chicken to make a sandwich. A few seconds later, her mother came into the kitchen.

'Don't go stuffing yourself, Amy,' she said, 'I'm cooking dinner soon.'

'Dinner?' answered Amy, 'why, who's birthday is it?'

'Don't be sarcastic,' said her mother, 'I told you last week, one of your father's writing friends is over on holiday from Germany and your father has invited him for dinner. You may have heard of him, Lucas Klein?'

'Never heard of him,' said Amy. 'Do I really have to come?'

'Yes you do,' said her mum. 'It's not often we sit and eat together, and this man is a published author. He may be able to help your dad with his writing, perhaps even put him in touch with an agent.'

'Yeah, like that's going to happen,' said Amy. 'I can't believe my own father is writing romantic comedy.'

'Well, apparently that's what sells, Amy. That's his hobby and we should support him.'

'But, mum,' whined Amy.

'No arguing,' said her mother, 'I've made my decision. You go, have a bath, and wipe some of that muck off your face. I want us to make a good impression for your father. Dinner is at eight, but I want you down here at seven thirty to meet Mr Klein.

Amy finished her sandwich and stomped up the stairs to display her disgust.

'Right,' said her mother to herself, 'let's make a start.'

Upstairs, Amy switched on her computer. Within a minute she was scrolling down her social networking page. A few minutes later, a chat box popped up in the bottom right corner of her screen and two words appeared alongside a picture of a young man in full vampire make up.

'*Hi, Amy,*' it said

Amy smiled and typed her reply

'*Hi Scott, how are you?*'

Scott was one of Amy's best friends online and despite having never met; they spent almost every night talking. Scott lived in America and they had met through another group, made up of vampire fans.

'*I'm fine,*' said Scott, '*just finished work?*'

'*Yes,*' said Amy, '*just got home.*'

'*It must be fantastic working in a museum,*' typed Scott, '*so atmospheric.*'

'*It is sometimes,*' answered Amy, '*but mostly it's boring.*'

There was a pause in the messages before Scott typed again.

'*So, what are you doing tonight?*' he asked, '*off out with your mates*'

'*No, I can't tonight. I've got to have stupid dinner with family and one of dad's friends.*'

'*Sounds boring,*' said Scott.

'*Yeah, tell me about it. Apparently, he is some poncey author from Germany,*'

'*Really?*' typed Scott, '*I wonder if he's rich and famous. Perhaps you can get an autograph and sell it on E bay.*'

'*I wish*', typed Becky, '*I've never heard of him.*'

'*What's his name?*'

'*Lucas Klein,*' typed Amy.

Again, the screen went dead before Scott answered again.

'*Are you sure?*' he typed.

'*Yes; why?*'

'*Hang on.*'

The screen went dead again before Amy saw the message "*Scott is typing*" once more.

'*Amy; you there?*'

'*Yeah, still here.*'

'*OMG, Amy, you know who Lucas Klein is don't you?*'

'*No!*'

'*Only the bloody illustrator of the Vampire histories.*'

'*You are joking?*' typed Amy

'*No, I'm not, take a look for yourself.*'

Amy left the computer and searched under her bed, finally coming up with a large illustrated volume of short stories called the Vampire histories. Throughout the book were graphic images of various vampires doing what vampires do best, and at the bottom of each picture was the name Lucas Klein. Becky went back to the screen.

'*OMG,*' she typed,' *you're right. These pictures are awesome and this guy is going to be right here in my house tonight.*'

'*You are so lucky,*' typed Scott. '*Ask him to sign your book.*'

'*I will,*' said Amy.

'Amy,' shouted her mother from downstairs, 'have you run your bath yet?'

'Not yet,' she answered. 'Why?'

'I'm out of onions,' answered her mother. 'Could you nip down the shops, please?'

'Just a minute,' answered Amy and typed once more.

'*Gotta go,*' she typed, '*I'll message you tonight and tell you how it went. Bye.*'

'*Bye, Amy,*' typed Scott and the screen went blank.

Two hours later, Amy heard her parents greeting their visitor downstairs and she put on the last of her makeup. Her mother had brought up a nice plain dress for her, but Amy had other ideas. With a deep breath, she ran her hands down her sides and looked into the full-length mirror. Gone were the loose fitting folds of black that totally swamped her slim figure, replaced with a slim line version, which hugged all her curves in the right places. Admittedly it was black but at least she had discarded the army boots and replaced them with a stylish pair of high-heeled shoes. Her hair was straightened and fell over one shoulder while a red rose over her ear matched perfectly the ruby red necklace draped around her neck. The overall effect was very sophisticated and while she had foregone her usual obsession with black makeup, the subtle dark colours she had used, still gave the impression of moodiness, albeit tinged with style. Satisfied with the look, she made her way downstairs and walked nonchalantly into the lounge.

Her mother was taking the coat of a tall young man, no older than twenty-five years old. He was dressed in a pair of black trousers, a white pressed shirt, and a smart grey jacket. His hair was slightly unkempt and he brushed the fingers of one hand through it to try to sort it out. Overall, Amy was very impressed and found herself blushing slightly as he caught her eye.

'Hello, dear,' said her mother, 'you look nice. This is Mr Klein, your father's friend. Mr Klein, this is Amy, our daughter.'

'Hello, Amy,' said the man; his words clear despite the German accent, 'please call me Lucas.' He held out his hand and shook hers gently.

'Hello, Lucas,' said Amy. 'Pleased to meet you; I am a great admirer of your work.'

'Really?' interrupted her mother, 'you've read some of his books?'

'I can't say I have,' said Amy, 'but I have seen some of his illustrations. They are lovely, so atmospheric.'

'Ah, I take it you are talking about the Vampire histories,' said Lucas.

'Oh, I should have known,' said her mother with a smile, 'vampires. I do not know what it is with teenage girls these days. They all seem obsessed with them. And not even proper ones either, these days they seem to be good guys and sparkle in the moonlight. Give me Christopher Lee any day.'

'It's a very popular genre, at the moment,' said Lucas. 'Everyone seems to be either writing vampire books or making vampire films. There are even whole organizations dedicated to the study of them.'

'Study of what?' asked Amy's father coming in from the kitchen with a tray of glasses.

'Vampires,' said her mother. 'Lucas was just saying they are extremely popular at the moment.'

'Oh, not that nonsense again,' said her father. 'No offense, Lucas, I know you write books in that genre and have done some illustrations, but I have no time for them, myself.'

'Dad prefers sloppy romance books,' said Amy reaching for her glass.

'I know,' said Lucas, 'we share the same editor. So, how is the writing going, Ben?'

'Okay,' said Amy's father, 'I have the final edit and just need to make a decision about which way to go.'

Amy lost interest as the conversation drifted toward writing, as it always did when any of her fathers' writing friends came around. She walked out of the kitchen, and leaned against the worktop, watching her mother finish the preparations for dinner.

'He's a bit nice, isn't he?' said Amy.

'Who Lucas? I suppose so.'

'How old do you think he is?' asked Amy.

'Too old for you, dear,' laughed her mother, 'so get those thoughts out of your mind.'

'I'm sure, I don't know what you mean,' said Amy, making a show of examining her own fingernails at arm's length.

'Oh, Amy,' said her mother, 'you look so nice and you've gone and spoiled it with that black nail varnish.'

'I think it looks lovely,' said Amy, 'anyway, as long as Lucas likes it, who cares?'

'Amy,' laughed her mother, 'now, stop it. Come on, you can help me lay the table.'

The next few hours went by far too quickly for Amy, as though she usually found this sort of evening boring, the combination of Lucas's charming personality, his lovely accent and of course, his boyish good looks made her glad that her mother had insisted she attend. Eventually, they all sat in the lounge, the men sipping brandy, while Amy and her mother finished off the wine.

Conversation focused on the state of the publishing industry and again Amy was getting bored until unexpectedly, it once again turned to her favourite subject, Vampires.

'Of course, you do know they actually existed?' said Lucas.

'Poppycock,' laughed Amy's father.

'It's true,' said Lucas, 'I don't mean the Hollywood versions or even the sort that Bram Stoker wrote about. No, I'm on about the ones that countless cultures from around the world have believed in since records began.'

'Really? I thought that all the stories came from the time of Vlad the Impaler.'

'It's true that Stoker got the name for his character from that era,' said Lucas, 'but the belief in vampires, as we now call them, existed long before that.'

'How interesting,' said Amy's mum.

'Yes, they were even known in cultures as diverse as the Greeks and the Romans. I'm not saying they had fangs and drank the blood of young maidens, but it seems that in all cultures there seems to be some sort of monster or demon who rises from the dead to kill the living and drink their blood. It's quite an easy tale to conjure up, really,' he continued, 'If you think about it logically, it preys on some of humanity's greatest fears. The raising of the dead, the drinking of blood, and a demon you can't kill, it's all perfect to frighten any civilization. Even today, with all our scientific knowledge and the amazing technology we have, there are still people who not only believe in them, but actually indulge in vampire like activities.'

'Surely not,' gasped Amy's mum.

'Oh yes. Like I said there are hundreds of different groups who run around dressing like their favourite vampire character or join social network groups, that sort of thing.'

'Yes, but we did that sort of thing as teenagers,' said Amy's father, 'though with us it was punk rock.'

'I agree,' said Lucas, 'but the people who I am talking about, go much, much further. Some of them even drink human blood as part of secret ceremonies. Nothing to do with killing people, I hasten to add. At least, I hope not, but they have their own little ceremonial traditions that you have to undergo to join their gang, so to speak.'

'You're not serious?' asked Amy's mother.

'I sure am,' said Lucas. 'I even joined one once in the name of research. Very interesting too, but when the self-styled vampire queen, a seedy stripper from Hamburg, if I recall correctly, cut her thumb with a knife and ordered me to drink her blood, I legged it.'

'No, seriously,' said Lucas when they had stopped laughing. 'There are discoveries being made even today, proving that the belief in vampires was rife throughout history. Graves have been found in Ireland, where the bodies had been decapitated, and the head placed between the corpse's knees, a typical method of immobilizing a vampire in that culture. Other graves have been found on the continent where the bodies had been weighed down with giant boulders, before being buried, in the hope that they wouldn't be able to rise again.'

'But it's absurd,' said Amy's father. 'How could they believe all that stuff?'

'Don't forget, people were very superstitious and believed in all sorts of things.' He leaned forward to emphasize his point, 'Imagine that you lived five hundred years ago in Eastern Europe and a young woman died and was buried in a coffin as you would expect. However, a few days later, something happened to make the villagers exhume her, and you found that not only did she seem just to be sleeping, but also she appeared to be well nourished, had grown a set of long teeth and there are stains around her mouth where she appears to have been drinking blood. Not only this, but when a stake is driven into her corpse to make sure she is dead, she groans as if in pain. Think what impact that would have made on simple superstitious villagers.'

'But surely that's all just rumour and hearsay?' said Amy's dad. 'Stories passed down from generation to generation and exaggerated as they went.'

'No,' said Lucas, 'there are actual documents from that time recording exactly those circumstances. Obviously all those symptoms can now be explained by science, but still.'

'How can they be explained?' asked Amy, transfixed by the depth of knowledge shared by this gorgeous man.

'Well, when a body dies, Amy, there are still all sorts of chemical reactions going on, and along with the gases given off by the decomposing process, they can combine to give skin a ruddy complexion. Bodily fluids can bubble up to escape through the mouth, and as one of the first parts of the body to decompose is the soft tissue around the lips and gums, the process can exaggerate the size of the teeth. As far as crying out when speared by some implement is concerned, well that's just an escape of gases built up in the body due to the decomposition process. It's even thought that gas escaping past the larynx in a corpse, makes a sound similar to groaning. Imagine how all that must have looked to the superstitious folk of back then.'

'They must have been terrified, 'said Amy's mother. 'Poor devils.'

Amy stared at her mother in disbelief at the understatement and they all burst out laughing.

'Anyway,' said Lucas, 'the point is, I don't think you should be too harsh on Amy, as there are millions of people out there just as fascinated by the tales of the undead, and I am proud to be called one of them.'

Amy was thrilled with the support from this strange man, and she was very disappointed when the time came for him to go. After he had gone, the family sat back in the lounge drinking coffee.

'Well, that was nice,' said Amy's mum. 'Was it what you expected dear?'

'Not really,' said Amy's dad. 'He was a lot younger than I expected and seemed a bit too focused on all that vampire stuff for my liking. Still, he gave me the number of his agent and promised he would put a good word in for me, so that's good.'

'I thought he was brilliant,' said Amy, blowing over the surface of her coffee.

'Yes, we noticed,' said her mum, 'you didn't take your eyes off him all night.'

'Don't be silly,' said Amy.

'She's right,' said her dad. 'It was a bit awkward at times to be honest, but still; I don't suppose we'll see him again. Right, that's me done, I'm off to bed. I have an early start tomorrow.'

'Hang on;' said her mother, 'I'll come up with you. The dishes can wait until tomorrow. Amy, would you lock the doors before you go to bed, dear?'

'Okay,' said Amy, and continued to sip her coffee as her parents went up the stairs. A few seconds later, she took out a small card from her pocket and her heart raced as she read it properly for the first time. It was a very simple card, with just a name on one side and a phone number on the other. She memorized the number and then turned the card over to read the name, Lucas Klein, and a thrill ran up her spine as she remembered the way he had secretively passed it to her under the table at dinner.

Amy locked the doors and made her way up to bed, knowing full well that she wasn't going to get much sleep that night.

Chapter Ten

London 2012

The rain was falling quite hard as the taxi pulled up outside a set of wrought iron gates in the Kent countryside. The driver looked over his shoulder to speak to his foreign looking passenger.

'Here we go,' he said. 'Sorry about the run-around, but it's the first time I've been out here and the Sat-Nav is knackered.'

The passenger glanced up at the meter. Seventy-seven pounds, it said, and although he couldn't prove it, he had an inkling that the driver had taken advantage of his passenger's ignorance to make the journey longer. He hated England and hadn't been here for many years. It seemed that every time he came, it was raining.

'Are you sure this is the place?' he asked.

'Mulberry Lodge,' said the driver, 'that's what it says on the gate.'

'Can we go in?'

'The gates are locked; hang on, there's an intercom. I'll see if they'll open up.' He wound down the window and leaned out to press the button on the post alongside the driver's door.

'Hello, Mulberry lodge,' said a distant voice.

'Yeah, hello,' said the driver, 'I'm in a taxi and I've got a passenger who wants to come in.'

'What's the passenger's name?' asked the voice.

The driver turned around and spoke to his passenger.

'They want to know your name,' he said, and when he had the answer, he leaned out again and pressed the button. 'The passengers name is Samari,' he said, 'Doctor Samari.'

'Okay, come on in,' said the voice and the electronic gates swung open gracefully before them.

Ten minutes later, Doctor Samari was standing in the sumptuous entrance of a grand manor house, situated at the end of a long, tree-flanked driveway. He placed his suitcase against the desk and waited politely as the receptionist finished a call. Eventually, she looked up and beamed a winning smile at him.

'Hello,' she said, 'you must be Doctor Samari, welcome to Great Britain.'

'Thank you,' he said, 'I believe I am expected.'

'You are,' she said, 'and everything is ready for you. We have given you a lovely room in the west wing, overlooking the gardens. It is a private wing, so you shouldn't be disturbed by any of the guests.'

'Guests?'

'Yes, we call them guests, their families prefer that. And to be honest, when you are paying as much as they are, then they are entitled to be called whatever they like.'

'I'm sorry,' said Samari, 'I don't understand.'

'Oh, I'm sorry,' said the receptionist, 'I thought you would have been informed. Mulberry lodge is an exclusive retreat for the elderly and the infirm. The only difference is that these are the families of the rich and the famous. They get to see out their days in the best surroundings money can buy and receive the best medical treatment in the world. I assumed that, because of your title, you were coming to work here.'

Samari thought quickly before answering.

'That may be the case,' he said, 'but this is a fact finding visit. Anyway, it's been a long journey and I am very tired, so could someone show me to my room?'

'Of course, Dr Samari,' she said, 'I'll get someone straight away. Oh, one more thing, I have a message from Mr Leatherman. He said that he's running late, but he will be in touch as soon as possible.'

'Thank you,' said Samari, and taking the key, followed the porter to the far staircase.

Fifty miles away, Becky was at home preparing dinner. John had finally turned up a few weeks earlier, and they had both spent the day together wandering around various antiques shops and museums, enjoying a relatively stress free day. It had been three months since their adventure in Egypt and they had spent a lot of time since, asking discreet questions about any new finds discovered in Egypt. But apart from those that were well known throughout the science world, nothing had emerged out of the ordinary. Gradually, John's interest in what had happened waned and Becky knew that if she approached the authorities, they would have asked too many questions. Just the fact that she had taken part in an illegal dig could cost her career. Subsequently, she had stopped asking questions and although it hurt, Becky knew that her father would have preferred it that way.

Back in her sitting room, the phone rang and she hurried in, wiping her hands on a tea cloth as she went.

'Hello;' she said, 'Becky Ryan.'

'Hi, Becky' said a voice, 'it's Amy. Sorry to bother you, but something has happened at the museum and I thought you should know before you come back in tomorrow.'

'What's happened?' she asked, intrigued at the concern in Amy's voice.

'Becks, you know that set of twelve Ushabti that we placed on display a couple of months ago?'

'Yes, what about them?'

95

'Well, we had a visitor to the museum today, and he made a complaint about the authenticity.'

'Why?' asked Becky. 'We know they are genuine, they came from the Cairo museum. In fact, both my father and Montague authenticated them in Cairo. There's no way they can be false.'

'Look,' said Amy, 'that may be the case, but all I know is that Montague is furious and he wants you in his office first thing in the morning.'

'Shit,' said Becky as the seriousness of the situation sank in. 'Okay, Amy, thanks for letting me know. I'll see you in the morning.'

'Bye, Becky,' said Amy and the phone went dead.

The following morning, Becky was at the museum early. She had had a restless night, and although she was sure there had been a mistake, Montague was well known for his short temper. If she had made a mistake, the very least she could expect was a severe dressing down. The security guard let her in and she swiped her card at the reader before making a way across the hall toward the staff stairs that led down to the vaults. As she approached the door, a voice echoed around the large marble chamber.

'Miss Ryan,' boomed Montague's voice.

'Shit,' mumbled Becky to herself, she had been hoping get some answers before facing the curator. She looked up toward the domed ceiling high above and saw Montague leaning over a balustrade on the second floor.

'Mr Montague,' she said with a false smile, 'you're in early.'

'As are you, Miss Ryan. Nothing to do with a certain mix up I suppose.'

'I don't know what you mean,' she said innocently, not wishing to get Amy in trouble for tipping her off.

'Becky,' said Montague, 'I know how loyal that girl is to you, quite an admirable trait for someone so young. I would be very surprised if you didn't get a call last night bringing you up to speed.'

Becky knew it was pointless bluffing any more. Montague was too astute for that.

'Look, I don't know what has happened...' she started, but was cut off by his booming voice once again.

'My office, Miss Ryan,' he said. 'Straight away, if you please,' and disappeared from view.

The other staff arriving for their days shift, questioned her silently with their eyes.

'What's up?' whispered one as she passed.

'I don't know?' she said, 'but I am about to find out. Wish me luck.' With that, she headed toward the wide sweeping staircase that curved around the entrance hall to reach the upper floors. A minute later, she knocked on the door and entered Montague's office.

'Sit down,' he said. 'Look; I'm not going to beat around the bush here. Yesterday I was put in a very awkward position. One of the visitors to the museum complained that one of the exhibits in the Egyptian display was a fake. Now, at first, as you can imagine, the duty warden dismissed his concern, but the person in question turned out to be an archaeology student and insisted he was right. In fact, he made such a scene that we had to call security to calm him down. Anyway, he stood his ground and insisted he speak to someone in authority. By now, a crowd had gathered around and he was causing quite a stir. As it was your day off, the only other Egyptologist available was me, and I had to leave a very important meeting to come down and speak to him.'

'But surely you put him right?' suggested Becky.

'Oh, at first I did,' said Montague. 'In fact, I virtually staked my reputation on it. I also assured him that I had personally confirmed the provenance back in Egypt.'

'So what happened?'

'Let me answer that with the question he asked me, Miss Ryan. What is the earliest recorded Ushabti ever found in Egypt?'

'It was during the middle kingdom, about the middle of the fourteenth dynasty, if I recall correctly.'

'You do indeed recall correctly,' said Montague, 'approximately two thousand years BC in fact. Second question. What do you know about Khufu?'

'Early kingdom Egyptian king,' she said, 'responsible for building the great pyramid of Giza. What's all this about?'

'Again, you are correct,' said Montague, ignoring her question, 'and I would expect no less from someone of your pedigree, but what concerns me is this. If you are so sure of your facts, then why is one of the Ushabti that you gave me to display in the great hall labelled thus.' He slid a printed description of an Ushabti across the table toward her. It was mounted on an information plaque typical of many of the exhibits.

'Forget the detail, Miss Ryan, just read the heading.'

Becky picked up the plaque and read the inscription.

'Early example of funerary Ushabti, uncovered in the burial chamber of Cheops.'

Becky looked up, aghast at the obvious mistake.

'But that's wrong,' she said. 'Cheops was also known as Khufu, but his mummy has never been found. His empty chamber was found in the great pyramid, but that was built over five hundred years earlier, during the fourth dynasty.'

'Exactly,' said Montague. 'The practice of leaving Ushabti in tombs didn't even start until the time of Mentuhotep II at the earliest. Even I know that, but more importantly, so did the student. As soon as he pointed it out, I

97

knew he was correct and had to apologize and save whatever respect I could.'

'Mr Montague, I am so sorry,' said Becky, 'I have no idea how this happened.'

'Nor have I,' said Montague, 'I checked those Ushabti myself before they left Cairo and I know they are authentic. There is no question about their provenance, so the mistake must be in the labelling, and that, Miss Ryan, is your department. I don't know what happened, but I want a report on my desk by the end of the day. Now, if you don't mind, I have work to do.'

Becky didn't answer, but left the office as quickly as she could to make her way down to the vaults. She had given Amy the job of typing up the inscriptions, but there was no reason Becky could possibly imagine why the girl would deliberately type an incorrect label. Despite making no sense, Becky could see no other possibility, especially as Amy was the only other person with access to the specialist digi-printer in her office.

'Oh well,' she thought as she reached the office, 'there's only one way to find out.' She opened the door and walked in to confront her young, but trusted assistant.

Samari was pleasantly surprised at the flavour of the black tea that he sipped from his cup. He stood in the window, and looked out over the elegant gardens, enjoying the equally surprising sunlight. Perhaps his visit to England wasn't going to be so bad after all. He had slept well, breakfasted in his room and was now immaculately dressed in a smart suit, waiting for the knock on the door that he knew would come very soon. Sure enough, as he was pouring a second cup of tea, the door knocked and Samari answered it, relieved that he was about to find out what this was all about.

'Dr Samari,' said Leatherman, 'how are you?' The arrogant Englishman walked into the room and straight past the doctor without offering his hand.

'I am well,' said Samari, closing the door, 'though keen to find out what this is all about. The last time we met wasn't the most pleasant experience of my life, and if I recall correctly, there was even a threat of violence.'

'Yes, an unfortunate circumstance that I now regret,' said Leatherman. 'The thing is, the situation has changed and we need your services again. Obviously you will be handsomely rewarded, but again, secrecy is of the utmost importance.'

'And why should I help you?' asked Samari, 'You made it clear last time, that my services were no longer required.'

'I did and that is regretful, but to answer your question, you don't have to help us. You can leave whenever you want, with no pressure. However, I don't think you will do that.'

'Why not?'

'The very fact that you are here in the first place, tells me otherwise,' said Leatherman, 'You want to be part of this project as much as we do.'

Samari sighed. It was true. The implications of this project were so important, he would do anything to be part of the inner circle of those who knew exactly what was going on.

'Okay,' he said eventually. 'Suppose I agree, what is it you would have me do?'

'All in good time, Doctor,' said Leatherman. 'First of all, I think we should familiarize you with your surroundings. Please, come with me.'

Samari grabbed his jacket and followed Leatherman out of the room.

'So,' he said, 'what exactly is this place?'

'Home for the elderly,' said Leatherman. 'One of many that our sponsor runs, but this one is unique, exclusive to the rich and the famous. Totally secluded and away from prying eyes or unwanted attention. It has beautiful gardens, luxurious rooms and qualified medical staff on hand day and night. We have rock stars, politicians, or simply the stinking rich, all of them seeing out their days side by side in the lap of luxury. No expense is spared, but of course, it all comes at a price.'

'Is this what funds his other activities?' asked Samari.

'This and other interests,' said Leatherman. 'Let's just say our sponsor is not short of a bob or two.'

'Who exactly is our sponsor?' asked Samari.

'Really, Doctor,' answered Leatherman, 'you know better than to ask that.'

They continued to the rear of the building until they reached a lift in one of the staff corridors.

'Old service lift,' said Leatherman, 'but we have put it to better use.' He pulled out a single key connected to a chain and unlocked the door. 'Come on,' he said, 'you are about to be shown the inner sanctum.' They entered the lift and pressed the lower of the only two buttons available. The lift lurched downward for a few seconds before lurching to a halt.

'This way, Doctor,' said Leatherman, and they walked down a well-lit corridor, stopping before a closed door. 'Here we are,' he said, 'I suggest you suspend belief, for what you are going to see over the next few minutes, will blow your mind.'

Becky sat at her desk in her office, while Amy sat opposite, a look of concern on the young girl's face.

'Amy,' began Becky, 'I want you to think back a few months to when we documented the Ushabti.'

Amy nodded.

'Do you remember using the digi-printer to write up the descriptions?'

99

'I do, it was a Tuesday night. You were going to do it, but you had a dentist appointment the following day, so I came in early and did it for you.'

'That's right,' said Becky, 'and don't get me wrong, I really appreciate it, but the thing is, one of those inscriptions is seriously wrong and the only person who had the opportunity to print them on the right background is us. Now, I know I didn't do it, so I have to ask you. Did you allow anyone else down here?'

Amy looked stunned.

'No, I didn't,' she said, 'and I am quite hurt you would even think that.'

'Please don't take this personally, Amy, I'm not accusing you of anything, it's just that someone put the wrong information on an exhibit and embarrassed the curator. If nobody else came down here, then it must have been one of us, and I know it wasn't me.'

'No, I did the typing, Becky, I grant you that, but I only did what you told me to do.'

'I didn't tell you to write anything like that, Amy, I asked you to type the transcripts of each artefact as supplied with each one in its own box. Those documents would have been meticulously researched before packaging and sent over here.'

'And that's exactly what I did,' said Amy. 'I copied each document religiously and placed it alongside each Ushabti so I wouldn't get mixed up.'

'Amy,' said Becky, 'you can't have. Those documents were researched and checked by both Montague and my father back in Cairo. There's no way they would have made a mistake like that. Look, I'm not angry with you; I just need to get to the bottom of this. Did someone put you up to this as some sort of practical joke?'

Amy glared, tight lipped at Becky, and stood up as if to leave the room. Instead, she walked to the filing cabinet and searched for a few seconds before pulling out a file. As she passed the desk, she threw the file on the surface, tears flowing down her face.

'I can't believe you think I would do that, Becky,' she sobbed. 'You have trusted me from the day I started and I thought we understood each other. I would never do something like that to you. I respect you too much. All the inscriptions are in there, all I did was copy them.' With that, Amy turned on her heels and ran out of the office crying.

'Amy,' called Becky, but the young girl ignored her and ran through the vaults back up to the main museum.

'Shit,' cursed Becky to herself, 'I could have handled that better.' She picked up the file and pulled out a handful of documents. It took a few minutes to locate the right ones, but she soon had twelve, A4 sheets of clearly typed notes spread out on her desk. Each one was the same as the other with several lines of description relating to whatever Ushabti they came with. There were dates, descriptions and backgrounds to where each was found and at the bottom of each sheet, were two typed names and two signatures in black ink; Andrew Montague's and her father's, David Ryan. She picked up the one regarding the supposed Khufu Ushabti and read the description again. With a sinking feeling, she realized that Amy had been telling the truth, the description was indeed wrong, and yet both men had signed it.

She stared at the document for a long time, bewildered how this could have gotten past not one, but two Egyptologists. It just didn't make sense. For an age, she stared at the words, the signatures, and the totally ridiculous claims. Finally, she gave up and got herself a drink of water, before sitting back down at her desk. Suddenly, as if it just jumped off the page, she noticed an obvious mistake in the signature of one of the men. She checked all the other eleven signatures before returning to the disputed document and sure enough, there it was, a missing 'e' at the end of Montague's name. She read it again, 'Andrew Montagu.'

'What sort of man misspells his own name?' she thought.

She retrieved a magnifying glass from a drawer and examined both signatures in more detail. Instantly, she could see that the same hand had written both names and when she compared them to the other documents, it was obvious which one was false, Montague's. Becky stared down in confusion. The document with the wrong information had been signed by her father, and, if she was correct, he had apparently gone on to forge the other man's signature. It didn't make any sense. Why would someone as respected as her father go to so much trouble to sign a document that was not only totally rubbish, but obviously so, to anyone with a hint of knowledge about Egypt?

Becky paused as something started making sense in her mind.

It wouldn't be obvious to everyone, just to someone who knew about Egypt. Someone like her.

'Oh, my God,' said Becky out loud. 'He meant me to see it. This must be the message he said he would send.' She grabbed the letter and stared hard at the contents, before picking up the phone and dialling a number.

'Hello, John?' she said when someone answered.

'Hi, Becky,' came the answer, 'everything okay?'

'I'm not sure,' said Becky, 'I know it's early but I need to see you, I think I found my father's message. Can you get over here?'

'Um, sure. Where shall I meet you?'

'Come to the customer reception and ask for me. I'll come up to collect you when you arrive.'

'Okay,' he said, 'Give me an hour.'

'Thanks, John,' she said, 'see you then.' She hung up the phone and looked again at the letter. The more she thought about it, the more she knew she had to be right. There was no way her father would have signed a dodgy description without a good reason and that reason had to be before her very eyes.

Just over an hour later, she met John in the main hall and took him back toward the staff stairwell.

'Where are we going?' He asked.

'Down to my office, why?'

'Is that okay?'

'You are still an Egyptologist, John,' she said, 'and as such, a perfectly legitimate visitor. If anyone queries your visit, I will tell them I am seeking another opinion.'

As they walked, Becky explained her findings, and by the time, they reached her office, he was fully aware of the situation. She sat at her own desk while John rolled Amy's chair from the far side of the room.

'So,' he said, 'where is it?'

Becky slid the document across the table top and John read it several times before putting it back down.

'What do you think?' asked Becky.

'I don't know,' said John. 'It doesn't make sense.'

'Perhaps he wanted to point us in the direction of the pyramids,' suggested Becky.

'No, too blunt,' said John. 'There's something else here, I'm not sure what it is, but I agree, I think he's done this deliberately to tell you something.'

Becky got up and pulled some books from a bookshelf.

'What are they?' asked John.

'Reports on all the kings of the 14th dynasty,' said Becky, throwing one of the books toward him, 'come on, start reading. There must be something in here somewhere.'

For the next hour or so, they each pored over the documents, trying to find anything with the remotest link to Cheops or the great pyramid. Finally, Becky pushed the book away from her in frustration.

'Oh, for heaven's sake,' she said, 'this is getting us nowhere. If he wanted to send me some sort of hidden message about the pyramids, why link it to an artefact that was never in them in the first place.'

John looked across at her, his eyes widening.

'Of course,' he said, leaning back in his chair, 'how bloody stupid of us. The answer is there all along, staring us right in the face.'

'Where?' asked Becky, 'I don't understand.'

'Becky, this hasn't anything to do with Cheops, the pyramids or anyone else in the 14th dynasty for that matter. Your father sent you a message that he knew you would immediately question, a wrongly labelled Ushabti. The only thing is, you looked in the wrong place. All this time you have been questioning the letter when what you should have been checking is the artefact itself.'

'The Ushabti?'

'Yes, the bloody Ushabti. Think about it, he knew the package was coming to you and he must have reckoned that you would be the one who would read the documents. By placing an incorrect description against something you knew about, he was obviously hoping that you would examine the doll, not the letter.'

'You think so?'

'One way to find out,' said John. 'Where are they?'

'I'm not sure,' said, Becky. 'They were in the display, but I doubt they are there now.'

'I know where they are,' said a voice and they both turned to see Amy standing in the doorway.

'Amy,' said Becky, 'I didn't know you were there. I am so sorry, Amy, I should have known better than to blame you. Please forgive me, I was wrong and I am very, very sorry.'

Amy gave Becky a slight smile.

'No problem,' she said before adding, 'I heard what you were saying, and I know where the Ushabti are. They are upstairs in Montague's office. He told me to take them up there after the argument with the student.'

'Shit,' said Becky. 'How am I going to get at them now?'

'I still have a key,' said Amy, 'I could let myself in and get them if you like.'

'No, they will be too heavy for you to carry,' said John. 'Anyway, we only need the one. It would be easier if one of us goes up there and see it for ourselves.'

'Then I will go,' said Becky, 'the staff are used to seeing me walking around the place, you will get challenged.'

'I have a better idea,' said Amy, 'I have to take some papers up to him anyway since he has a meeting at twelve. I could hang around up there until he's gone, let myself in his office and bring the one you need back down here. Nobody would ever know and we could change it back before anyone realizes.'

'It could work, I suppose,' said John.

'Of course, it will,' said Amy.'

'I suppose it might,' said Becky, 'but why are you offering to do this, Amy, especially after the way I have treated you?'

'I know you wouldn't be doing it if it wasn't important, Becky,' said Amy.

'Oh, Amy,' said Becky, 'that's really kind of you.' She got out of the chair, walked up to Amy, wrapped her arms around her, and gave her a massive hug. 'I have been such an idiot.'

'Okay,' said Amy pushing her away gently, 'don't go on about it, you're getting embarrassing now.'

Becky smiled; this was the Amy she knew and had become fond of; the self-conscious, seventeen year old with a typical teenage attitude.

'Okay, Amy,' she said, 'I'll tell you what. You do this, but if you are caught, you are to say that you acted on my instructions, is that clear?'

Amy nodded.

'I mean it, Amy, if anything goes wrong, all you have to do is say that I wanted the Ushabti back for examination and told you to go and get it. Clear?'

'Crystal,' said Amy.

'Okay, you go and borrow the Ushabti and we will wait down here. Be careful, Amy,' she said.

'Wish me luck,' answered Amy and walked out of the office and into the vaults.

'What now?' asked Becky.

'Now we wait,' said John.

Chapter Eleven

Itjawi - 1245 BC
The Caverns of Sekhmet

Ramesses' mind was racing. He was deep in the caverns of Sekhmet and had just been told that the immortality he craved was outside his reach. He wanted to fall on the frail form of Sekhmet and tear her apart for leading him down this false path, but knew the isolation from his bodyguards put him at risk.

'You are quiet, Ramesses,' said Sekhmet 'yet I see murder in your eyes. Do not strain to conceal such burning emotion, for I read the soul as easy as you read the proclamations of your false prophets. Declare your will, Ramesses, I seek amusement.'

Ramesses stared at her with hate in his eyes and venom in his words.

'For three seasons I have knelt before you, Sekhmet,' he growled, 'ever since the governor of Itjawi made representation to stop you and your sisters slicing through the population like a farmer's scythe. Each time, you have received sacrifice from me and during my battles, I allowed you to feast on the dead of friend and foe alike. I have stopped the masses from tearing down this place with their bare hands, and all for what. To see you stand there and gloat in your revelation that it has been for nothing. You have belittled me, Sekhmet, played with me as a cat does a mouse.' He retrieved his blade and held it at his side in a threatening manner. 'Your soul may be immortal, Sekhmet, but your body is frail. What is to stop me from piercing your black heart with my blade right now and ending this earthly existence?'

Sekhmet laughed again.

'Oh, Ramesses,' she said, 'do you not listen to anything I say? You can fall upon me right now if you so wish. If it makes you feel better, carry out your threat, for I have suffered worse in my life.' Suddenly, she seemed to glide effortlessly over the floor and into the light of the burning bulrushes. She grabbed his wrist holding the knife and lifted the blade up until it pressed against her own chest. 'Don't you think I have thought of release, Ramesses, dreamed of it, begged for it, even sought it out by my own hand, but always the hunger pulls me back.'

Ramesses held back the urge to flee as he gazed closely into the hag's eyes close up for the first time. The effect was mesmerizing, as the blackness seemed to be an empty void of nothing that threatened to drag his soul into their endless depths. The yellow skin over her skull was parchment thin and bore the wrinkled lines of age from unknown eons of time while the stink from the rotting flesh between her jagged teeth was nauseating.

'Do it, Ramesses,' she whispered, pushing against his blade, 'kill a goddess. You are the all-conquering Ramesses, smiter of the Hittites and ruler of all lands. Thrust your blade, great king and be rid of the one being in this world who would call you servant.'

Despite the urge to do as she bid, Ramesses stepped back, breaking her evil stare.

'No, Sekhmet,' he said, 'I will not take this route. I am not just a great king, but also a great ruler. A sovereign does not take the life of a subject with his own hands and that is what you are, Sekhmet, a subject. I am Ramesses, the greatest king that ever lived and I decide when someone dies or someone lives. Today, it is my decree that you live.'

Sekhmet looked down at the floor for several moments before lifting her head to stare at him once more. This time, Ramesses felt a twinge of fear as the look on her rotting face was one of evil and impending danger.

'Your arrogance knows no bounds, Ramesses,' she said. 'Yet it is I who decrees that you live this day, not the other way around.' With a flick of her hand, she sent a signal to the shadows and a group of bedraggled women in stinking shrouds emerged from the darkness to fall upon the tethered slaves. Knives slashed across veins, rocks smashed in skulls and jagged teeth ripped at throats as the sisters tore the men apart in their terrible need for blood and flesh. Within seconds, the brutality ended, and Sekhmet's acolytes either lay or knelt around the mutilated corpses like a pride of lions around the kill. The noise of the assault was gone, only to be replaced by the sounds of teeth, tearing through flesh and tongues lapping at flowing blood.

'When the hunger rises, Ramesses, it cannot be stopped. Even now I feel the aches that announce the onset of my eternal desire and you should go before my need to feed outweighs my need to talk.'

'One more question,' said Ramesses, 'and I will be gone from this place. If this was the case all along, then why ask me here? If immortality is beyond me, then why tell me all that you have?'

'I have said before, Ramesses, your arrogance amuses me, yet there is something else about you. A sense of destiny that I have rarely seen before and I believe you will truly be the greatest mortal man ever to reign over these lands. A king so powerful, that all will tremble at your whim and with such a man, my sisters can once more take our rightful place in the temples of the gods. We are the true immortals, Ramesses, not the images of the false priests or the tales told to children, but nightwalkers. We see the same men born, live and die while we do not age, yet it is us who are banished to hide amongst the rocks of the wastelands. I cannot give the gift you seek as it is not mine to give. Yet there are other gifts that are within my power.'

'Such as?'

'My sisters and I can become part of your rule, Ramesses, becoming a silent blade to all upon whom you cast a disapproving eye. An instant and terrible retribution that calls in the dead of night yet is gone again by rise of the sun. Imagine hundreds of your enemies dying in a single night, yet no guilty hand upon which to lay blame. No fortress could withstand our silent assault and the people of your enemies will turn on their kings to rid them of the curse that takes the lives of their children. Nations driven by fear will fall to their knees and beg you to accept them as subordinate. No wars, Ramesses, no expensive armies to empty your treasure houses, just endless tribute to build your palaces dedicated to your name. This is the gift I offer, Ramesses, invisible wings of death that will sweep you on your way to become truly, the greatest king this world has ever seen.'

'And what would you expect in return?'

'Only that already offered. Give me and my sisters the tomb of Amenemhat and freedom to take our place amongst your people.'

Ramesses stood for an age, staring into the black pools of hell that passed as eyes in this creature of the night. Finally, he spoke once more, breaking the unearthly silence between them.

'At the next full moon, I will break the seal of Amenemhat myself. Bring your people, Sekhmet, for now it is I, who offers everlasting life.'

'Then leave this place, Ramesses,' said Sekhmet, 'for my hunger is upon me.' She disappeared into the shadows and Ramesses turned to make his way back through the tunnels.

Soon he was outside, breathing deeply of the cool night air. Atmar appeared out of the darkness and stood slightly distant, staring at his king in a strange manner.

'Is it done?' asked Atmar.

'Do not fret, Atmar,' said Ramesses, 'I am still the same person that entered this cursed place. I am untouched by her curse, yet I am not disappointed. My greatness will be nonetheless, yet still be holy in the sight of Ra.'

'Then it was a wasted trip?' asked Atmar.

'Oh no,' said Ramesses, 'in fact it was far more productive than I could ever have desired. Come, we need to get from this place before the nightwalkers emerge. We have preparations to make.'

'Preparations?'

'Yes, we have a long dead king to visit.'

Yafeu, the stonemason, stood in front of the official of the king's court. He had deliberated long and hard before making the decision to report the death of Serapis to the authorities. Like everyone else, he had heard the legends of the nightwalkers, but had always put it down to unsubstantiated stories. Now, having seen the evidence with his own eyes, his days were filled with worry, and his nights were filled with terror. His son had fled the town to escape his debts, and because of the sleepless nights, Yafeu had lost work at the quarries. He knew he couldn't go on much longer as he was, and had finally decided to report what he had seen to the local priest. At first the priest was sceptical, but when the reports of the missing trader had started coming in, he had referred Yafeu to the court of the king.

The king's official had listened carefully to the stonemason's detailed representation, before leaving him alone in the antechamber. Yafeu was exhausted and though he knew there would be a price to pay for the intended crime, the thought of being sought out by the nightwalkers was far, far worse. Finally, the official returned and spoke to him again.

'I have consulted with the appropriate authority in such matters,' said the official, 'and your story intrigues us. There are many stories of these so-called nightwalkers and it is the king's wish to allay the fears of his people. In his mercy, the king's authority feels that although you went out that night with dark intentions, you ultimately committed no crime. However, as there was intent, it would not be in the interests of justice should any man feel free to set out to commit a crime without fear of retribution.'

Yafeu's heart sank.

'Your punishment will be to attend the tomb of Amenemhat at dawn, and there you will be tasked to work under the attention of the priests attending the majesty of the old king's memory. There are various tasks therein that have need of your skills and you will fulfil that need until further notice. You will not receive recompense for this work; though you will receive food and shelter. Such is the punishment bestowed.'

Yafeu looked in amazement. In the greater scheme of things, this decree could hardly be deemed as punishment. The work suited his skills and he would be under the supervision of the priesthood while working in a holy place. Surely, even the nightwalkers would hesitate at the door of a Pharaoh's tomb.

'If there is nothing more,' said the official, 'then you may leave. Present yourself at the tomb of Amenemhat at dawn.'

Yafeu left the temple in a much lighter frame of mind. He knew he had escaped relatively lightly, and as long as he could make it through one more night, then surely his burden would ease.

Three weeks later, a team of donkeys pulled a solitary covered cart through the backstreets of Itjawi, containing a creature older than the pyramids. In the surrounding streets, fleeting shapes of half-seen figures, seemed to float from shadow to shadow, following the route of the cart. All the citizens of Itjawi stayed within their homes and the streets were empty by king's proclamation.

Finally, the cart left the dusty streets of the main town behind and trundled onto the paved roadway leading to an enormous temple complex. Statues of Amenemhat lined the roadway along with Stelae recording the tales of his reign, tribute to the great achievements of the long dead king. As the cart entered the archway of the outer courtyard, a thousand priests prostrated themselves on the ground in supplication, lying in silence as the cart made its way to where a solitary man waited before the temple itself. Finally, the cart stopped and a few moments later, an old woman descended from beneath the cover accompanied by a beautiful young girl. Together, they walked up the steps toward the waiting man.

'A momentous occasion, Ramesses,' she said.

'As befits your kind, Sekhmet,' said the king.

'And who are these people?' she asked, half turning to gaze over the throng, now face down in the enormous courtyard.

'They are the priests allocated to revere your name and see to your whims.'

'I need no priests,' she said.

'What goddess does not have priesthood?' he asked. 'They will look after your needs and protect you during the hours of the day when you are at your weakest.'

'And if my sisters are tempted by the blood within their veins?'

'They are yours to do with as you wish,' said Ramesses. He turned his head toward the girl.

'It is good to see you again, Nephthys,' he said.

'And you, great king,' she answered.

Ramesses saw that veins of black had appeared in her eyes and looked over at Sekhmet quizzically.

'It was time;' said Sekhmet, answering the unanswered question, 'a new era demands a new goddess.'

'She will be a suitable successor,' said Ramesses, 'but we delay, your temple awaits.' He stood to one side and allowed the two women to walk through the enormous doors. Inside, they entered a lavishly decorated labyrinth, lit by rows of oil bowls with floating wicks.

Outside, twenty nightwalkers glided between the prostrate figures, the lightness of their footfall gentler than that of a desert cat. Hungry black eyes peered down at the men at their feet, but without the say of Sekhmet, their blood would remain un-tasted. Each walker made their way toward the labyrinth that was to become their home, but as they walked, one paused and stared at the nearest priest lying at her feet. Slowly, she reached out a bare foot and pulled back the edge of his robe, unveiling a military sword strapped to his waist.

Her hellish eyes widened in anger and she snarled out a warning to her sisters.

'Treachery,' she hissed, and all around the men leapt to their feet, throwing off their robes to reveal the full leather armour worn by the king's elite troops.

'We are found out,' shouted Atmar, discarding his own disguise. 'Cut them down. If any escape, then we will all die.'

With a roar, the soldiers fell upon the women, showing them no mercy and though it took many sword thrusts to have any impact, eventually the force of numbers took their toll. Within minutes, every nightwalker had been hacked into pieces by the soldier's blades.

'Bring the brushwood,' ordered Atmar and a line of slaves ran into the courtyard, each carrying a tied bundle of firewood. Quickly they built a bonfire as Atmar gave his orders to the captain of the guard.

'On pain of death, you will carry out these orders exactly as I say. First, set the fire ablaze and keep it going through the night. Cut every one of these women's bodies into pieces small enough to fit into a fist. When that is done, throw the pieces into the flames. Repeat it with any of our own dead and wounded.'

'Our wounded, Sire?' asked the captain.

'Yes, anyone who has as much as a scratch on their skin must be executed straight away and fed to the flames. Do not fail me on this, Captain, or you will share this fate. When it is done, have every man strip and check them yourself for any hidden wound. If they bleed, they die; it is as simple as that. When you are sure there are none with so much as a bruise, burn your uniforms. Fresh clothes are located in wagons nearby. I cannot emphasize this enough, Captain, no matter how long it takes; I want nothing left of this night, but ashes smaller than the finest flour. When it is done, you will divide the ashes into no less than a thousand sacks and send each off to a different fate. Spread them on seas across the known world, bury them deep underground, or pour them to the seven winds. I care not, but ensure that there is never more than one sack disposed of in each location. Then I want a list of where everyone went and who carried out the task. This is something we cannot afford to get wrong. Have I made myself clear?'

'You have, Sire.'

'Then let it be done. Now, get me ten of your best men and follow me.'

Ramesses continued into the labyrinth with Sekhmet and Nephthys, unaware of the carnage that was happening outside. At every junction, stood a long-robed priest holding a torch and though the king knew that each was really a trusted soldier, he still felt very vulnerable now that he was so close to the prize. Finally, they rounded a corner and stood before a sealed door, complete with funerary inscription.

Here lies Great King Amenemhat III
Slayer of the bewitched
Protector of the innocent
King of Kings
Death falls swiftly on all who disturb his sleep

A nearby stonemason passed him a hammer and Ramesses turned to Sekhmet.

'I am a man who keeps his promises, Sekhmet,' he said and smashed the age-old seal with a single stroke of the stone hammer.

Two of the disguised soldiers pulled the door open and stood to one side to allow the party through.

'Light,' Ramesses ordered, and the stonemason grabbed a burning torch from the wall.

'Lead the way,' ordered Ramesses and the man stepped into the room, closely followed by Sekhmet and the girl.

Yafeu the mason held the torch up high as he walked deeper into the tomb. His heart was racing, as he realized he was honoured to be the first man to step inside this place for over five hundred years. Close behind, he heard the footfall of the two women as he continued along the spectacularly decorated corridor. Suddenly, a great crash echoed through the chamber and all three spun around to see the cause. Yafeu's heart leapt as he saw the door had been slammed into place behind them. Sekhmet and Nephthys stayed still, but Yafeu ran back to the door in terror.

'Wait,' he shouted, banging on the door, 'what are you doing? Open the door.' He continued to bang on the door until a soft voice behind him spoke.

'Be silent,' hissed Sekhmet.

Ramesses' face appeared in a hole in the wall above the door, formed just the previous day at the command of the priests. Yafeu stepped back and held up the torch so they could see the king.

'So this is the way of a so-called great king,' said Sekhmet, her voice dripping with venom, treachery and deceit. 'All this time I had you marked as different, Ramesses. Yet you are no better than all the rest.'

'On the contrary, Sekhmet, I have already succeeded in doing something that no other man, king or god has managed to do.'

'And what is that?'

'Wiped your kind from the face of this land.'

'There will always be my kind, Ramesses. My sisters will drink your blood before the sun rises.'

'Your sisters already burn in my soldiers' fires,' said Ramesses.

'You lie.'

'It is true, but your belief is not something that matters.'

'You claim greatness, but what sort of king goes back on an agreement?' asked Sekhmet.

'I have honoured my agreement,' said Ramesses, 'and delivered my promise. Are you not within the tomb of Amenemhat?'

'But we agreed.' said Sekhmet, 'We would become your blade, defeating your enemies without the need for war.'

'I made no such agreement.' said Ramesses, 'Scour your memory, for this was an offer made, but not accepted. I did think about it, Sekhmet. For a long time I deliberated over your proposal, but when all is considered, what is a king without a war? Be grateful, Sekhmet, I have allowed you and the girl to live. All of your other sisters burn as we speak. At least you will have eternity to ponder on my greatness.'

'Without blood, we will wither away,' said Sekhmet, 'eternally dying, yet never dead. Why would you inflict such a fate on any being?'

'Don't preach morality to me,' hissed Ramesses. 'How many people have you sent to hell in your time?'

'Then at least release the girl,' shouted Sekhmet. 'Leave me here to rot, but let Nephthys go.'

'It is too late,' said Ramesses, 'I have seen her eyes, and she is as you. No, Sekhmet, your time is done. As soon as I leave this place, my armies will destroy the temple above, leaving no trace of its location. This whole valley will be filled in and planted over with crops. Mention of Itjawi will be forbidden on pain of death, and within a generation, no one will know this place even existed.'

'That is impossible,' said Sekhmet, 'you can't fill in an entire valley.'

'*I am Ramesses*,' shouted the king, 'and I will do as I wish. Even as I speak there is a workforce of a hundred thousand approaching this place. My troops are evacuating the town and within one cycle, this valley will be nothing more than a forbidden memory. That is my wish, and my wish is law.'

Silence fell again and Ramesses took a deep breath, before speaking calmly once more.

'So, Sekhmet,' he said, 'it seems that despite your inability to die, it is I who will become immortal. In a thousand years, my name will still be spoken, yet you will be nothing but dust beneath the shifting desert sands. I have prevailed, Sekhmet, I am the master and you are the servant. In my kingdom, I have the ultimate power of life and death over my people, and today, my decree is that you die. The blood of the mason may sustain you for a while, but die you will, Sekhmet, and one day you will be as insubstantial as the dust on the floor.'

'My kind do not die, Ramesses, for there will always be another. Do your worst, treacherous king, I spit on your name.'

'So be it,' said Ramesses and his face disappeared from the hole. He climbed down off the ladder and turned to the soldiers alongside him. 'I am done here,' he said. 'Seal them in.'

Two more masons approached with mortar and limestone blocks to block up the hole.

'Wait!' shouted Yafeu, banging on the inside of the doors again. 'What about me? You can't leave me down here with them.' He sensed someone behind him and spun around, holding the burning torch before him. The younger woman stood two paces away from him, her head slightly tilted as she stared at him.

'What's the matter?' he asked, 'why are you looking at me like that? Oh my god, what's wrong with your eyes?'

'Not yet, Nephthys,' whispered Sekhmet's voice from the darkness, 'we have to make him last.'

Chapter Twelve

The British Antiquities Museum - 2012

Amy lingered on the second floor balcony. She had delivered the paperwork to Montague and had taken the opportunity to spot the Ushabti collection while she was there. After she left the office, Amy waited, knowing that his meeting was overdue. Sure enough, Montague left the office a few minutes later, and quickly made his way downstairs. Without hesitation, Amy unlocked the door and made her way over to the side table where the exhibits lay. All twelve were in their tiny, coffin-like boxes and though they all looked similar to Amy, one was without its inscription. She took the Ushabti from its box and made her way back downstairs as quickly as possible. Within minutes, she was back in Becky's office, her heart racing, yet revelling in the subterfuge.

'Amy' said Becky with relief, 'what happened, are you okay?

'Fine,' said Amy, 'he just took a bit longer to leave than I thought he would.'

'Do you have it?' Asked John,

Amy reached inside her wrap and pulled out the Ushabti, placing it on the table.

'There it is,' she said. 'Fill your boots!'

Both Becky and John crouched down and stared at the small figure with interest.

'See anything?' asked John.

'Nothing,' said Becky. 'Looks fine to me.'

'Almost too fine,' said John, picking up the clay doll. He turned it over and over in his hands, before making a statement that made Becky's heart sink.

'Do you know what, Becky?' he said, 'I think we've been had. This Ushabti is fake.'

'Fake? No, it can't be. The Ushabti is genuine, it's just the inscription is wrong.'

'I don't think so,' said John. 'If you look carefully, you can see the marks on the head where the clay burs were filed off after firing. I've seen this before, it's the type that's mass produced in the back streets of Cairo and touted to every tourist that ever sets foot in any city in Egypt.'

'It can't be,' said Becky and took the Ushabti from John. For a few moments, she was quiet, but eventually, she replaced it on the table and sat down with a sigh.

'I don't understand,' she said, 'how can it be fake and such a bad one at that? Both my father and Montague verified them alongside the experts from the Cairo museum. There's no way this cheap imitation would have got past them.'

114

'Unless…' started John

'Unless what?'

'Becky,' said John, 'didn't your father say he had let himself back into the museum on the night of Samari's supposed attack?'

'Yes, but he didn't say why.'

'No, but what if he went in to swap the Ushabti after they had been verified. He could have let himself into his office and simply opened the package ready to be shipped to the UK, before replacing the original with this fake.'

'Why would he do that?' asked Becky. 'Surely, you don't think he stole the original to sell it.'

'No, I don't,' said John, 'I think he used this modern one as a message and put in the false description, knowing you would probably see it for what it is.'

'But there's nothing on it,' said Becky.

'Look at the base,' said John.

Becky picked up the doll again and turned it over. Though it seemed the same as the rest, there was a slight difference in texture. She rubbed it with her thumb and grains of sand fell on the table.

'It's coming off,' she said. 'It's as if it is glued on.'

'I think it's a false base, Becky,' said John. 'The message isn't on the Ushabti, but in it!'

Becky grabbed the paper knife on the desk and started to scrape the rest of the base. Within seconds, she unveiled a hole in the base seemingly filled with wax.

'Whatever is in there is well protected,' said Becky.

'Let me see,' said John and took it off her. He peered at the wax plug and before Becky could do anything to stop him, John banged it on the edge of the table, smashing the clay outer casing.

'John, what are you doing?' exclaimed Becky.

'Becky, it's worth about ten pence in a boot sale,' he said. 'Don't be silly.'

He continued to peel away any remnants of clay, until he was left with a wax cylindrical tube about six inches long and two inches across.

'What is it?' asked Amy, as John held it up to the light.

'I can't see,' said John, 'the wax is obscuring whatever is inside. Put the kettle on, will you?'

'You want tea?' asked Amy, incredulously.

'It's not for tea, Amy,' said Becky, 'it's for hot water to melt the wax without damaging whatever is inside.'

'Oh,' said Amy and filled the kettle as asked.

A few minutes later, Becky and Amy sat at the desk, while John stood at the sink, trickling hot water onto the wax cylinder. Gradually the wax dripped away and he uncovered what had been hidden inside.

'Oh, my god,' said John, with his back still toward them.

'What is it?' asked Amy and ran to the sink to see what he had uncovered.

John stepped aside as Amy stared into the sink.

'Yuk,' she said, 'that's disgusting.'

'What is it?' asked Becky, and as Amy stepped aside, she too could see the message her father had sent. It wasn't a typed piece of paper, or even writing of any sort, but the last thing she had expected to see. An ancient human finger.

Fifty miles away, Samari stood in the doorway of large room lit by dozens of overhead lights. The walls were tiled floor to ceiling and a non-slip vinyl covered the floor. Banks of computers lined the walls along with all sorts of machinery, much of which Samari didn't recognize. The whole effect was very clinical and the room was spotlessly cleaned with a hint of disinfectant in the air. Three technicians in white overalls busied themselves taking notes between machines and calibrating dials. One turned to greet the visitors and came over.

'Dr Samari,' she said 'we have been expecting you.'

'You have?'

'Of course, and I suppose you are impatient to see the subject.'

'Subject?'

'Dr Samari isn't fully aware of his role here yet, Jenny,' said Leatherman, 'but I am about to put that right.' He turned to Samari. 'Doctor, please take a seat and I will bring you up to speed.'

They both sat at a table and Jenny brought a couple of coffees in cardboard cups.

'First of all,' said Leatherman, 'tell me what you know so far, and then I will fill in the gaps.'

'Well,' said Samari, 'following Doctor Ryan's illegal discovery of Amenemhat's tomb, we found the king's sarcophagus had already been opened and his body discarded across the chamber. In addition, at the far end of the tomb, we found the skeletal remains of a woman who had obviously died of old age. Many of the bones had apparently crumbled to dust; however, within the coffin itself was a nondescript body, with seemingly no royal connections whatsoever. As there had been no obvious forced entry to the tomb, we assumed that they had been brought to the tomb hundreds of years after Amenemhat's interment, perhaps as a living sacrifice. We believe that both women had been brought through the main entrance and the door subsequently resealed.'

'And the body in the coffin?' asked Leatherman.

'Like I said, the body was obviously female and still wore the remnants of a simple linen dress. The corpse displayed the typical aging process to be expected of a someone entombed for over two thousand years,

116

yet the flesh had been naturally mummified from the dry environment, a condition not completely unknown in other tombs.'

'But this was different?' suggested Leatherman.

'It was,' continued Samari, 'though mummified, there seemed to have been no decomposition. Everything seemed to be in place, including organs, eyes, and brain. Obviously we did not do any invasive surgery, but our initial examinations were very exciting.'

'Because?'

'Because to the best of my knowledge, nothing like this had ever been found before; it was almost as if the subject had died and became instantly preserved by the unique conditions in the tomb. This meant that the entire make up of a person who lived over two thousand years ago could be examined in great detail.'

'So you called us,' said Leatherman.

'I did, for two reasons. First, to my shame, I saw an opportunity to make some money on the artefacts prior to making the discovery public. There was so much there, I knew that it would become worldwide news very quickly and I wanted a slice before the museum world started circling.'

'And the second reason?'

'There was something about the body in the coffin. I believed I had discovered a previously unknown mummification process and wanted my name to be associated with it. I knew from my dealings with your organization in the past, that not only did you have an interest in gene science, but you were also crooked enough to smooth any, shall we say, shady dealings. Subsequently I took a tissue sample and sent it to you. Within weeks the place was swarming with technicians, I was paid off, and you threatened me with a gun. After that I heard nothing until you phoned me a couple of weeks ago.'

'Seems correct to me,' said Leatherman, 'So let me bring you right up to date. First, you are right that we have an interest in gene therapy. In fact it is fundamental in our sponsors business. This building has an interesting history. It was built in the nineteenth century and was the country residence for some rich aristocratic family. In the First World War, it was used as a hospital for casualties of the Somme, and the government in the Second World War sequestered it again, albeit for a different purpose. The room we stand in now was constructed at that time and was a tactical centre for the control of England's aircraft. After the war it fell into disrepair before our sponsor bought it and turned it into what it is now, a luxury home for the elderly.'

'Our sponsor has a string of such properties,' continued Leatherman, 'and his company is at the forefront of medical research. In particular, bearing in mind our clientele, he is particularly focused on the aging process, or should I say, slowing down the aging process.'

'That's impossible,' said Samari.

'Perhaps,' said Leatherman, 'but suffice to say, that is the focus of our research. There are people in this world that will pay an absolute fortune for even the possibility of a few extra years, so when you put that alongside the wallets of the giant drug corporations, you can see it is a very lucrative business.'

'And have you been successful?' asked Samari.

'A little,' said Leatherman, 'but nothing worth writing home about. However, all that changed when you sent us that sample. You see, what you sent us was far more than a new mummification process, it was something we had never seen before.'

'What did you find?'

'Well, bearing in mind that this body had been dead for over two thousand years, imagine our surprise when under the microscope, we found cells that had not deteriorated at all. Yes, they were surrounded by mummified or dead tissue, but amongst them all, there were some cells that were still alive. Dormant, admittedly, but alive.'

'You must be mistaken,' said Samari. 'Your testing process must have been flawed.'

'That's what we thought,' said Leatherman, 'so we tested again and in all scenarios the results were always the same. That body in the tomb, contained live tissue. You can imagine how we felt; it was like finding the Holy Grail. All we had to do was identify the gene sequence in those cells and there was a possibility of replicating the DNA and finding a cure for the aging process. Imagine that, Samari, no more old age. Imagine how much the oil sheiks and corporate billionaires would pay for such an option.'

'I don't know what to say,' stuttered Samari, 'It's too much to take in.'

'I know;' said Leatherman, 'anyway, suffice to say our sponsor pulled out all the stops to obtain that corpse. The corporation kicked into gear like a military machine and we moved the operation out to Egypt immediately. However, it soon became clear that we were working with more than we had bargained for and we had to bring the body back here to our laboratories where we have the best scientists and technology available.'

'The mummy is here?'

'Sort of,' said Leatherman. 'Anyway, over the last few weeks we have had spectacular success with our experiments and have moved forward at a pace we could only dream of. However, we have now come across a problem that needs your particular skills, hence the phone call.'

'Considering what you already have here,' said Samari, 'I can't imagine what it is I have that you need so much.'

'You are about to find out,' said Leatherman. 'Please come this way.'

118

He led Samari through a door at the far end of the room and into what seemed like a small cinematic auditorium. The room was well lit and a heavy pair of drapes covered where the screen should be.

'Please, sit down,' said Leatherman. Between the seats, two sets of strange headgear were sitting on a simple wooden coffee table. They were similar to baseball caps, but with visors made of transparent plastic.

'Doctor, when we brought back the mummy from Egypt, we took samples of the hibernating cells and tried to reproduce them. Everything failed. However, when we found that the veins were intact, albeit collapsed, we tried pumping a watered down version of plasma through them to encourage the release of any dormant cells so we could try to harvest them. What actually happened was beyond our wildest imagination. The veins immediately flexed enough to allow passage of fluid. Well, you can imagine our astonishment, but absolute delight. This meant that if we could transfuse real blood through the veins, hopefully, any dormant hibernating cells would react with the haemoglobin and we could extract them for our experiments. Subsequently, we increased the consistency until basically we had given the body a complete transfusion.'

'What happened?' asked Samari.

'At first nothing. We farmed the blood, but all we got back was the same blood cells we had pumped in. We tried repeatedly, but were ultimately stumped. That night we left the lab, very disappointed, but within a few hours, I had a phone call in my room from a very concerned technician, demanding I return to the lab straight away. Apparently, he had taken a fresh sample from one of the veins, but the composition had changed and was exhibiting traits none of us had seen before. First of all, it hadn't congealed, but still lay in a liquid form, and secondly, it was much thinner than what we would have expected. It was as if all the proteins had disappeared and what was left was almost water. Anyway, we arranged another transfusion and over a period of several hours, the same thing happened. The blood consistency seemed to thin out as if it was being absorbed through the walls of the veins. To back up these results, we found the moisture content of the body had also risen accordingly. Obviously we were ecstatic, as it seemed to indicate that the dormant cells must have been reacting with the blood, so we harvested the blood again to see if there were any cells attached, but once more, the tests were negative. All through the night, we pumped the body's veins with fresh blood, and each time it absorbed the protein, but despite everything, we could still not reproduce the cells in enough quantity to reproduce them in a Petri dish. However, what did happen was even more fascinating and we soon realised all we had to do was continue with the transfusions, and wait.'

'Why?'

'Well, what we think happened is that those elusive dormant cells not only interacted with the blood transfusions, but actually used them as nourishment and started to reproduce. As soon as we realised this, we continued to pump in fresh blood every hour, each time removing the thin waste that it replaced. The effects were astonishing; within days, the moisture content of the flesh rocketed. Old skin cells fell away and the keratin re-grew. To all intents and purposes, the body was renewing itself.'

'This is preposterous,' said Samari, standing up, 'I don't know why you brought me here Leatherman, but whatever pathetic reason you have, I will not stay here and be made a fool of.'

'Sit down, Doctor,' said Leatherman, 'I know it is hard to take in, but you will see the evidence soon enough.'

Samari paused before taking his seat once more.

'Like I was saying,' continued Leatherman, 'the body was regenerating before our very eyes. The flesh filled out, the dead skin fell away and the hair grew. You can imagine how we felt, the dormant cells that we had been chasing were obviously doing their job and we knew that at last, the prize was within our grasp. All we had to do was identify and segregate the cells, harvest them and we would have the beginnings of a completely new science. Age control.'

'And have you been successful?'

'No, because something happened that was completely unexpected.'

'What?'

'Her heart started beating.'

Samari shook his head slowly from side to side.

'No,' he said, 'it can't have. That is not possible. I saw that mummy with my own eyes; it has been dead for over two thousand years. There is no way you could have resurrected her.'

'I agree,' said Leatherman, 'but we did. Don't ask me how, because at the moment we don't have the answers. All I know is that, somehow, against all our better knowledge and understanding, just by giving this corpse several simple blood transfusions, we have managed to resurrect life.'

'Impossible, impossible, impossible,' repeated Samari. 'It cannot be done, there must be some mistake.'

'I can understand your disbelief, Doctor,' said Leatherman, 'and I'm not sure that I believe it myself. However, I think you have heard me talk long enough. Perhaps it is time you saw it with your own eyes. He reached out for the headgear on the table. You will need these,' he said, 'There's a switch on the battery pack at the back. Flick it up and pull down the visor.'

'What are they for?' asked Samari, examining the headgear.

'Think of them as infrared goggles,' said Leatherman, 'Best we could do in these circumstances. We intend to build filters into the glass as soon as we can, but these will have to do for now. The room containing the subject is only lit by infrared light and the only way we will be able to see her, is through these.'

'Why infrared?' asked Samari, pulling down the visor. 'Does the light destroy the cells?'

'Oh no,' said Leatherman, 'nothing like that. It hurts her eyes.'

Samari's head spun to one side and stared at Leatherman in astonishment.

'What?' he gasped. 'You mean, she is conscious?'

'Don't believe me, Doctor,' said Leatherman. 'See for yourself.'

Dr Samari turned back to see the two curtains sliding away from the wall to his front and immediately another room sprang into view behind a glass screen. The inner room was filled with a red glow and though it took him a few seconds to adjust, Samari could make out a single hospital bed in the centre. On a table to one side, stood a clear jug of water and a tray with various items of food, while toward the rear of the room, stood a freestanding screen.

'Doctor,' said Leatherman, 'what you see before you is an examination chamber. Without the equipment you now wear, it would appear completely dark. The water and food on the side tables are replaced daily, but never consumed. The subject is conscious, mobile and sentient, however, despite our best efforts, we cannot get her to eat or drink.'

'Then how is the body sustained?' asked Samari.

'At first we had to give her a transfusion every night, but that became too cumbersome. Eventually we tried pouring the blood into a jug for her to drink, and while that had some success, she deteriorated quickly, until we had to transfuse again. Finally, one of the techies suggested a solution, and whilst it sounds like something from a horror film, it turned out to be the answer we needed.'

'What was it?' asked Samari.

'Watch,' said Leatherman, and both men stared at the seemingly empty room, waiting for something to happen.

The lab technician holding a box approached the side door leading into an inner chamber He lifted a sliding hatch in the bottom of the door and tipped something inside before retreating to the back of the chairs. Samari stared, and instantly saw a typical laboratory white rat, sitting up on its haunches, its nose twitching at the smell of the food at the other side of the room. As it scurried along the bottom of the glass toward the table, another movement caught Samari's eyes and he saw a hand appear from behind the screen. Within seconds, the rest of the body appeared and Samari's head spun toward Leatherman in confusion.

'Surely that's not her?' he said.

'I assure you it is, Doctor.'

'But, she's so young!'

'I know; the transformation is astonishing.'

'This doesn't make sense,' said Samari. 'How can that cadaver now look like this?'

'I wish I had the answers,' said Leatherman. 'All we know is that the cells seem to have regenerated to the state they must have been in, before the mummification process started. What you are looking at there is a walking factory of regenerative cell never seen before. To put it bluntly, Samari, she is worth billions.'

Both men turned back toward the glazed chamber as the woman walked slowly from behind the screen. She was just under six feet tall and though her hair was untidy, it was quite thick and very dark brown. Her face was young, though very pale, and a simple hospital nightdress covered her slender body. The nails on both her hands and feet were very long and quite yellow. Her gaze was focused on the rat and she walked slowly toward it, her feet seemingly gliding over the vinyl.

'Don't forget,' said Leatherman, 'it's pitch black in there, yet it seems that she can see the rat easily.'

The girl got closer and as the rat sat up once again to sniff up at the food on the table, she leapt forward and grabbed it with both hands.

Samari was transfixed. He had hardly seen her move, yet she was now standing upright and holding the rat up in front of her, examining her prize. Holding the rat's head in one hand and the back legs in the other, she pulled them in opposite directions to expose the chest, before opening her mouth wide and crushing the animal's chest with her teeth. Immediately, the rat stopped struggling and she rammed the open cavity hard against her mouth to extract as much blood as possible. Some ran down onto her chest as it escaped from the sides of her mouth, but she held it there until she had extracted all the blood she could. Finally, as if to finish off the disgusting display, the girl tore apart the body and pulled out the entrails, stuffing them hungrily into her mouth. Samari stood up and walked down the few steps to the glass in order to get a closer view. Close up, he could see that despite the girl's appearance, she was actually quite beautiful.

'This is incredible,' whispered Samari again. 'Is she some sort of offshoot of our own species?'

'So many questions, Doctor,' said Leatherman, 'but as yet, I have few answers.'

The girl finished her horrible meal and threw the fur and bones toward the back of the room. Slowly, she walked toward the glass and though the focus of her eyes was above Samari's head, she lifted her hand up and placed it gently on the glass.

'Oh, my god,' said Samari, 'can she see us?'

'No, it's a two way mirror, yet every time she is active like this, I swear she knows we are watching her.'

'And do you always feed her like this?'

'No, the rat is just a snack for your benefit. Her hunger is insatiable and she has dispatched many animals so. Cats, dogs, we even put a fully-grown pig in there, but she dispatched each with as much ease. It seems as long as there is a pulse, she sees it as food.'

'And humans?'

'We can only assume so.'

'So how do you get in there to undergo experiments and the like?''

'She is averse to light,' said Leatherman, 'When we need to sedate her, we armour up with protective suits and flood the chamber with light. That is why the screen is there, to give her a place to shelter, while we do what we have to do.'

'This is amazing,' said Samari and placed his hand on the glass, mirroring the girl's own. Her head tilted, as if she sensed something, and she was straining to hear anything she could.

'So, am I to assume that you want me to examine her,' he asked softly, staring into the girls black eyes.

'Oh no, Doctor, we have all the scientists and doctors we need. You have been invited here to carry out a role that we never expected to need in our wildest dreams.'

'And that is?'

'It's very simple, Dr Samari,' said Leatherman. 'We need a translator.'

Yet again, Samari stared at Leatherman in astonishment.

'You mean she speaks?'

'She does,' said Leatherman, 'and we can't make out a word she says. As far as we can tell, it's Egyptian and we would love to find out what she is saying.'

'But, why me?' asked Samari, turning back toward the girl.

'Well, we can't really go to a normal translator, can we?' said Leatherman, 'this is still top secret, and don't forget, we smuggled her out of the country. You already have your hands dirty in this, so we thought we would keep it in the family, so to speak.'

'What do you want to find out?'

'Anything and everything - who she is, where did she come from? How did she get in there? How can a diet of blood sustain her? You name it; we want to know about it. I realize it may take time, but we think that if you can win her trust, she may tell you something we can use.'

'And how am I going to do that?' asked Samari, fearing the answer.

'You are going in there,' said Leatherman.

Chapter Thirteen

British Antiquities Museum

John, Becky, and Amy sat around the desk, each staring at the severed finger that was now lying in a steel specimen tray. Becky donned a pair of latex gloves and using a pair of large tweezers, lifted the finger up to the light to examine it closer. The index finger was grey with age and the skin very dry. The nail was elongated and a dirty yellow. It had been severed at the third knuckle from the nail and the bone joint could still be seen amongst the dried flesh.

'Why would he send me this?' she asked.

'I have no idea,' said John.

'Is it real?' asked Amy

'It's real,' said Becky. 'You can see the end of the bone where it seems to have been twisted away from the knuckle.'

'Ouch,' said Amy. 'That must have hurt.'

'Not really,' said Becky. 'The body this came from has been dead thousands of years. It has come from a corpse or a mummy.'

John's head shot up and stared at Becky.

'What did you say?' he asked.

'This finger has come from a body that has been dead for hundreds, if not thousands, of years,' said Becky.

'Becky, you know what you have there,' said John, 'Don't you remember, back in the tomb of Amenemhat? The body in the sarcophagus only had a thumb and three fingers on the left hand. The index finger was missing. Your father must have snapped it off when he was in there and sent it to you.'

'Why on earth would he do that?' asked Becky.

'I have no idea,' said John. 'Can I take a look?' He donned his own gloves, but didn't bother with tweezers. He turned the finger repeatedly in his hands, taking particular notice of the torn end.

'Do you have a microscope?' he asked.

'Yes, but it's not very powerful,' said Becky and went to the store cupboard to retrieve a very basic microscope.

'Thanks,' said John and placed the finger on the stage of the scope, arranging it so the torn end was directly beneath the objective lens. He fiddled with the adjustment knob to bring it into focus and gazed into the viewfinder for a long time.

'That's strange,' he said.

'What is?' asked Becky.

'Take a look at the bone edge,' he said, 'Tell me what you see.'

Becky stared at him before peering through the viewfinder and adjusting the focus to suit her own eyes.

'Clean and dry joint,' she said, 'with filaments of what seems to be micro tendons around the edges.'

'Exactly,' said John, 'micro filaments. Those filaments are tiny hair-like substances that make up a ligament called the Volar Plate. It joins each part of the finger bones together, acting as a sort of hinge.'

'So?'

'Becky, Volar Plates are in continuous movement and need constant regeneration. They are reliant on a regular blood supply to keep repairing the used or damaged cells. Take away the blood supply, and they quickly die off. If this corpse was as old as you reckon, then there should be no trace of any Volar Plates, even a few weeks after death.'

'John, sorry, but I have examined enough mummies to know this finger has come from a corpse at least a thousand years old.'

'I'm not saying you are wrong, Becky, but I am beginning to wonder if this is some sort of elaborate hoax.'

'What do you mean?'

'You saw that Mummy back in the tomb,' he said. 'It certainly looked ancient, but there must have been a good reason for all those wires and tubes. It would be pointless on a cadaver, but as we saw, the body seemed to have retained a level of moisture content. I have no idea why, but I suspect someone put that body in there fairly recently to try to pull the wool over someone's eyes.'

'You think so?' asked Becky.

'It's the only possible answer,' said John, 'Volar Plates do not survive after death.'

'Well there's one way to find out,' said Becky.

'And what's that?'

'Full cell analysis,' said Becky. 'Send a sample up to the lab and ask them for a full report. They can tell us an approximate death date. One way or another, we will know by tomorrow.'

'Won't that be placed on record,' asked John.

'No, leave it to me. One of the techies up there has been nagging me for a date for months. I'll ask him for a favour.'

'That's very noble of you,' laughed John. 'To go out on a date with a geek in the name of research.'

'Who said he was a geek?' asked Becky. 'All I said was he is a technician. He's quite cute, actually.'

'Excuse me,' said Amy. 'Sorry to interrupt, but could someone please tell me what the hell is going on here?'

Becky stared at Amy for a second, before turning her attention to John.

'We should tell her,' she said. 'After all, without her help we wouldn't have this.' She nodded toward the finger. 'And anyway,' she said with a smile, 'she is my assistant and I trust her one hundred percent.'

125

'Okay,' said John.

'Sit down, Amy;' said Becky, 'it's quite a long story.'

After Becky had finished bringing Amy up to date, there was a long silence while the girl absorbed the information.

'Well,' said Becky eventually, 'do you think we are mad?'

'No,' said Amy, her eyes still wide with wonder, 'I know there are things in this world that we don't understand. Wouldn't it be great if we were the ones to discover something?'

'I wouldn't get too carried away just yet,' said John, 'this isn't some 'Curse of the mummy's tomb' film we have here. I still think there is some sort of trickery going on and the sooner we bring it to light, the better.'

'Right,' said Becky,' in that case, let's get it up to the lab.'

'Hang on,' said John, 'why can't we just cut a bit off and send it up. They only need a tiny piece, surely?'

'I know,' said Becky, 'but all the outside has been contaminated by our DNA. They will need to cut it in half and reach the untainted cells to have an uncontaminated sample. Don't worry, I send this sort of thing up all the time. They won't suspect a thing.' She picked up the finger with the tweezers and placed it in a plastic bag. 'I'll take this up, and you take the Ushabti back up to Montague's office before he returns.'

Almost before she finished the sentence, all three realised the problem and looked down at the broken pieces of the false doll strewn across the floor.

'Shit,' said John, 'I never thought about that.'

'What are we going to do now?' asked Becky.

'I have an idea,' said Amy. 'Don't we have other Ushabti down here?'

'We do,' said Becky. 'There are a few of our own in aisle three.'

'Then give me one that is similar and I can take it up to his office.'

Becky looked at John.

'What do you think?' she asked.

'Do you think he will spot the difference?' asked John

'I wouldn't think so,' said Becky, 'not unless he looks at it close up. He's already done all the necessary checks back in Egypt, so he wouldn't have paid them much attention back here. Besides, the one we took was a modern fake, at least this one will be genuine.'

'I don't see how we have any other alternative,' said John.

'Then what are we waiting for?' asked Amy. 'You go and pick one that fits the bill and I'll take it up.'

A few minutes later, all three left the vaults and walked up the stairs to the upper floors. John was leaving to go back to his shop, and Amy was taking the replacement Ushabti to Montague's office. Becky carried a plastic bag containing a three thousand year old finger to the lab.

'I've had calmer days,' thought Becky, and after saying goodbye to John, entered the admin wing where the labs were located.

'Hello, Sandra,' said Becky as she entered the Lab, 'is Craig about?'

'He's over there,' said the female researcher, 'go on over.'

Becky walked over to the man with his back toward her. He was leaning over a microscope.

'Something interesting?' asked Becky.

The young man turned around and smiled at her.

'Hello, Becky,' he said, 'how are you?'

'Fine,' said Becky. 'Thought I would pop in and catch up.'

'Good to see you,' said Craig. 'Coffee?'

'I'd love one,' said Becky.

Five minutes later, they were wandering around the laboratory, while Craig explained what they were working on.

'This is quite interesting,' he said, 'DNA harvesting from a snow leopard. There's only approximately thirty five left in the wild. We are helping a wildlife organization build a library of DNA for every threatened species on the planet, and they asked us to do the snow leopard.'

'Interesting;' said Becky, 'and this one?'

'This is part of a mammoth calf found under the ice in Siberia. It is the same sort of thing really, though obviously, they are already extinct, so a lot harder to get a full sequence.'

'You love your job, don't you?' said Becky.

'It's fascinating,' said Craig. 'Under the microscope, a different universe unfolds and when you learn how to understand it, it gives you a whole new perspective on life. Sometimes, I have my eyes glued to the lens for hours on end without realizing it. The worst part is writing up the notes.'

'I know how that feels,' laughed Becky.

'Anyway,' said Craig when they had finished the tour, 'what can I do for you, Becky?'

'I'm that transparent, eh?' asked Becky.

'You are a bit,' laughed Craig. 'Come on spit it out.'

'The thing is, Craig,' said Becky, 'I need an analysis done on something, but at the moment it needs to be kept a bit quiet. It's early days, but I don't want to risk my work getting out. Do you know what I mean?'

'I understand,' said Craig, 'but why can't you just go through the usual channels? We are bound by confidentiality clauses, after all.'

'I know,' said Becky, 'but this artefact has been loaned to me from another museum, and if anyone finds out, then we'll all be in trouble. Look, I don't want to get you into any bother, Craig, so if you feel awkward…'

'No, it's okay,' said Craig. 'As long as it doesn't take too much time, I'll see what I can do. What exactly is it?'

Becky pulled out the bag and showed the contents to Craig.

'I want to know, if this fake?' said Becky, 'and if possible, could I have a full cell analysis on the blood. We think it's a hoax, but want to find out quietly.'

'Ah,' said Craig, 'I see; you don't want the hoaxer to know you are onto them.

'Something like that,' said Becky. 'So do you think you can do it?'

'No problem,' said Craig taking the bag, 'come back tomorrow at the same time and I'll have the results for you.'

'Thanks, Craig,' said Becky, 'I'll do that. Look, I'm free on Saturday and there's a good band in the local pub. Perhaps we can have that drink we keep talking about?'

Craig's face lit up.

'Thanks, Becky,' he said, 'I'd love that.'

'Great,' she said. 'See you tomorrow.'

Amy checked all around the landing before entering Montague's office. Immediately, she made her way over to the row of twelve Ushabti and filled the one empty box with the one from beneath her wrap. Satisfied it did not look out of place, she left the table, but before leaving the office, she took the opportunity to have a look around. Montague was the highest level you could get in the museum and it wasn't often you got to see inside his office unless you were high up or in trouble. Amy was neither, so she was fascinated at the level of luxury the office enjoyed. All around the walls portraits of people she had never heard of stared down with accusing faces, and on every flat surface, stood an ornament or carving from cultures all across the world, dating from prehistory through to the modern age. Four soft chairs were positioned around a coffee table to one side, standing on a beautiful Persian rug, but dominating the room by far, was an enormous mahogany desk where Montague carried out his day to day work. Amy reckoned it was at least the size of their dining table at home and the wood gleamed with a deep shine from hundreds of years of care. She went up to the desk and swept her hand gently across the smooth surface, daydreaming about the day when she might work behind such a desk. As she walked along the front of the desk, her eyes caught a name scribbled on the memo pad along with the name of a hotel. She frowned as she read the name, because as it seemed familiar, she struggled to recall where she had heard it. Without giving it much more thought, she left the room and returned downstairs to carry on with her day job. Becky was already there.

'Okay, Amy?' asked Becky.

'Yeah, no problems,' she said, 'I must have been a female spy in a previous life.'

'A femme fatale?' suggested Becky.

'Yeah, something like that,' said Amy. 'So, what are you going to tell Montague?'

128

'The truth,' said Becky, 'well, sort of. I'll say that you typed up the inscription on my instructions and that the original must have been replaced somewhere between here and Cairo by persons unknown, which in essence, is also the truth.'

'But won't he say that you should have noticed?'

'Probably, but I will play on the fact that I have been a little tired recently after the death of my dad and that I made a mistake.'

'Will you lose your job?'

'No, nothing like that,' said Becky. 'I know Montague and he respects people who front up and admit their mistakes. I'll probably get a ticking off, but that will be it, really.'

'So what are you going to do next?' asked Amy.

'I'm not sure,' said Becky. 'I suppose I'll wait for the results first, and then try to work out why my father sent me a false finger. If John is correct, I suspect my father found out about some sort of fraud at the museum and sent it to me as evidence. Perhaps it was over something so controversial that it could have damaged the museum's reputation.'

'You think so?' asked Amy.

'I don't know,' said Becky with a sigh, 'but hopefully this will all become clear in the next few days.'

They spent the rest of the day working as normal, and soon Becky found herself letting herself back into her flat to be greeted by her cat, another day over. The evening went as normal, but just as she was about to have an early night, there was a knock at the front door.

'Oh, for heaven's sake, Smokey,' she said to the cat, 'who on earth could that be at this time of night?'

She opened the door to the full extent of the security chain and was surprised to see Craig standing outside, his collar turned up against the rain.

'Craig,' she said, 'what are you doing here?'

'Hi, Becky,' said Craig, 'I'm sorry to call at this time of night, but I have to talk to you.'

'Why, what's so important that it can't wait until tomorrow?'

'It's that finger, Becky. I managed to do some work on it and quite frankly, I can't believe what I am seeing.'

'Oh,' said Becky, 'I suppose you better come in.' She undid the chain and Craig walked into the flat, removing his coat as he did so.

'You look soaked,' said Becky. 'Take a seat, and I'll get a towel and some coffee.'

Five minutes later, they were sitting opposite each other in Becky's lounge. Craig sipped his coffee as Becky waited patiently for him to explain. Finally, she could wait no longer and asked the question burning on her lips.

'So, Craig, what is so important, that you dragged yourself halfway across London in the pouring rain to tell me?'

Craig put his cup down and stared at her.

'Becky, I don't know what you are involved in,' he said, 'but whatever it is, it scares me.'

Chapter Fourteen

Mulberry Lodge

Samari looked at Leatherman with a look of disbelief on his face.

'Oh, no I'm not,' he said. 'You have just told me that thing in there is capable of tearing me limb from limb.'

'It's not as bad as it seems,' said Leatherman. 'Our technicians go in there all the time. Hell, I've even been in there once myself. Obviously we don't expect you to waltz in unprotected; we have safety systems in place.'

'And what are they?' asked Samari.

'First of all, you will wear protective equipment. We have had suits made up from a material similar to police officers' bullet-proof vests. It is flexible yet armoured. Your face will be protected with a helmet, which has a neck guard that falls to the shoulders. Every inch of you will be covered and as she only uses her teeth and nails as weapons, you will be fully protected. Secondly, there is a bank of ultraviolet lamps along the wall above the entrance door, they are the nearest thing to sunlight and she hates them. Whenever we go in we use them to control her, making her retreat to behind the screen, so we can do whatever needs doing. There are four levels in all, and level one is infrared as you see now. We call this the darkness setting and it seems to put her at ease the most. We suspect the reason is that she has been used to total darkness for thousands of years. She cannot see the infrared, but obviously we can observe her, albeit with goggles on. Level two is low level blue lighting we call moonlight. It enables us to observe her freely and it seems to have no adverse effect on her. Level three is daylight, which she avoids by going behind the screen and level four we call sunburn. Sunburn is full power ultraviolet and will only be used in an emergency. It has an immediate debilitating effect on her, causing the skin to burn and we suspect, left in this level of intensity, she would probably die or whatever the equivalent is in her species.'

'Have you ever used sunburn?' asked Samari.

'Only once,' said Leatherman. 'The first day we entered the room, she attacked the technicians. The suits ensured they were safe, but we flicked the sunburn switch and she recoiled as if we had poured boiling water over her. It seems like she is a quick learner, because after that, she never attacked any of our staff again.'

'If I agree,' said Samari, 'how do I know that someone will react if there is an emergency?'

'There are two levels of safety, Doctor. First, there will always be a technician sitting at the controls you see there. Every second is recorded on CCTV, and at all times they will be in contact with you via a radio system, reacting to your instructions. You shout sunburn, and we'll roast her. Secondly, just in case the technician has a heart attack or something, there is

131

a red button placed in each corner of the room. Hit that, and it's toast time again.'

'You have a nice way with words,' said Samari.

'Facts are facts,' said Leatherman. 'She can't take ultraviolet light, and is floored the second we switch it on. We are not in the business of hurting our people, Samari. The safety measures are fool proof.'

'Not in the business of hurting people,' Samari sneered. 'Forgive me my cynicism, Leatherman, but don't forget it was only a few months ago that you placed a 9mm bullet on my desk.'

'That was different,' said Leatherman. 'Then you were an outsider and it was a bluff to ensure you kept your mouth shut. Now you are part of the team and we look after our own. So, what do you think? Do you fancy being the first person in history to talk to someone who lived thousands of years ago? Or should I book you a flight home?'

Samari turned his gaze to the girl once more. She was curled up on the floor like a puppy, yet her black eyes were wide-open, seemingly staring right through him. He knew it was an opportunity too great to miss.

'Okay,' he said eventually, 'I'll do it.'

An hour later, Samari stood with his arms outstretched as a team of technicians helped him into his protective suit. The gloves were made from a thin Kevlar link, while the main body of the suit was padded with a fabric, which was interwoven with stab proof Kevlar strands. The helmet was again predominantly soft and slipped over his head like a balaclava, though it had a perspex face visor built in at the front. The wide neck protection fell down past the shoulders and was clipped onto the chest with lever clips Overall Samari felt like one of the bomb disposal experts he had seen so many times on the news. As he was being dressed, he stared at the girl in the cell. The infrared light had now gone and had been replaced with a dark blue glow that was just adequate for him to see clearly without the aid of special goggles.

She was sitting at the back of the cell with her arms around her knees and though she was perfectly still, her black eyes were wide open. Finally, when he was done, he turned and looked at his back up team. Immediately in front of the window, two men sat at the control desk and Samari could see the four buttons in the centre of the console, black for night, blue for moonlight, green for daylight, and red for sunburn. Alongside the main console were two TV monitors, one showing a full image of the girl's cell, while the other was split into a four-screen mode, reflecting each view of the four cameras situated high in each corner of the cell.

The row of chairs in the small auditorium were beginning to fill up with staff, and at the back of the room, Samari could see Leatherman in deep conversation on his mobile phone.

'That's it,' said the supervisor technician, 'you're ready. We fed her just before you came back in, so she will be in a good mood, but don't do anything sudden or unexpected.'

'Can you test the lights please?' asked Samari.

'They are working fine,' assured the technician. 'As you can see, we are currently in moonlight mode.'

'I'd like to see the rest of them,' said Samari.

'Okay,' said the technician through a forced smile and turned to address the men at the console.

'Give her the warning,' he said, 'then go to daylight.'

Samari looked into the cell, as a small amber light, started to flash. The girl looked up sharply.

'Whenever we change the settings, we give her a warning,' explained the supervisor.

Inside, the girl stood up and looked toward the door in anticipation, before taking shelter behind the screen.

'Going to daylight,' said one of the controllers and pressed the green button.

Immediately the blue lights extinguished and the room lit up as bright as any office.

'And sunburn?' asked Samari after a few seconds.

'We only use sunburn as punishment,' said the technician, 'And she hasn't done anything wrong.'

'Show me sunburn,' repeated Samari.

'But she will be confused,' said the technician and looked up toward Leatherman.

Leatherman nodded silently and the supervisor turned back to the controllers.

'Initiate sunburn,' he said, 'Two second blast.'

The controller hit the red button and the room lit up like nothing Samari had ever seen. In reflex, he turned his head away, as the brightness hurt his eyes. Two seconds later, the controller hit the green button and the room returned to daylight.

'Wow,' said Samari, 'I see what you mean.'

'That's why we don't like using it without cause,' said the supervisor. 'She is affected even behind the screen, and is probably confused now.'

'Point taken,' said Samari, 'So just to confirm, in an emergency, all I have to do is either call out or hit one of those red buttons in there.'

'Correct,' said the supervisor. 'The light will come on and the automatic door locks will disengage to allow you to get out. At that point, she will be screaming in agony on the floor. So, are you ready?'

'As ready as I will ever be,' said Samari and stepped up to the door.

'Right, take your time and no sudden movements. This is first contact, so be gentle and try to establish an element of trust. We don't expect too much on this visit, but just want to send the message that any subsequent visits from you are friendly. Okay with that?'

Samari nodded.

'Right,' said the supervisor, and turned to the men at the console. 'Open the outer door.'

Samari heard a clunk and the door in front of him opened. He stepped in to a small entrance chamber, and waited for the sliding door behind him to close, before the inner doors opened. With a deep breath, he stepped into the cell, and as the door closed behind him, stared around taking in the surroundings.

From this point of view, everything seemed different. First, it seemed much bigger, but he soon realised it was due to the viewing window appearing mirrored, which gave a false sense of size. The next thing to hit him was how bright it was inside, it had seemed a little dimmer from the other side of the glass, but the main thing that he wasn't expecting was the awful smell. The room reeked of gone off food, human waste and something else. While he couldn't put his finger on it, he suspected that it was the smell given off by the girl, a stink of what remained of any dead flesh that still hadn't regenerated. He controlled the urge to gag and a second later, a voice came over the tannoy.

'Are you okay, Doctor?'

'Fine,' said, Samari. 'Just getting used to my surroundings.'

'Good, just let us know when you are ready to proceed.'

Gradually Samari got used to the smell and a few seconds later, he gave the instruction.

'Okay,' he said, 'go to moonlight.'

'Going to moonlight,' confirmed the voice, 'like we said, take it steady and no sudden movements.'

Immediately the bright lights dimmed until the cell was almost dark and a blue glow permeated the entire room.

'What do I do now?' asked Samari, 'Do I go over?'

'No,' came the reply, 'that is her safe place; she may see it as a threat. Just remain patient and she'll come to you.'

Samari waited until finally, a moment or so later, the girl appeared from behind the screen and stared at him. Samari gulped involuntarily and took a small step forward.

'Steady,' said the metallic voice, 'wait for her.'

Sure enough, the girl walked forward and stopped before him. She glanced up nervously at the lights, before walking slowly around him. Samari realised he was sweating through nervousness, and although he knew he was safe, he still felt uncomfortable when she was out of his sight.

'Don't worry,' said the metallic voice, 'We are watching her. If she tries anything, we hit the fry button.'

A few seconds later, the girl came back into view and stood directly in front of him, staring into his eyes.

'Oh, my god,' said Samari, 'her eyes are unbelievable.'

'Yes, they are quite unique,' said the voice. 'Completely black.'

'No,' said Samari as he met her gaze, 'not completely black, they have a slight tinge of red. It's difficult to explain, but probably the darkest shade of red you could have on the spectrum, before it tips over into black.'

'Really?' said the voice. 'We hadn't noticed that. Well done, Doctor. You have been there two minutes and already we have new information.'

The girl raised her hand and touched the visor gently before touching her own face to feel the difference.

'There is no doubt there is a high level of intelligence there,' said Samari. 'I'm going to try to speak to her.'

'Okay,' said the voice. 'Recorders are on.'

Samari took a breath and speaking in Egyptian, greeted the girl.

'Hello,' he said.

The girl took half a step back and her head tilted like an interested puppy.

'Hello,' said Samari again. 'My name is Doctor Samari. I am here to help you.'

The girl's eyes narrowed and he could see her silently forming the words with her mouth.

'Samari,' he said again, 'I am Doctor Samari.'

The girl's mouth formed the words again, though this time she made a sound.

'Doctorsamari,' she said, the two words merging into one.

'Yes, Doctor Samari,' he replied, 'it may be easier to just say Doctor.'

'Doctor,' she said, though this time much clearer.

'You,' he said, pointing at her chest, 'what is your name?'

Again, her eyes narrowed as if deep in thought. Finally, she spoke again.

'Nephthys,' she said.

'Good to meet you, Nephthys,' said Samari and then clammed up, unsure what to say next. Before he could say anything, Nephthys broke the silence.

'Are you a god?'

Samari was taken aback. Although the dialect was somewhat removed from modern Egyptian, he found he could understand the words quite comfortably.

'No,' he said, 'I am a man.'

'Why are you dressed so?' asked Nephthys.

'For my protection,' said Samari. 'In case you try to harm me.'

'My mother is a goddess,' said Nephthys, 'A nightwalker who dominated these lands for more years than there is wheat in the fields.'

'Who is your mother?' asked Samari.

'Sekhmet; bringer of death, granter of life, provider of immortality.'

'And is she a goddess?'

'She is a nightwalker,' said Nephthys, 'as am I. Why do you not know her name and cower in fear before me?'

'It is a tale too long to tell at the moment,' said Samari, 'but tell it, we will. First, I would like to know you. Where have you come from?'

Nephthys didn't answer, but kept staring at him.

'How old are you, Nephthys?' asked Samari. 'When and where were you born?'

Again, Nephthys remained silent.

'Why do you not answer?' asked Samari. 'Do you not understand?'

'I understand your words, but the questions make no sense. I am of here and I am of now.'

Samari nodded, thinking furiously. Obviously her awareness seemed to have just continued from the time she had lost consciousness thousands of years ago. If he revealed any information regarding dates and circumstances, it would only confuse the issue. He knew he had to be careful in the way he framed the questions.

'Have you always been of Kemet?' he asked, using the ancient name for Egypt. 'Or were you born in a different land?'

'I was born in Kemet,' she confirmed, 'in Itjawi, burial place of the persecutor Amenemhat.'

Samari swallowed hard. This conversation was already opening up so many doors that he could hardly contain himself. Finally, he allowed himself to ask the one burning question, he wanted desperately to know.

'Nephthys, you have been in this place a long time.'

'I have.'

'Then tell me this. What king wore the two crowns of Kemet when you last saw the sky?'

Nephthys' eyes narrowed in anger and Samari could see he had touched a nerve.

'Is he your master?' she hissed. 'The false god who has as many tongues as thrones. He is nothing but a serpent, and he will be cast into everlasting servitude at my kiss.'

'I know no master,' said Samari, gently, trying to calm her down. 'You have been here for many years and a new king sits on the throne. I would like to know the name of the one who was king when you came here.'

'Ramesses,' she spat, 'the second king who has borne that name. He of a treacherous heart and false tongue. He tricked us into this place, slew my sisters and condemned my mother and me to a thousand lifetimes in the dark

136

with nought, but a single slave to sustain us. When I leave this place, I will unleash my wrath upon his form with the fury of a thousand years.'

Samari's heart was pounding. If what this girl was saying was correct, she actually lived during the reign of Ramesses II. It was unbelievable. Here was someone who not only lived and breathed over three thousand years ago, but also experienced the reign of the greatest Egyptian king ever to have lived. Not only that, but she was conscious, sentient and understandable. The implications were incalculable, this creature would be able to recount stories that even the best Egyptologists could only guess at. The tinny voice came back over the air.

'Is everything okay, Doctor?' it asked.

'Everything is fine,' he said.

'We can hear her talking to you. Do you understand her?'

'I do,' said Samari, 'I will be out soon. Give me another two minutes.'

'What are these strange sounds you make?' asked Nephthys. 'Are they the words of demons?'

'I am speaking to others like me,' said Samari, 'in our own language.'

'I see no others,' said Nephthys.

'They are beyond these walls and are able to hear my words through…um,'

'Magic?' she interjected.

'Yes, sort of,' said Samari, 'we call it Radio.'

'Then you are demons.'

'No, we are men.'

'My kind feed on men,' said Nephthys.

Again, Samari gulped.

'We thought as much,' said Samari, 'and that is why we are being careful. We want to talk to you, learn about you and find out what we can do to make your time here as comfortable as possible.'

'Then why do you burn me?' asked Nephthys glancing up at the lamps above the door.

'It is only for protection,' said Samari. 'We know you can do us great harm, so if you attack us, it is our way of defending ourselves.'

'It is the way of things,' said Nephthys. 'We are the predator, you are the prey. It has always been and the way it is now.'

'But it doesn't have to be,' said Samari. 'I and others like me are men of great learning. We have knowledge we can share with you and in return, you can tell us things that we don't know. That is why I am here, to establish that you are willing to talk and not attack us.'

'Why should I trust you?' said, Nephthys. 'When the last man we trusted betrayed us and wiped our sisters from the face of the earth.'

'I understand your reluctance,' said Samari, 'but I am not Ramesses. His time has gone and we are now a land of learning. We want to understand and work alongside you in peace, learning from each other.'

'Are these the words of your king?'

'We have no king,' said Samari, 'though the highest among us here agrees with my explanation.'

'And can you give me a throne to rule all men?'

'I can't,' said Samari. 'There is much for you to learn about this place, but it will take time. I am happy to teach you, but I need your trust.'

'You ask for my trust,' said Nephthys, 'yet you come here with weapons of light and armour of cloth. Where is your trust, doctor?'

Samari stared at her for an age before replying.

'If I display my trust,' he said, 'will it be offered in return?'

'It will,' said Nephthys.

'Then I offer my ultimate trust,' he said and started to unbutton the neck guards around his shoulders.

'Doctor, what are you doing?' asked the tinny voice.

'Don't worry;' said Samari into his microphone, 'I know what I am doing.'

'Doctor, stop. That is an order; do not remove your protection.'

'Be quiet,' snapped Samari, 'this is my choice.'

'Doctor,' said the voice, 'if you remove your protection, she will kill you.'

'I don't think she will,' said Samari, staring into the girl's eyes.

'Stand by for sunburn,' said the voice.

'No!' snapped Samari. 'Leatherman, if you are listening, stand down your men. Do not go to sunburn, I repeat, do not go to sunburn. It is essential we stay on moonlight if we are to gain her trust. If I am wrong, then I will pay the price, but that is my decision.'

Outside the Cell, the technician turned to face the back of the room where Leatherman stood alongside another man who had entered the room at the last minute. A quiet conversation took place between Leatherman and the visitor before Leatherman made his decision.

'Give him what he wants,' he said.

A silence followed before Samari spoke again over the intercom.

'Well,' he asked, 'what's it to be?'

'We have had confirmation from Mr Leatherman to maintain moonlight,' said the technician. 'I hope you know what you are doing, Doctor Samari.'

'So do I,' said Samari and continued to unclip the helmet.

Finally, all the clasps were undone and Samari spoke again in the language that Nephthys understood.

'You asked me to display my trust, Nephthys,' he said, 'so I will entrust you with the most precious thing I have.'

'And what is that?' asked Nephthys.

'My life,' said Samari and lifted off the helmet.

Both people stared at each other, meeting the other's respective gazes. Nephthys stepped closer and leaned slightly forward, her nose twitching as she took in his scent.

'It has been a long time since I tasted the blood of man,' she said hoarsely and moved in closer.

Samari felt the sweat running down his back, knowing that if she struck now, there would be no time for the staff to save him, sunburn or not.

'You have no idea how much I desire to rip out your throat, Doctor. To enjoy the flow of your blood pumping into my mouth while your heart still beats, and to taste the saltiness of your flesh as I tear through your muscle to feast on your organs.'

'Then I ask you not to take out your hunger on me, Nephthys,' he answered, his voice shaking, 'For if you make me your victim, then those who watch will know they can never trust you again and you will be locked in this place for evermore.'

Her face drew close to his and her tongue emerged to lick the side of his neck.

'I can hear your blood, Doctor. I can see the pulse as your heart sends it through your veins.'

'Don't do it, Nephthys,' he said.' You asked me for my trust and I have given it freely. You have many things we desire, and in return, I can help you get out of here.'

Nephthys stepped back and stared at him.

'I have been in this place for a long time, Doctor. Why would you let me out?'

'You don't belong here, Nephthys,' he said. 'You belong back in Egypt amongst our own people. We will look after you there and our people can learn many things from you.'

'We are not in Kemet?'

'No, we are in a place far removed, and it is wrong.'

'Then we will work together to kill those who imprison me,' said Nephthys. 'When will you set me free?'

'Nephthys, I have to go,' he said, 'my people are expecting me, but I will return as soon as possible. In the meantime, promise me this. Do not attack anyone who enters here. Be subservient to their whims and cause no concern. I will try to ensure they burn you no more, but you must cede dominance, for they have more ways of killing you than you can imagine. This is just the beginning, Nephthys, there is so much more to come. The next time I come, I will wear no armour, but will bring gifts of information. This way we will win the trust of others and as you grow stronger in body, you will grow stronger in knowledge. You ask me to demonstrate my trust, Nephthys, now I need yours.'

After a few moments silence, where Nephthys' eyes seemed to bore into his soul, she finally spoke.

'I have waited an eternity, Doctor, living only in my dreams. A little while longer makes no difference. Go in safety and return in safety. I will not take your life, but there are more questions, than there are stars above Kemet. I would have answers.'

'As would I,' said Samari. 'Now, you should go behind your screen until I leave or they may turn on the lights.'

Nephthys walked backwards until she reached the screen.

'Do not let too much time pass before we speak again, Doctor,' she said, and with that, she stepped behind the screen.

Samari turned and walked to the entrance.

'Open the door,' he said, 'but remain in moonlight.'

'Against regulations, Doctor Samari,' said the tinny voice.

'Screw regulations,' he said, 'I made her a promise, now let me out.'

The light remained blue as he stepped through the airlock and he stepped back into the auditorium to a round of applause from the gathered technicians. As the door closed behind him with a satisfying clunk, Samari bent over and promptly threw up on the floor.

Chapter Fifteen

Outskirts of London

Becky looked at Craig in confusion. Obviously he was worried, but why he was so wound up over a simple finger off a cadaver was beyond her.

'What do you mean?' she asked.

'Becky, that sample you gave me earlier is either unique in this world, or the most elaborate hoax I have ever seen.'

'Sorry, I don't follow,' she said.

'Look, Becky, if you are part of something that I should be aware of, please have the courtesy to tell me. I will keep my mouth shut, I promise, but please don't take me for a fool.'

'Craig, you are making no sense,' said Becky. 'Why don't you start at the beginning and tell me everything you have found?'

'Okay,' sighed Craig and took another sip of coffee before continuing. 'After you left this morning, I finished the tests that I was doing and found I had some time on my hands, so I prepared the sample you gave me. I placed the finger in a sterile pod and sliced it in half, taking uncontaminated tissue from the centre. As soon as I confirmed the sample was clean, I ran a series of tests, thinking I would find one of three things. One, that the tissue was ancient and from a corpse long dead. Two, that it was no more than a few hundred years old and the result of a natural decaying process, or three, it is from a relatively modern body, altered to present a false aging process as part of some unknown hoax.'

'And which did you find?' asked Becky.

'That's the thing,' said Craig, 'basically, I found all three.'

Becky looked on uncomprehendingly.

'I don't understand,' she said, 'please explain.'

'Well, first of all I did a tissue sample.' said Craig. 'I confirmed it was human tissue, and in the first results, it seemed that the subject probably died a few decades ago. However, further analysis shows there are cells present that are several hundreds of years old and on top of that, even more cells that are in a state of decay that suggests the sample is from a body that died thousands of years ago. It doesn't make any sense.'

'Do you think it is a fake and has been made deliberately to look like that?'

'Absolutely not,' said Craig, 'the structure is perfect and far too detailed to reproduce, unless of course, you consider cloning, but the age of the cells preclude that.'

'Then what do you make of it?' asked Becky.

'I had no idea,' said Craig, 'so I carried out a full suite of tests.'

'And your results?'

'Are astonishing.'

'Do you have a report with you?'

'I have better than that,' said Craig, lifting his bag from the floor, 'I have brought the experiment with me. Could we use your table?'

'Of course,' said Becky.

Craig opened his bag and pulled out an electronic microscope, passing the lead to Becky to plug in. Delving further into his bag, he pulled out a lidded plastic container and placed it alongside the microscope. He retrieved a blank slide and after pricking his finger with a pin, he smeared the blood on the glass and placed it on the shelf of the scope. After focussing the instrument, he stood up from the table so Becky could take his place.

'Take a look,' he said, 'and then tell me what you see.'

'I know what I will see,' said Becky.

'Humour me,' said Craig

Becky peered into the viewfinder and focussed the microscope for her own eyes.

'As far as I can make out,' said Becky, 'it is a collection of healthy blood cells.'

'Good,' said Craig. 'We have established our benchmark. Now, how long do you reckon it will take for the cells to deteriorate?'

'With no oxygen supply? A few minutes maximum.'

'That's what I thought,' said Craig. 'Now, replace the slide with this one.'

He gave her two slides stuck together labelled with a capital 'A' in marker pen. Becky removed the top slide and placed the bottom one under the microscope.

'Now, tell me what you see,' said Craig.

'Another cluster of blood cells,' said Becky, 'though abnormal in shape. They look grey in colour and seem to have some sort of thin protuberances coming from the cell walls. Similar to a parasite, but inside the cell walls themselves.'

'Very good, Becky,' said Craig. 'The strange cells you see are indeed dead blood cells, but have been genetically altered to a different form. I have run various tests and the nearest infection I can find is a virus known as Neurotropic Lyssavirus, more commonly known to you and I as rabies.'

'Rabies doesn't infect blood cells,' said Becky, 'it is a stand-alone virus that infects the neurological cells, infecting the brain and spinal cord.'

'I know,' said Craig, 'but for some unknown reason, the virus has taken this cell as a host, and it was the probable cause of the cell's death. However, there is something else there. Those strange things sticking out from the cells are the external extremities of the Sporozoites of Plasmodium cells, otherwise known as?'

'I don't know,' said Becky.

'The malaria parasite,' said Craig. 'The dead cells under the scope are the unfortunate host of both a parasite and a virus. The exact genome type for either are unknown to me, or indeed any reference book I have referred to. However, suffice to say they are very similar to the rabies virus and the malaria parasite, both within the same cell.'

'What are you getting at?' said Becky.

'First of all,' said Craig, 'I have never come across this sort of infection before. Two separate infections, both latching onto a blood cell and living long enough to alter the actual structure of the host. It is amazing and any haematologist would find enough data on this cell alone fascinating enough to fill an entire book of genetic research.'

'But why?' asked Becky. 'We hear of this sort of thing all the time these days. Scientists are splicing genes together, cloning sheep and even transfusing artificial blood into humans until such time as the right type becomes available.'

'I know,' said Craig, 'but the combination of these two infections seemed to have altered the actual state of the host cell. It must have taken a whole raft of coincidences for the host to be in just the right state, but happen it did, and when they merged in the bloodstream, something astonishing happened.'

'What?'

'It would seem that not only did they transform the genetic structure, but the cell retained enough of its previous identity for the host body not to reject it.'

'Okay,' said Becky, 'I can grasp it so far, but surely if that were the case, then perhaps the subject died from the infection?'

'No, I don't think it did,' said Craig, 'I think the infection actually worked in the host's favour and made it stronger, with a much more effective cell regeneration rate.'

'You don't know that,' said Becky.

'Oh, but I do,' said Craig. 'And I can prove it.' He reached into his bag once more and withdrew a syringe. He squeezed another drop of blood from his thumb, and drew a tiny drop into the end of the syringe, before giving it to Becky.

'Now,' he said, 'look at the dead cells again, but this time, add a drop of healthy blood. Tell me what you see.'

Once again, Becky did as she was asked, and added Craig's blood to the slide already on the bed of the scope. The deep red of the oxygenated fresh blood stood out against the grey of the dead infected cells, and just as Becky was wondering what it was she was supposed to be seeing, a tiny movement caught her eye. Over the next few seconds, she stared into the microscope in astonishment as the supposedly dead grey cells, gradually absorbed the red cells. Within a few minutes, all the red cells were gone and the grey cells had taken on a pink hue. She looked up and stared at Craig.

'That's mad,' said Becky, 'I thought those cells were dead.'

'As did I,' said Craig, 'but keep looking, the best is yet to come.'

143

Becky returned to the microscope and stared down at the infected strange cells. Again, she waited patiently and was soon rewarded with movement. As she looked, some of the cells started to stretch and within moments, many had duplicated themselves and though Becky had seen this process many times before, the implications of this process blew her mind.

'Oh, my god,' she whispered,' they've split into exact replicas, not only of the cell, but the infections as well. How can that be?'

'I know; it's the strangest thing I have ever seen.'

Becky stood up and faced Craig.

'Am I understanding this correctly?' she asked. 'That sometime in the past, a person with normal blood cells was infected with two different diseases at the same time, and due to circumstances we will probably never understand, they combined to create a completely new type of blood cell that fed on the host.'

'That's about it,' said Craig.

'But that would have killed the host,' said Becky, 'once the remaining blood was used up, then there would be no more left to nourish those that are infected.'

'You are right, except for two things. First, if you were to keep watching the sample, you will see the cells eventually stop reproducing and start to feed on each other. The last cell that survives this microscopic cannibalism seems to withdraw into a sort of hibernation until a fresh source of blood is provided, which brings me onto the second thing. All you have to do to start the process all over again is introduce a fresh source of blood.'

'Yet, that last cell never dies?'

'Not unless you take positive intervention. Extreme heat seems to be the most effective. As with most things on this planet, if you burn something, the actual structure of the item itself is destroyed. A sort of natural disinfectant. The other thing is ultraviolet light. It has the same effect, but without the accompanying heat that fire brings, it takes a little longer to have an effect.'

'So how long will these cells last if they are left alone?'

'I can't be sure,' said Craig, 'but that finger contains many such dormant cells and depending if what you say is true, may have lain that way for thousands of years. Don't you get it?' he continued, 'What you have here, Becky, is a blood cell that doesn't die and is able to reproduce itself very easily. It is a cycle of never ending cell renewal that needs no gene manipulation, just a source of oxygenated haemoglobin to enable reproduction. Imagine the implications, Becky, a potential cure for blood diseases, organ repairs or even cells within the rest of the body. Hell, the possibilities are endless and in theory, if manipulated correctly, they could even replace dying cells in every part of the body, slowing or even halting the aging process.'

Becky stared at Craig in disbelief.

'No,' she said, 'that's impossible.'

'That's what I thought,' said Craig, 'but I reproduced that experiment over a dozen times today. The results are robust and they happened the exact same way every time I tried it. The cells are dormant until the addition of fresh blood. As soon as that happens, they absorb the blood and reproduce. Continue to add more blood and the process repeats, but withdraw that source of blood and any cells touching each other turn cannibalistic, leaving only the strongest. That last remaining cell then withdraws into a state of hibernation.'

'But how is that possible?' asked Becky.

'Oh, it's possible,' said Craig. 'We already know there are fish eggs, seeds and even some actual animals that lay in a state of dormancy for many years, but these are by far exceeded by bacteria that have been found on the seabed beneath the arctic oceans. Some of those have lain dormant for millions of years until climatic conditions are suitable for reproduction.'

'Millions of years?'

'Millions of years,' confirmed Craig, 'so the thought of a cell staying dormant for a few thousand isn't that great a stretch of the imagination.'

'This is unbelievable,' said Becky, her mind racing.

'I know,' said Craig, 'and that is why I asked if you were involved with some sort of organisation carrying out this sort of research.'

'I'm not,' said Becky, 'I promise you. All I know is that I was sent that finger by…' She hesitated, unsure of how much to tell the young man, 'by somebody, and though he knew it was special, I doubt he knew all this.'

'Where did he get it?' asked Craig.

'Off a body in Egypt,' said Becky.

Craig spluttered, choking on his coffee.

'A body,' he gasped, 'you mean you have the rest of the corpse?'

'I don't,' said Becky, 'but someone else does.'

'Who?'

'I'm not sure,' said Becky, 'but I've got a good idea. Look, Craig, thanks for this. I'm not sure what we have here and I know I am going to have to go to the authorities about this, but can I ask that you keep all this to yourself at the moment? I think this is going to blow up in my face, and if it does, I don't want to drag you down with me.'

'Don't worry,' said Craig, 'when I get back, I'll destroy all the evidence. Do you want the finger back?'

'No, burn it,' said Becky, 'but could you do one last favour?'

'Sure.'

'Could you prepare a vial of these sample cells for me? I'll put them in my safe, and if it all falls apart, at least I can prove my story with them. Call it an insurance policy.'

'Will do,' said Craig, 'but after that, I'm out. Wherever this is leading, I don't want any part of it.'

'Understood,' said Becky.

'The samples will be ready tomorrow,' said Craig, 'collect them at midday.'

'Thanks, Craig,' said Becky and walked him to the door. As he went to walk away, he turned one more time.

'Oh,' he said, 'one more thing, our date on Saturday.'

'What about it?' asked Becky.

'I'm a little busy,' said Craig. 'Could we put it off until a later date, you know, when all this is over?'

'Of course,' said Becky. 'No problem. Goodnight, Craig, and thanks again.'

She closed the door and leaned against it, overwhelmed by the information she had just received.

Finally, she walked into the room.

'I've got to speak to John,' she said to herself and picked up the phone.

Amy got out of the taxi and nervously stood in front of the restaurant doors. She had been out to eat many times with her family, but this was by far the most famous restaurant she had been to, and the very first as a venue for a date.

She placed the change from the taxi driver in her purse and took a deep breath before walking up to the doors. The new dress she had bought for the occasion was figure hugging and though it was indeed black, it was far removed from the gothic influence she favoured. Her hair had been done and she looked every inch the elegant young lady. If her mother had seen her, she would have been very proud, but that hadn't happened, as nobody knew she was even here. Nobody that is except Lucas Klein, and hopefully, he would be waiting inside.

Since the night of the dinner party, they had talked constantly on the phone, messaged each other on the social network pages and even talked face to face via webcam. They had got on like a house on fire, and when he had actually asked her on a date, Amy thought her heart would break through her chest; such was her excitement.

She had suggested the cinema, but Lucas had insisted on a fancy restaurant, so here she was. She knew she looked great and felt even better. This was special and unlike the two other dates she had in her life, this was going to be very grown up and sophisticated. She stepped through the door and was immediately met by the Maître d.

'Good evening, Madame, do you have a reservation?'

'Yes, I believe the table is booked in the name of Mr Lucas Klein.'

'Of course,' said the waiter, 'Mr Klein is expecting you, please follow me.'

They walked through the restaurant toward the cubicles along the wall and Amy smiled when she saw Lucas stand up as she approached.

'Hello, Amy,' said Lucas. 'You look beautiful.'

'Hello, Lucas,' said Amy. 'Thank you, you look quite smart yourself.'

'Please, let me take your wrap,' said Lucas and took the thin garment from around her shoulders.

'Would you like some drinks?' asked the waiter.

'If you could just give us a minute,' said Lucas, 'we'll have a look at the wine list and call you over.'

'Of course,' said the waiter and left the table.

'Wow, you look incredible,' said Lucas.

'You've already said that,' giggled Amy.

'I know, but still. I was expecting an awkward teenaged Goth. Instead I get a beautiful and sophisticated young woman. I am entranced.'

They settled down for the evening and although Amy was already overwhelmed by the occasion, it got better and better as the night went on. All too soon, it was over and Lucas saw her to her taxi.

'Please,' he said, as the car pulled up, 'can I see you again soon?'

'Yes,' said Amy, 'I would like that.'

'When?'

'Whenever you like. Tomorrow?'

'I was hoping you would say that,' said Lucas. 'Tomorrow would be fantastic. I am flying back to Germany in a few days.'

'Oh,' said Amy, with a hint of disappointment in her voice, 'won't I see you again after that?'

'Of course,' said Lucas, 'I am in London every couple of months, and now that I know you are here, I will probably be back even more.'

Amy smiled.

'Well, that's okay then,' she said, 'where shall I meet you?'

'Shall I pick you up?'

'No,' she said a bit too quickly, 'my parents don't know yet, so if you don't mind, perhaps we could meet somewhere else.'

'Oh, I see,' said Lucas, 'Ok, I'll tell you what. Meet me at the local train station at seven, but don't dress up, just wear something warm.'

'Why, where are we going?' asked Amy.

'It's a surprise,' said Lucas and leant over to give her a peck on the cheek. 'Goodnight, beautiful Amy, I will see you tomorrow.'

'Good night, Lucas,' she said and got into the taxi. As it drove off, she recalled the entire evening minute by minute, and realised it had probably been the best night of her life.

Chapter Sixteen

Mulberry Lodge

'So,' said Leatherman, 'you were chatting away in there like a couple of old apple women. What did she have to say?'

Samari and Leatherman were sitting in a tiny office somewhere in the basement area of the lodge. After he had been sick, one of the technicians had taken him to the washroom to clean up and then brought him to Leatherman's office.

'To be honest, not much,' said Samari. 'There was a lot of confusion at first, as we struggled to find common ground, but eventually we got there.'

'What did you find out?'

'Well the most astonishing thing,' said Samari, 'is that she believes she is from the time of Ramesses II. That's over three thousand years ago.'

'And do you believe her?'

'I don't know what to believe at the moment,' said Samari. 'With everything you have told me today, and then meeting that girl, I suppose anything is possible.'

'What about her condition, did she shed any light on that?'

'Condition?'

'Yes, the reason for how she has lived in that dormant state for so long.'

'No, not really, though she has stated that she is one of the Nightwalkers, whatever that means, and as such, is immortal.'

'You took a great risk in removing your helmet,' said Leatherman, 'I have seen her tear the throats of animals wide open.'

'I know, but it was essential that I gained her trust. That was the only way I could do it, but it worked. What we have to do, Mr Leatherman, is give some ground. She has promised not to attack anyone if the room remains on moonlight.'

'We can do that,' said Leatherman, 'but any funny business and she gets zapped.'

'Understood,' said Samari.

'So is that it?' asked Leatherman.

'More or less,' said Samari. 'I'll write up a transcript, but the main thing today was initial contact and to gain her trust. I feel we have achieved that, and now the worst is over, I think there is so much more she can give.'

'Like what?'

'Think about it,' said Samari. 'If she is telling the truth, then this girl grew up in the time of Ramesses II, the greatest king in Egypt's history. She would have first-hand knowledge of the way they lived, their political systems, and day-to-day struggles of everyday life. All we have at the moment are carvings on walls and relatively few records etched onto fragile

148

papyrus. Everything else is speculation from people such as me, who add two and two together, often getting five and accepting that as true. This girl will not only have actual evidenced information from her own time, but accurate cultural memories about their own history at that time. Her knowledge would be priceless and give us a picture of what life was really like.'

'How would this be priceless?' asked Leatherman.

'Are you serious? Think about the access rights, the sales of documentaries and interviews across the globe. When Tutankhamen's tomb was unveiled, the whole world went Egypt mad and that was in the time before media. Imagine what would happen if we presented this girl to the world, along with supporting evidence proving that she is genuine. It would be the greatest moneymaking scheme of all time.'

'There may indeed be some value in that,' said Leatherman, 'but I suspect that it will be pocket change compared to the main product.'

'The main product?'

'Yes, the main reason you are here,' said Leatherman, 'all this history stuff is all very interesting, but you are missing the whole point. If this is all genuine, then this girl has the secret to everlasting life, or as near to it as we are likely to get. That is the main focus here, Samari, if you want to pan for gold dust in a stream of historical information, that's fine, but don't lose sight of the main seam of solid gold that we require, immortality.'

'Then, what is all this for?' asked Samari. 'Why do you want me to befriend her?'

'Because we want her on our side,' said Leatherman. 'We need samples of her blood and plenty of it. We can do that in two ways. Either with her cooperation, where she will live comfortably in secure surroundings and be looked after in return for regular donations, or the other option where she will be strapped down and milked of her blood as we see fit. We are not animals, Doctor Samari, so we would prefer the former. However, this is too great a prize to be bothered with the human rights of someone who could hardly be called human at all. One way or the other, we will get what we want, so it is up to you and her to decide which way it is going to be. However, the clock is ticking.'

'How long do I have?' asked Samari.

'One week,' said Leatherman. 'After that, it is out of my hands.'

When the meeting was over, Samari returned to his room and took a shower. After lunch he strolled around the extensive gardens enjoying the rare English sunshine. The guests at the lodge were also taking advantage of the sunshine and many old people walked along the paved paths between perfectly manicured lawns. Some walked with friends, some walked arm in arm with nurses, while others sat on benches, reading or just enjoying the sun. Overall, it was a very quiet scene and Samari couldn't fail to be impressed with the standard of care that they seemed to enjoy.

Suddenly, a commotion filled the air and all heads turned to see an old lady sprawled on the floor alongside her tipped wheelchair. Samari was the closest and ran over to help.

'Are you okay?' he asked.

'I'm fine,' said the woman struggling to sit up. 'My brake must have slipped and I came off the decking.'

'Take your time,' said Samari, 'you've taken quite a fall.'

'Nothing is hurt, except my pride,' she said.

Two nurses arrived and checked her over before helping her back into the wheelchair.

'Do you want to go back to your room, Mrs Leighbourne?' asked one.

'Not at all,' said the woman,' I'm fed up of being stuck inside. This young man can push me around the garden.'

The nurse looked at Samari inquisitively.

'Is that okay?' she asked.

'Of course,' said Samari, 'I could do with the exercise.'

The nurses went back to the others, while Samari headed off down the path, pushing Mrs Leighbourne's wheelchair.

'So,' he said as they started out, 'I always wanted women to fall at my feet, but this isn't quite what I expected.'

'I'm sure that with that dark skin and delicious accent, you have had your fair share of conquests, young man,' she said. 'What's your name?'

'Doctor Samari,' he said, 'but you can call me Geb.'

'Pleased to meet you, Geb,' she said, 'and you can call me Mrs Leighbourne.'

Samari stifled a laugh at the woman's formality and continued on their joint journey around the garden.

'I take it that you are you a resident here?' asked Samari.

'Unfortunately, yes,' she said.

'Why unfortunately? Don't you like it?' asked Samari.

'Oh, the standards are okay,' she said, 'it's just the loneliness.'

'Don't you have any visitors?'

'Nope, I am the only Leighbourne left on this planet,' she said. 'When they bury me, it will be the last of our line.'

'Really?' said Samari. 'That's quite sad.'

'Well, I'm an only child, never had any children of my own and my husband died several years ago. Luckily enough, he left enough money for me to see out my days here. Still, it won't be long now.'

'What do you mean?' asked Samari.

'Terminal cancer, Geb,' she said, 'the big C. Given me three months max, and then it's checkout time.'

'Oh, I'm sorry, Mrs Leighbourne,' said Samari, 'I didn't know.'

'Don't be sorry,' she said, 'I am eighty years old and I am very tired. I don't mind dying, in fact, in a perverse sort of way, I am quite looking forward to it. I just hope it's not going to be too painful. Anyway, don't you read your patients notes?'

'I'm not that kind of Doctor,' he said, 'I have a doctorate in Egyptology.'

'Oh, that's where you are from,' she said, 'I thought I recognised the accent. What is a doctor of Egyptology doing in death's waiting room anyway?'

'It's a long story,' laughed Samari, 'so I have a better idea. I bet you have had a wonderful life, why don't you tell me some of the exciting things you must have seen on your journey?'

'I suppose I have, really,' she said, and for the next two hours, Doctor Geb Samari spent quality time with a lonely old woman, listening to the stories of a life well lived.

Over the next few days Samari spent more and more time with Nephthys and though it was still tense in the beginning, after a while the tension eased and the meetings were very productive. Samari had persuaded Nephthys to sit across a table from him while he made copious notes in his diary. After the sixth day, he again sat in the cell, though this time only wore white clinical overalls. Nephthys stood against the far wall watching him closely as he entered the room.

'Doctor,' she said, 'our talks grow more frequent.'

'Are they too much?' asked Samari.

'No. They hold much that is interesting, yet I feel there is more to come. Your words are guarded as if there are things you would have me not know.'

'You are very perceptive, Nephthys,' said Samari, 'and you are correct. There are things still to be said but they are not withheld to trick you, I worry only for you. This place is not what it seems and the world around you has changed. If I told you everything straight away, you would label me a liar.'

'Would they be lies?'

'No.'

'Then speak them.'

'They would bring you stress.'

'Then that is my choice.'

Samari fell silent for a while. There was something about her that was different. Her skin seemed to have more colour and the hair growth was more pronounced. In addition, there was a calmness about her that he had not seen before.

'Okay,' he said eventually. 'I will tell as much as I can, but in return, you must tell me something that no other person in this world knows.'

151

'I have told you much already, Doctor.'

'Yes, and it is fascinating, but our world eats knowledge like locusts eat the crops of the Nile. I seek something that will set me apart in this world of knowledge.'

'Now, I see,' said Nephthys, 'you are indeed like other men but while they seek crowns of gold, you seek a crown of a different sort?'

'Something like that,' said Samari.

'All men covet so,' said Nephthys, 'and when you place knowledge against riches, it is the coin that outweighs the papyrus.'

'Not so with me, Nephthys.'

'It is true of all men,' said Nephthys, 'and I will set you a test that I know you will fail. Will you take this test, Doctor?'

'I have strength in my own convictions,' said Samari. 'Ask your questions.'

Nephthys left her position against the wall and walked slowly past him. He glanced nervously over his shoulder as she passed but remained where he was.

'I will offer you a choice of information, Doctor,' she said as her hand caressed his throat, 'and you can pick which one you want me to reveal. Whichever you choose, I will answer truthfully. Both answers can change your life in ways you can never imagine, but you can hear only one.'

'And what do you want in return?' asked Samari.

'Nothing more than that already promised. I have been patient, but the time approaches when you must help me leave this place.'

'You know I want to take you back,' said Samari, 'but it is very difficult. The land we are now in is very far away from Kemet and I fear we will not make it.'

'Hear my words first,' said Nephthys, 'and make your choice later.'

'Go on.' said Samari.

'My first gift will be one of knowledge, Doctor. I will tell you all there is to know about my kind, where we came from, how it is we survive and what it is like to be forced to sleep for a thousand years. I will tell you what it is like to walk on both sides of death and see what lies on either side. I have seen what awaits mortal man across the divide, and though it is something your kind are not meant to see, I will share this knowledge with you to do with as you wish.'

'And the second choice?' asked Samari.

'The gift of gold,' said Nephthys, 'a treasure unimagined in any mortal's wildest dreams. In the mountains to the east of the Nile, lies a single tomb, carved so deep into the mountains, that after you enter, it takes half a day to reach the burial chamber. The king buried therein has taken a treasure so vast, that it makes every king thereafter seem like a pauper in comparison. He was the greatest ever to walk the lands of Kemet and makes Ramesses look like a thief in the night.'

'And who was this king?' asked Samari.

'Khufu,' said Nephthys, 'King of kings.'

'But didn't Khufu build the great pyramid?'

'He did, but he saw the greed in his people and turned his eyes elsewhere even before it was finished. His body lies to the east in a location unknown by any mortal.'

'And how do you know this?' asked Samari.

'For I have been there,' said Nephthys. 'During his reign, he treated Sekhmet with respect and allowed the nightwalkers to share in the bounty of his lands. There were temples in Sekhmet's name and Khufu paid tribute at her feet. When he died, Sekhmet repaid the debt by ensuring his body was safe for eternity. She and her sisters guarded the tomb for a generation until the earth moved and rocks covered the entrance. Only one way in remains and it is by this route my mother took me as a child to pay tribute at the feet of Khufu.'

'You saw the treasures yourself?' asked Samari,

'I did.'

'And how much was there?'

'It was spread in ten chambers, each ten times the size of this,' said Nephthys.

'And Khufu?'

'Lies there still.'

'How do you know that? It could have been robbed.'

'No man could find it, for no man goes there. All who built the tomb were interred within and those who sealed the tomb were killed by the sisters. My mother chose the place well, for it is a place of death.'

'Yet you know where it is.'

'I, and only I, have that knowledge.'

'And you would share it with me?'

'Release me from this place and I will take you there. I have no use for memories of dead kings, or golden statues. My need is freedom and for that I would pay the earth.'

Silence fell as Nephthys walked back to the wall at the rear of the cell.

'Consider carefully, Doctor;' she said, 'knowledge of life after death, or a treasure unparalleled. Either is available, all you have to do is open the door.'

Samari's mind was spinning. What she was offering was beyond his wildest dreams, but the trade-off was a price too high. How could he let her loose? She would be a killing machine in an over populated world. Yet, was that his problem? There had always been killers and even if she did kill people, it would be the merest fraction compared to wars, starvation and disease. Who was he to assume the role of the world's protector? With either gift, his life would change out of all recognition. The meaning of life, or a lifetime of luxury?

Finally, he stood up.

'There is much to consider, Nephthys,' he said, 'I will back this evening with an answer.'

'Do not ponder too long, Doctor;' she answered, 'for there are other deals to be made.'

'What do you mean?' asked Samari.

'Be gone, Doctor, for I tire of your questions.'

Samari left the cell and made his way back to his room, confused and scared, yet excited beyond all reason.

Later that evening Samari made his way down to the canteen for his evening meal. Even here they had spared no expense and those who were able enough, could eat their meals in a restaurant atmosphere. For the last few evenings, he had joined Mrs Leighbourne for dinner. Each enjoyed the other's company and though he avoided the real reason he was here, he still was still able to share the many fantastic stories of Egyptian history he had learned throughout his career. In return, he heard Mrs Leighbourne's tales of the worldwide travel she and her husband had enjoyed throughout her life. He looked over to the table they normally shared and was surprised that she wasn't there as she was a stickler for timekeeping. He called one of the nurses over.

'Has Mrs Leighbourne been in already?' he asked, 'It's not like her to be late.'

'Oh, Doctor Samari, I am so sorry,' she said, 'didn't anyone tell you? Mrs Leighbourne passed away this morning.'

'Oh no,' he said, 'that's awful. I thought she had a few months left?'

'These things can strike at any time,' said the nurse. 'She had a poor night and never really woke up. Her poor heart finally gave out about ten this morning and she died peacefully in her sleep.'

Samari sighed deeply.

'Oh well,' he said, 'at least she wasn't in pain. That's the only thing she was worried about.'

'She was an extraordinary woman,' said the nurse. 'Can I get you anything?'

'No thanks,' said Samari, 'I'll grab a sandwich and take it back to my room. Thank you.'

The day's events had a sobering effect on Samari, and he lay on his bed in his room, staring at the ceiling while wrestling with his conscience. This whole immortality thing was tearing apart everything he believed in. He was an Egyptologist and spent his life studying the dead and their surroundings. It was the way of things, the way it should be. People, animals, plants, they all lived and died before being replaced with the young and the healthy. Just take Mrs Leighbourne for instance. She was a prime example of someone who would have benefited from some miracle drug that could replace the cancerous cells or prolong her life, but even she had stated she welcomed the eternal sleep that death brought. Death was as natural as birth. It was inevitable, it was natural and more than that, it was right. Yet to be in a position to understand how to slow that process down was a privilege and surely he had a duty to the human race to explore this opportunity that lay before him.

On the other hand there was a powerful argument against there being be an elixir of eternal life. The world couldn't take it. The rich and the powerful would keep it for themselves. Power would remain in the same hands for generations and with absolute power came absolute corruption. But even if the outcome was different and the drug became widely available; what then? The world could hardly maintain the population as it stood now. Millions already went hungry and the human race was stripping the planet of resources faster than they could be replaced. What would happen if you threw immortality into the pot? Birth rates would continue to rise, yet there would be far less death and disease, ideal in principle but disastrous in practice. The population would implode and the human race would be wiped out apart from a few privileged individuals. No, whichever outcome came from this, it could only end in disaster.

Then there was the lure of Khufu's tomb. He already knew that many Egyptologists had long thought Khufu was buried elsewhere, and if Nephthys could show him where he lay, then the world would benefit enormously with the expansion of knowledge. Fame and fortune would follow and though that was secondary in Samari's thoughts, he had to admit, the thought of worldwide recognition did make him smile.

For hours, the thoughts raced around his mind until finally he made a decision. He would accept the offer of Khufu's tomb and somehow take the girl back to where she belonged. He wasn't sure how that could be done yet, but the decision was made. He just wanted to do one thing first and then he would go down to the basement and tell her she was right. Men chose wealth over knowledge every time. He walked down to reception and spoke to the girl on the desk.

'Hello again,' he said, 'I wonder if you could help me, please? ' One of my friends passed away today and I understand you have a chapel here where people can pay their last respects,'

'That's right we do,' said the girl. 'It's in the east wing but you have to make an appointment as sometimes there are other families there.'

'Okay,' he said, 'I may be too late but could you check if Mrs Leighbourne is still there and if so, could I book fifteen minutes as I would like to pay my last respects.'

155

'Just a second,' she said, consulting a diary on her desk. 'Oh yes, here we are, Mrs Agnes Leighbourne, died early this morning. Oh, sorry, Mr Samari, It seems Mrs Leighbourne's body has already been collected earlier today.'

'Oh, I see,' said Samari. 'Could you let me know what undertaker took her? Perhaps I could pay my respects at the chapel of rest.'

The girl read the notes.

'Right,' she said, 'there is no record of an undertaker on file as apparently the body was taken away by private ambulance.'

'Really?'

'Yes, that's quite normal. Sometimes the families of the deceased make their own arrangements and transport the body to a funeral home closer to the family home.'

'I thought she didn't have a family?'

'According to this, it was organised by her husband, Mr Ivor Leighbourne.'

Samari's brow furrowed in confusion.

'Okay,' he said, 'thanks. Perhaps I will contact him.' He walked away from the desk deep in thought. He recalled that Mrs Leighbourne had told him that she had no surviving family. Why would she have said that if her husband was still alive?'

'Oh well,' he thought. 'People's domestic arrangements were often strange.'

He continued down to the basement lab where only one technician was on duty.

'Hi, Lewis,' said Samari, 'on your own?'

'Yeah, everyone's left for the evening and I've got the graveyard shift.'

'Okay to go through?' asked Samari.

'Yeah, sure. You are not going in the cell though, are you?'

'No, I just need to make some observations for about an hour and I'll be done.'

'Okay, give me a shout if you need anything.'

Samari went in and sat in one of the chairs, facing the viewing window. As the cell was now on permanent moonlight, he didn't need the infra-red goggles. Nephthys was sitting at the back of the cell, staring into nothing, as was her habit.

'Who are you?' he asked quietly to himself, 'what are you?'

For an age Samari watched Nephthys, and though she sat motionless, he was fascinated with everything about her. For the first time, she seemed to look healthy and had a self-satisfied look on her face. He couldn't put his finger on it, but there was something definitely different about her. Finally he stood up to leave but as he turned away, he spotted something in the corner of the auditorium which made him stop dead in his tracks; Mrs Leighbourne's wheelchair.

He stared at the wheelchair in confusion. Why would it be all the way down here, and why would they need a wheelchair at all? It didn't mean sense, unless...

'Oh dear god no,' he said and turned to stare at the cell once again. Surely they wouldn't have given the body to Nephthys?

He walked back down to the viewing window and peered into the room. The cell floor looked very clean with no sign of blood but that in itself was strange. There was always mess on the floor; in fact, he had never seen it so clean. It was if it had been recently mopped.

No matter how much he tried to avoid the subject, his suspicions kept coming back. Mrs Leighbourne had said she had no family and he had no reason to disbelieve her. He knew Leatherman had no scruples and if Leatherman knew Mrs Leighbourne had no family, then when she died, it would be a perfect opportunity to see Nephthys do what nature had intended her to do. Samari contemplated opening the door and asking Nephthys himself but suddenly realised there was a far better option. He walked over to the technician's desk and sat in front of the CCTV monitor. After a few minutes, he worked out how to rewind the recordings and set it to earlier in the afternoon, before forwarding it at double speed. The screen was showing the cell from the point of view of the furthest camera, and showed Nephthys sitting in her normal position against the wall, bathed in the blue Moonlight setting. After a few seconds, the screen changed and an orange light started flashing. Samari changed the play to normal speed and watched in growing horror as the scenes from earlier in the day unfolded before his eyes.

Chapter Seventeen

London

Becky was at her desk in her office when John finally returned her call. She briefly explained what had happened the night before and they agreed to meet for lunch so she could fill him in on the details and agree what they should do next.

Amy was at her own desk and Becky had been pleasantly surprised when the girl had turned up for work in a pair of jeans and a nice top.

'Amy,' she had said, 'you look lovely, what's happened to all the black stuff.'

'I thought it was time for a change,' said Amy.

'Well, you look lovely,' said Becky, 'and it suits you.'

'Thanks,' said Amy and returned her attention to her computer screen.

'Looking forward to tonight,' she typed.

'Me too,' came the reply in the message box.

'Amy,' said Becky, interrupting the love struck teenager's online conversation, 'I may be a bit late this afternoon. Could you do me a favour, go up to the lab sometime after lunch and pick up a package from Craig?'

'Sure,' said Amy. 'Is it the results from the finger?'

'It is,' said Becky, 'though to be honest I don't really know what to make of it.'

'You've seen the results already?'

'Sort of, Craig came around last night to run through the results himself.'

'Really?' said Amy with renewed interest. 'What did he have to say, is it a fake or do we have a real life 'Curse of the Mummy's tomb' on our hands?'

Becky turned her chair and explained to Amy everything that had happened. The girl listened intently and when Becky had finished, she stared at her boss with excitement in her eyes.

'Oh...my...god!' She exclaimed, pausing between each word.

'What's the matter?' asked Becky. 'You look like you have just won the lottery.'

'Becky, don't you realise what you have just described?'

'Enlighten me,' said Becky.

'A living organism, that feeds on the blood of others, gaining strength to ensure they live forever.'

'And?'

'Becky, you are describing a vampire.'

'Oh, for heaven's sake,' said Becky, 'that is ridiculous.'

'Feeds on blood?' asked Amy.

'Yes but…'

'Lives forever?'

'I know but…'

'Dies in sunlight.'

'Amy…!'

'Did you try Garlic?' asked the girl.

'Amy, stop it. You are being ridiculous. We are talking about simple blood cells. Each is a microscopic individual entity that is a tiny part of a much bigger picture.'

Amy smiled.

'You have just described a human,' smiled Amy. 'Oh my god, Becky, you need to get a crucifix.'

Becky laughed out loud this time.

'Amy, I can just about get my head around the scientific aspects. The one thing I totally reject without fear of contradiction is that there is any link whatsoever to any religious doctrine.'

'Okay,' said Amy, slightly disappointed, 'but still, the rest all adds up. I think that somewhere back in Egypt, that doctor who framed your father has the body of a vampire on his hands.'

Again Becky laughed out loud.

'Oh Amy, if only you were right. Imagine the shock on Samari's face when she sunk her fangs into his scrawny neck.'

The smile on Amy's face disappeared instantly.

'What did you say?' she asked.

'What's the matter?' asked Becky. 'I just joked that it would be funny if Samari met his end at the hands of some Hammer Horror monster.'

'Who is Samari?' asked Amy.

'That's the name of the man who framed my father. Why?'

'I saw his name written on a memo pad up in Montague's office,' said Amy. 'I knew I had heard it before but couldn't recall where. I must have heard you mention it down here, on the phone or something.'

'Well,' said Becky slowly, 'I don't suppose it means anything. Montague knows Samari from Cairo. I suppose it could be just coincidence that you saw his name.'

'Might be,' said Amy, 'but it was written above the name of a hotel. Somewhere called Mulberry Lodge.'

'Mulberry Lodge?' said Becky. 'That doesn't sound like an Egyptian name to me. In fact, it sounds positively English. Do you think Samari could be over here?'

'Possible,' said Amy, 'why?'

'Because if he is, I want to meet him face to face and find out exactly why he framed my father.'

'Do you think he'll tell you anything?'

'Probably not, but it would be worth it to see the look on his face when he realises he hasn't got away with it. I wonder where this Mulberry Lodge is?'

'There's one way to find out,' said Amy, and she swung her chair back to face her screen.

'What are you doing?' asked Becky.

'I'm going to do what I do best,' said Amy, 'research.'

Half an hour later, Amy picked up her note book and turned her chair away from the computer.

'Becks,' she said, 'it's been a pain but I've finally got somewhere.'

'There are a lot of hotels called Mulberry lodge, I assume,' said Becky.

'Yes, quite a few, but not many in the London area. Anyway, I checked out as many as I could but couldn't find a record of any Samari being in any of them. However, during my search I found a Mulberry Lodge not far from here, but it's not a hotel, it's a retirement home.'

'What made you look at that?' asked Becky.

'I don't know, really,' said Amy, 'but the website seemed interesting so I had a look. It seems that it is solely for the rich and the famous and is one of a chain owned by the Bearing's group, which in turn is a subsidiary of Glencol pharmaceuticals PLC.'

'And?'

'Well, that's where it gets interesting. I did a search on the company and found the board of directors. One of them is a major shareholder, and goes by the name of A. R. Montague.'

'Andrew Montague?' asked Becky.

'The one and only,' said Amy. 'Anyway, I phoned the lodge and gave my name as Susan Samari and asked if I could speak to my father.'

'What happened?'

'The receptionist said she'd see if she could find him for me. As soon as I heard that, I hung up. It seems like we've found our man.'

'Wait a minute,' said Becky, 'Let's take stock here. Are we saying that Samari is not only over here, but also a guest of Montague's in a lodge owned by a company where Montague is a major shareholder?'

'Seems so,' said Amy.

'It still doesn't mean Montague is involved in any of this,' said Becky, 'but considering Montague has stated to me that he didn't believe any of the accusations made against my father, it is a bit two faced of him to now work with Samari.'

'What are you going to do?' asked Amy.

'I'm meeting John for lunch and then I am going to go over there and pay Mr Samari a visit,' said Becky.

'Do you want me to come with you?'

'No, you go and pick up my parcel. I'll go and meet Samari and see what he has got to say for himself.'

'I'll go straight away,' said Amy.

Five minutes later, Amy returned with a small plastic box. Becky unclipped the clasp and opened the box to see a clear plastic vial sitting within a bed of preformed sponge. The contents were a very dark red and obviously in a liquid form.

'Looks like blood,' said Amy.

'That's exactly what it is,' said Becky, before snapping the lid shut. 'Right, you put this in the safe, I'm off to try and make some final sense of all this. Wish me luck.'

'Becks, before you go,' said Amy, as she took the plastic box from her boss, 'can I finish early tonight? I'll make sure the notes are done for Monday's meeting but I'm going out and need to get ready.'

'Really?' smiled Becky, 'hot date?

'Sort of,' said Amy, blushing furiously.

'Anyone I know?' asked Becky.

'No, he's not from around here, but he's really nice. Not even my parents know yet, but I really like him.'

'Okay,' smiled Becky, 'but on one condition.'

'What's that?' asked Amy, a slight look of concern on her face,

'That you tell me all about it on Monday,' she said. 'Now, go and make yourself beautiful for that lucky man.'

'Thanks, Becky,' said Amy. 'Good luck with Samari and have a nice weekend.'

A couple of hours later, Amy finished her work for the day and put on her coat. As she walked out she switched on her phone and smiled when she saw four missed calls from Lucas. She pressed recall and her face lit up even more when she heard his sexy German accent.

'Amy, hi, I was beginning to think you were avoiding me.'

'Not at all,' said Amy, 'there's just no signal in the vaults so it's pointless switching the phone on.'

'Oh, I see,' said Lucas. 'Are we still on for tonight?'

'Absolutely,' said Amy. 'In fact, I've managed to get an early finish so I've got plenty of time to get ready.'

'Excellent,' said Lucas.

'There is something else, Lucas,' said Amy, 'you will never guess what happened today.'

'Surprise me,' said Lucas.

'Well, I can't say too much,' said Amy, 'but what if I was to tell you that vampires were real?'

'Then I would say you are preaching to the converted and we have already had this conversation at your house.'

161

'No, I don't mean the stories from folklore,' said Amy, 'I mean real, flesh and blood creatures that lived, breathed and needed blood to survive.'

'Then in that case,' laughed Lucas, 'I would say that perhaps you have had a rather long liquid lunch and the wine had flowed too freely.'

'No, seriously,' said Amy, 'today the museum carried out a test that shows they actually did exist, and more importantly, they have the evidence to prove it.'

'Amy, please,' said Lucas, 'you know my fascination with this subject, so please don't patronise me.'

'Lucas, I know how much you are interested, and so am I. That's why I am so excited. When I heard the news today, I could hardly believe my ears. Apparently they found an old body in Egypt and have managed to get a tissue sample analysed. Honestly, Lucas, the results are conclusive. The person that the sample came from needed blood to survive and lived for thousands of years.'

'Are you sure about this, Amy?'

'Absolutely, and I can prove it.'

'How?'

'I can't say now,' said Amy as she walked out of the museum doors, 'it's too complicated but I will explain everything later.'

'Well, I'm not going to get too carried away, Amy,' laughed Lucas, 'and I am sure whatever it is you have got is fascinating, but let's wait and see.'

'One more thing, Lucas,' said Amy, stopping at the foot of the museum steps. 'About tonight.'

'What about it?'

She looked around to see she was not overheard before lowering her voice.

'Um, the thing is, my parents are going away and I have told them I am going out with a friend and then staying at her house.'

'So, you are not expected home this evening?' asked Lucas slowly.

'No, not until tomorrow afternoon, so, if you want to, you know, arrange a local hotel or something; that would be really nice.'

'Amy, are you sure?' asked Lucas.

'Positive,' she said, her face burning furiously, 'unless of course you don't want to.'

'No, I mean yes, of course I want to,' stuttered Lucas, 'it's just that I feel so, ah, honoured.'

'So you should,' laughed Amy, 'anyway, my bus is coming, I'll see you later. Bye.'

Becky waited outside the small antiques shop on the side road off Oxford Street. John locked the door and turned to join her.

'Right,' he said, 'I hope this is going to be worth it. Friday afternoons are sometimes quite busy for me.'

'Thanks for coming with me,' she said. 'I don't want you to lose business but I also don't want to waste this opportunity. If Amy is right, Samari could be less than fifty miles from here and he's got some explaining to do.'

'You don't really believe all that vampire crap, do you?' asked John.

'Of course not, but whatever is going on here, Samari holds the answers. I think this organisation is heavily into gene research and believe they have found some sort of rogue gene that may help in cell reproduction. Hell, they may even be right but the thing is, Samari is involved and if this company is anyway linked to my father's death, then I want to know about it. Come on, it'll be dark soon and I don't want to get there only to find he's gone out for the evening.'

'Hang on,' said John, 'we need to stop in at the grocers.'

'Why?' asked Becky.

'Garlic,' said John. 'You never know.'

'Okay, that's enough,' said Becky. 'This is serious. My father died because of this Samari guy and the last thing I need right now is you making light of it. Either you are in this with me or you're not. Your choice.'

'Sorry, Becky,' he said, 'of course you are right. Come on, I'll get us a cab.'

'Hang on,' said Becky, 'one more thing. Do you still have that necklace from Amenemhat's tomb?'

'I do, why?'

'If this all goes belly up and Samari denies everything at least that provides credible evidence that we were there. Somebody with Montague's credentials would recognise it as genuine almost immediately, and with him on our side, we have a chance.'

'Right,' said John, 'I'll go and get it.'

Five minutes later they were in the back of a taxi and on their way toward the outskirts of London.

Amy stood before the entrance to the tube station, waiting for the taxi she thought would be picking her up. Finally a car pulled up before her, a bright red Porsche. The passenger window wound down and she heard a voice calling from within.

'Taxi for Amy,' said a German accent.

Amy bent down and was shocked to see Lucas behind the wheel.

'Hi, Amy,' he said. 'Ready for a fantastic evening?'

'Lucas,' she said, in astonishment. 'Wow, this is fantastic, is it yours?'

'Only for a few days,' said Lucas. 'It's my guilty pleasure when I am over here.'

'It's gorgeous,' said Amy.

'Well, don't just stand there,' laughed Lucas, 'get in.'

Amy threw her overnight bag over the back of the seat and climbed in besides him. They drove off with a wheel spin, making the passers-by tut with disapproval, and soon they were on the way out of London, laughing together as they left the smoky city behind them.

'Where are we going?' asked Amy.

'I thought we would have a drive along the coast,' said Lucas, 'stop off at a seaside resort, have some fun on a funfair, and try some of those English fish and chips you are so famous for and then head into the country. I've rented a little cottage in the middle of nowhere. Is that okay?'

'Sounds fabulous,' said Amy, 'go faster.'

The next few hours went by in a blur, for Amy. The ride was exhilarating, and even when they were booked for speeding, as soon as the policeman left, they doubled up laughing as if it was the funniest thing in the world. They spent hours in the funfair in Southend and then sat on a bench overlooking the sea as they ate their chips from the paper.

'Enjoying yourself?' asked Lucas.

'I am having a wonderful time,' said Amy, 'but it's getting a bit cold, how far away is this cottage?'

Lucas gazed at her and smiled.

'About half an hour,' he said and threw the last of his paper into the bin. 'Are you ready to go?'

'I am,' said Amy and stood up before holding out her hand for him to take.

They walked hand in hand back to the car and shared a lingering kiss before driving to the cottage.

An hour later they had unpacked their small bags and Lucas had built a fire in the hearth of the small cottage. Two glasses of wine were sitting on the table between them and Lucas was transfixed as Amy retold the story she had heard earlier.

'Wow, that's some story,' said Lucas, 'but at the end of the day, it could be just one big set of coincidences.'

'I know it sounds wild', said Amy, 'but even you said the legends of vampires were based on fact.'

'Yes, but the facts I was on about were stories of people who thought there were vampires, not actual beings.'

'But what if there were such things, Lucas?' said Amy, with an excited look in her eye. 'What if all of it is true and they did exist? Surely this is an opportunity too good to miss?'

'Opportunity for what?' asked Lucas.

'To prove to everyone in the world that vampires were real. Becky isn't some sort of mad scientist, Lucas. She is a serious Egyptologist who works in a Museum. Do you really think I would be talking like this unless I had seen the evidence with my own eyes?'

'You have?'

'I was sent up to the lab for the results,' she said, 'and I was given a package for Becky.'

'What was in there?'

'A small vial of black blood;' said Amy, 'and a hand written note.'

'What did it say?' asked Lucas, 'do you recall?'

'I can do better than that,' said Amy, 'I have it with me.' She pulled a note from her bag and handed it over.

Becky,

The sample you requested is enclosed. I have destroyed the other item as requested but cultured this sample from the cells therein. I don't know what you are involved in, and don't want to know, but whatever it is, it scares me. This sample is unique as it is alive, and continues to be alive even now, twenty four hours later. That's not natural, Becky. It goes against everything we know about nature.

Please be careful.

Craig.

When Lucas finished reading he looked at the back and then up at Amy.

'Is that all there is?' he asked.

'Why?'

'It could be about anything,' he said.

'I suppose so,' she said, 'but that's why I brought this.' She put a small plastic vial on the table.

'What is it?'

'The blood sample.'

'Why did you bring it with you?' gasped Lucas.

'Well, I knew that you were as interested as I am,' she said, 'and it isn't often we get to see real vampire blood.'

'Wow,' said Lucas, picking it up and holding it up to the light, 'It's almost black.'

'I know,' said Amy. 'Isn't it fantastic?'

'Well, there's still no proof it is the real thing,' said Lucas.

'I know, but I thought we could pinch a bit, and I could put this back before Becky knows any different. After that, all we have to do is get it sampled for ourselves and if it is genuine, let the world know that people like us were right all along.'

'You would do that?'

'Why not? The authorities always cover up things like this. Aliens, Atlantis, ESP, that sort of thing. Who are they to hide things like this from the people? We have a right to know I think it should be you and I who reveal it to the world. What do you think?'

Lucas looked at the vial once more before leaning over and kissing her deeply.

'I think we should go upstairs,' he said, and leaving the vial on the table, led Amy up to the bedroom.

Chapter Eighteen

Mulberry Lodge

Samari watched the CCTV monitor closely. The time display in the top right corner showed the recording was at 2pm that afternoon. The amber light flashing in the room meant someone must have been there and was about to change the settings. Sure enough, the dark blue room was suddenly lit up and he knew that whoever had been down there must have switched to daylight mode.

Nephthys had hidden behind her screen and within a few seconds, the doors opened and Samari could see two technicians struggling to drag something inside. Samari's worst fears were realised when he saw they were carrying the body of a woman between them. He used the controls to zoom in and sure enough, he recognised the dead face of Mrs Leighbourne.

'This is sick,' he said to himself, but despite his revulsion, he continued watching. The two technicians left the room, and Samari was about to fast forward the tape but paused as two different men entered the room. He recognised one immediately as Leatherman, but gasped in astonishment as the second man looked up toward the camera.

'Montague,' gasped Samari, recognising the manager of the British Antiquities Museum.

The two men crouched over the dead body, and Montague produced a syringe that he placed into Mrs Leighbourne's arm.

Samari was confused but suddenly it dawned on him.

'Oh my god,' he said to himself, 'she's not dead.'

The two men on the screen withdrew from the room, leaving the unconscious woman behind them in the cell. The lights remained on daylight as the drugs in the woman's bloodstream worked, and gradually she regained consciousness. Within a few minutes, she sat up and looked around in confusion. Samari turned up the volume until he could hear her speaking.

'Hello,' she said, 'is anyone there? Where am I? What is this place? Hello, can anybody hear me?'

Suddenly the lights turned off and the cell returned to moonlight. The old woman now looked afraid and called out again.

'Hello, I don't know what all this is about but can somebody help me? Please, I need my wheelchair.'

Samari saw Nephthys peer from around the screen. She stared at the old woman for a moment before taking a few steps forward and standing before her.

'Who are you, old woman?' she asked in her native Egyptian.

'I'm sorry, I don't understand,' replied Mrs Leighbourne in English. 'Can you help me please? I don't know where I am.'

Nephthys looked toward the mirrored glass.

'What is this trickery?' she asked.

Samari was surprised to hear a voice answer her in Egyptian over the tannoy system and though the speaker was obviously not fluent, Samari could understand the words, as indeed, could Nephthys.

'Nephthys, I am called Montague,' said the voice, 'and I am the leader of the people who hold you captive.'

'Then I will one day eat your heart,' snarled Nephthys.

'I understand your anger,' said Montague, 'and your captivity is indeed unfortunate but we believe that if we can work together, there may be an opportunity to change this state of affairs.'

'You speak the same words as Doctor,' said Nephthys. 'Where is he?'

'He is not here,' said Montague, 'and will soon be gone. His work is poor and we grow impatient. From now on you will talk with me.'

'Then show yourself,' said Nephthys. 'Let me stare into your soul to see the truth of your words as I did with Doctor.'

'I can't do that,' said Montague, 'however, to show you my eagerness to please, I offer you this gift.'

'The woman?'

'Yes, she is yours to do with as you will.'

'You bring me a sacrifice?'

'We do.'

'She is old.'

'Yet her heart still beats,' said Montague. 'If you work with us, there will be more such offerings and in time, we will arrange younger blood. In the meantime, this is a gesture of our commitment to you.'

Samari gasped as he realised what was unfolding before him. If he understood correctly, Montague had just committed to feeding live human beings to this creature. That could only mean that where he had guests with no family ties, then they would be used as sacrifice to her inhuman needs. In addition, he had just said there would be younger blood. How would he do that, Abduction? On the screen, Nephthys approached Mrs Leighbourne who was struggling to stand on her weak legs.

'What do you want of me?' asked Nephthys, as she circled the old woman.

'It is very simple,' said Montague, 'every week or so we will bring you sacrifice.'

'Week?' she asked.

'Sorry, I forgot our language is strange to you. Every few days you will have a sacrifice such as this. The following day you will allow us to remove some of your blood. It won't hurt and we don't need much. All we need is for you to allow us to secure you with binds while we extract what we need.'

'Excuse me,' said Mrs Leighbourne to the girl, 'please could you tell me what is happening here. I can't understand a word you're saying and I can't find my spectacles.'

Nephthys ignored the woman's strange words and spoke again toward the glass.

'You would have me make deals with demons who are afraid to show themselves,' she said, 'why would I allow this?'

'Because you have no other choice,' said Montague. 'Either you will agree or we will do it anyway.'

'You forget my strength, Montague,' Nephthys sneered. 'What soldiers would you pit against me? My fury would smite them before they got near.'

'It is you who forgets, Nephthys,' said Montague. 'We have the sunlight weapon that burns you. If you do not agree, we will remove your screen. You will be fed on rats and when we want your blood we will burn you until you are weak before taking what we want. These are your choices, Nephthys. I wish they could be different but they are not. The world has changed and is no longer as you remember it. We are the rulers now, and it is we who decide who lives or dies.'

'Hello,' interrupted, Mrs Leighbourne, speaking up toward the CCTV camera. 'I don't know who you are, but please can you help me. There seems to have been a mistake. Can you call someone please? I don't know where I am.'

'So what is it to be, Nephthys?' asked Montague. 'Choose your future.'

'Why do you want my blood?' she asked.

'We wish to study it,' said Montague, 'to see what it is that makes the nightwalkers immortal.'

'Many men before you have sought the secret, Montague. All have failed.'

'Like I said, times have changed,' said Montague, 'we have methods that would amaze you.'

'I will take your arrangement,' she said, 'but will not be bound.'

'We have to bind you,' said Montague. 'We know your strength and will not put our people in danger.'

'I will not be bound,' she said again, 'but will give you the blood you require.'

'How?' asked Montague.

'I will open my own vein and fill the clear cup that contains the water. I will do this only after you have offered sacrifice. These are my terms.'

There was a silence before Montague came back on the tannoy.

'Agreed,' he said. 'The next time we bring you fresh blood, we will require yours in return. Now we will go.'

The tannoy fell silent as did the cell. Mrs Leighbourne had found her glasses and bent over to pick them up before putting them on.

'That's better,' she said and shuffled around to face in to the cell.

Nephthys stood immediately in front of her and made the old lady jump in fright.

'Oh my goodness,' she said, 'you made me jump…Oh my god; your eyes are black…are you okay?'

Nephthys grinned and when Mrs Leighbourne saw her misshapen teeth, she caught her breath in fright.

'Who are you?' she gasped. 'What are you? Oh my god, somebody help, please, anybody…'

Before she could say any more, Nephthys grabbed her by the hair and yanked the old woman's head backwards to expose her throat.

'Rejoice,' snarled Nephthys, 'for your blood sustains a goddess.'

In front of the screen, Samari gagged as Nephthys sank her teeth into the old woman's throat and tore away the flesh over her jugular vein. The old woman's eyes widened in horror and a feeble cry of pain was drowned out by gurgling, as blood poured down her wind pipe. Immediately, Nephthys covered the severed artery with her mouth and hungrily sucked on a human's pumping blood, the first time she had done so for over three thousand years.

Samari stared at the screen in morbid fascination as Nephthys drained the old woman of blood. But if he thought that was bad enough, he was sadly mistaken. As soon as she had drained the body, she seemed to explode in a fit of rage and tore the old woman's body apart. At first, she used her teeth to tear through the soft belly and then used her sharp claws to rip open the flesh to expose the inner organs. Samari was horrified as she pulled out the liver and kidneys and took bites out of each in turn before placing them to one side and delving into the corpse once more. Horror after horror followed and within moments, the entire contents of the lower body were strewn across the floor and she tore frantically at the body before ramming her hand up into the chest cavity to reach the ultimate prize. With a flourish she pulled out the heart and stood up cradling it in both hands. Finally she faced the screen once more, drenched in blood, and though Samari knew all this had happened many hours earlier, it seemed she was addressing him directly.

'Behold my power, body-less demons,' she said, 'for such is the fate of all men.' She lifted up the old woman's heart to her mouth and ripped apart the blood-rich meat.

Samari turned off the recording and stared at the girl in the cell. There was no trace of the carnage of earlier that day, but there was no mistaking that she looked different, somehow healthier. For the next half hour, he sat there experiencing all sorts of emotions ranging from revulsion and hatred to pity and forgiveness. What he had just witnessed, more or less proved that she was indeed some sort of creature far removed from the human race, and indeed, meant that all the suppositions about immortality were probably true. If that was the case, what she had said earlier in the day was also probably true. She did know what lay beyond the grave and was also probably telling the truth about the last resting place of Khufu.

When he had come down to the cells, he had done so with every intention of trying to release the girl and whilst he knew the location of the tomb was probably a stretch of the imagination; he knew the tales she could tell about everyday Egyptian life would probably enthral him for the rest of his life. However, having seen the carnage that she had wreaked on Mrs Leighbourne, he knew that idea was no longer an option.

Despite the horror he had just witnessed, however, he also felt a pang of sympathy for the girl. She hadn't asked for this. It wasn't her fault she was as she was. She had been torn from somewhere that was intended to be her last resting place, dragged into a time she knew nothing about, thousands of miles from where she was born. Despite the knowledge she may hold, Samari knew that there was no way she would ever survive in the world as it was today. All around him Samari could see nothing but outcomes involving pain, despair and horror. The lives of thousands revolved around the ultimate destiny of this strange young woman and no matter which way he looked at it, there seemed no happy ending to the predicament. As much as he would have loved to spend the rest of his life talking to this living history book, he knew he couldn't take the risk. The world couldn't take the risk. With a heavy heart, he left the auditorium, knowing exactly what he had to do.

An hour later he entered the laboratory for the last time, this time carrying a holdall.

'Hello, Doctor Samari,' said the technician, 'back again?'

'Yes, not for long though.'

'No problem,' said Larry, 'go on through.'

'Larry, there's something wrong with the lift,' said Samari, 'I couldn't get it to work, so I came down the stairwell.'

'That bloody lift is a pain,' said Larry. 'I'll take a look.'

He left his chair and walked through the door into the corridor beyond. Samari slammed the door behind him and threw the bolt to lock him out. He reached into the holdall and retrieving the full petrol can that he had stolen from one of the garages, walked into the auditorium and down to the doors to the cell.

Nephthys heard a clunk and looked toward the door. Usually, the little yellow sun flashed before the mortals came in this strange place, but this time, someone was coming unannounced. She heard the second clunk and the inner door opened.

'Doctor,' she said, 'you have returned.'

'I have,' said Samari, 'but I do not come with good news, Nephthys, I am the bearer of destiny.'

'What are these words, Doctor? The last time we met, we spoke of knowledge and a future shared. You offered your throat and I honoured your trust. Why is it that your eyes are now heavy with sadness?'

Samari didn't answer, but opened the lid and poured the petrol over the floor. The effect of the fumes was instant in the confined space, and she stared at the growing pool of fuel with her deep black eyes.

'What is this poison that burns my eyes, Doctor?' she asked, looking up at him.

'It is release, Nephthys, release for you and possibly for me. I meant everything I said, yet there are others who do not share my views. They want to lock you in a place such as this, for all eternity, harvesting your blood to be used by mere mortals in a vain attempt to mirror your immortality.'

'I know of their desire for my blood,' said Nephthys, 'but they waste their time. Only nightwalkers enjoy immortality, man is nothing but prey.'

'I don't know if you are truly immortal or not,' said Samari, backing up toward the door, 'but I can't take that chance. Better to end this now, before any lasting harm is done.'

'Your liquid is meant to harm me,' said Nephthys. 'All your words of trust were nothing but lies. Yet again man proves he is not fit to stand alongside nightwalkers in this world. Amenemhat, Ramesses, Montague, Doctorsamari, all are nothing more than vessels of lies. There is only one being fit to rule these lands, teller of lies, and that is I, Nephthys, daughter of Sekhmet.'

'You may be right, Nephthys,' said Samari, 'and I wish there was some other way, but there is not.' He pulled out a lighter from his pocket, but in his haste, the lighter fell to the floor, before he had time to ignite the flint. For a second, they both looked at each other across the pool of petrol.

'What is that thing?' asked Nephthys.

'Nothing,' he said taking a step closer to the lighter.

'You said it was better to end this,' said Nephthys. 'You think you can harm me? Do you still not understand? Nothing can destroy nightwalkers, except the fire of the sun.' Her head spun toward the lighter again, as understanding dawned.

'Is that what your trinket is, Doctor, a machine of fire?'

The look in his eyes confirmed her suspicions.

'Oh, Doctor,' she said, her voice heavy with malevolence, 'you stupid man. You could have had it all, now there is nothing but death.'

Samari went diving across the floor and grabbed the lighter. He held it up before him.

'Stay away from me,' he said. 'One flick of my finger and this place will burst into the flames.'

172

'Then we will both burn,' she said.

'If that is what it takes, then it is a sacrifice I am willing to make. Your time is over, Nephthys. There is no room for your kind in this world anymore. We have enough troubles without things like you murdering old women.'

'You know of the woman?' said Nephthys.

'I saw you with my own eyes.'

'I have never hidden my needs, Doctor. It is your kind who spew lies as easily as her vein gushed blood. I am what I am, and you are what you are.'

While they were talking, Samari hadn't noticed that she had edged her way toward the open door. Too late, he realised her intention.

'No,' he screamed and dragged the wheel down on the flint. The spark ignited the fumes in the room and as the explosion of flame engulfed Samari in a burning furnace of pain, the same blast blew Nephthys through the door and into the auditorium.

Chapter Nineteen

Outside Mulberry Lodge

The taxi pulled away, leaving Becky and John outside the ornate gates.

'Put that card somewhere safe,' said Becky, referring to the taxi driver's business card. 'I don't want to be stuck out here if I can help it.'

'Me neither,' said John, 'so, shall we press the button?'

'Hang on,' said Becky, 'If Samari is indeed in there, I don't want him to know we are coming. Do you think there is another way?'

'I doubt it,' said John, 'though the walls don't look too high. We could climb over and sneak up to the building. Of course, if we are caught, we will be guilty of trespassing.'

'One more to add to our growing list of misdemeanours,' said Becky. 'Okay, let's do that, but not here, let's go up the road a bit first.' They walked along the perimeter before finding a place on the wall that was a bit lower than anywhere else. John helped Becky up before scrambling up himself and dropping into the wooded area on the other side.

'Watch your step,' whispered Becky, 'it's a bit rough underfoot.'

'It's going to be dark soon,' said John. 'Let's try to get through these woods while we can still see.' They crept slowly through the undergrowth, trying to avoid making too much noise. Ten minutes later, they crouched at the forest edge, gazing across well-manicured lawns to the impressive manor house a few hundred yards away.

'What do we do now?' asked Becky. 'We'll be seen if we walk across there.'

'Wait until it's dark,' said John, 'and see which areas are lit. Hopefully, there'll be some dark areas that we can use to get across.' They retreated back into the trees and sat against a large fallen tree.

'Warm enough?' asked John.

'I'm fine,' said Becky, 'I just want all this nonsense to be sorted out, once and for all.'

'I know how you feel,' said John, 'all of a sudden, it doesn't seem worth it. You are risking your job; I've risked my liberty entering Egypt illegally, and all for what? To prove some corrupt Egyptian official is hiding the existence of a tomb that will probably be revealed in a few years anyway.'

'And to clear my father's name,' said Becky.

'Of course,' said John, 'and I don't intend to back out now. It's just that sometimes, I wonder what your father would have made of all this.'

'Well, he went to a lot of trouble to let us know Samari was up to something,' said Becky, 'but even if he was wrong, at least I get to see Samari's face when he realises we are on to him.'

'And what do you think about the other thing?' asked John. 'You know, the idea that they may have found some sort of cellular cure for aging.'

'To be honest, I don't know what to think,' said Becky. 'On the one hand, the scientist in me tells me it is impossible and this is some sort of elaborate hoax, but on the other hand, those results from Craig were pretty conclusive, and he had no need to lie. If this is a hoax, somebody, somewhere, has gone to an awful lot of trouble and expense to make it as convincing as possible. Why on Earth would they do that?'

'I suppose if enough people fell for it, it may convince them to loosen their wallets and fund further research.'

'Possibly,' said Becky, 'but there are potentially some big names involved here. As much as I hate Samari, there was a time when he was one of the most respected names in Egyptology. He still is, in fact. And of course, then there's Montague.'

'Hang on; we don't know if he is involved yet,' said John, 'it could just be a coincidence. You would expect men of their stature to meet occasionally, let's not hang him just yet.'

Becky glanced up at him.

'Sorry,' said John, 'poor choice of analogy.'

'That's okay,' said Becky.

Silence fell for a few moments, before John spoke again.

'Hungry?' he asked.

'A bit. Why?'

'I have these,' he said, retrieving a couple of packages from his pockets. 'Not homemade, though. Bought them in the corner shop this afternoon.'

'They look damn fine to me,' said Becky, as she opened one of the sandwiches. 'Mmm, cheese and onion, my favourite.'

Half an hour later, they stood on the edge of the woods once again, this time in total darkness. In front of them, discreetly placed lights illuminated the topiaries of the gardens and up-lighters bathed the front of the manor in a warm red glow.

'Over there,' said John, pointing toward a hedge that ran alongside a path leading toward the building. Whilst the path was well lit with sunken lamps, the grass side of the hedgerow was in relative darkness, due to the shade it afforded. 'If we keep our heads down as we go,' he continued, 'we should remain out of site until we are close. After that, we need to take our chances and run across the last few yards to the house.'

'Some house,' murmured Becky.

'You know what I mean,' said John. 'Are you ready?'

'I suppose so,' said Becky. 'What do we do when we get there?'

'Take a look through the windows,' said John, 'see if we can get a clearer picture of what this place is. Right, stay close.' With that, he crouched low and ran to the hedge line, closely followed by Becky. They ran up toward the manor, keeping their heads low to avoid being seen from the windows. At the end of the hedge, they paused in the shadows to catch their breath.

'Look,' whispered John and pointed across the drive to a sign.

'Welcome to Mulberry Lodge,' read Becky, 'a quality home for quality people.'

'Wow,' said Becky, looking up at the three story façade, 'I wonder how much it costs to see out your days here?'

'More than you or I could afford, I would imagine,' said John scanning the front of the building. 'Most of the windows have their curtains drawn, so I don't think there's much risk of being seen from there. Can you see any CCTV cameras?'

'There's one there,' said Becky, pointing at a camera fixed to a bracket on the wall, 'and there's another.'

'Those two are okay,' said John, 'they seem to be fixed, but *that* one is on scan.' He pointed to a third.

'Scan?'

'It's swinging back and forth across one hundred and eighty degrees,' said John, 'I think there's enough time to get across the road, but we will have to move fast. You up for this?'

'Ready when you are,' said Becky.

John looked at the camera and timed its movement over a series of sweeps.

'Right,' he said, 'get ready, and when I say go, run like hell. Aim for that internal corner, the other side of the flowerbed. I think it will be hidden from any other cameras.'

'Okay,' said Becky.

John looked up at the moving camera.

'Get ready, three, two, one, go!'

They both burst from the shadow of the hedge and sprinted toward the protection of the internal corner where a wing met the main building. John was a few yards ahead of Becky, and though he made it to the safety of the wall easily, he stopped suddenly when Becky tripped and fell headlong into the flowerbed. He glanced up quickly at the camera, which was beginning its return journey. Becky had picked herself up and was limping as quickly as she could but John ran out and grabbed her, helping her to the safety the wall offered.

'Shit, that was close,' he said. 'Are you okay?'

'I think so,' she grimaced, 'but my bloody knee is killing me.'

They looked down at the tear in her jeans.

'You're bleeding,' he said, looking at the spreading stain appearing on the denim. He pulled out a Swiss army knife and cut away some of the torn fabric.

'I don't think it's too bad,' he said. 'At least it's not deep.'

'Hurts like hell,' she said. 'Haven't you got a first aid kit in that rucksack of yours?'

'No, sorry,' he said. 'Hang on.' He took off his ever-present hat and folded it over. 'Hold this against your knee for a few minutes, it should stop soon.'

'Are you sure that's hygienic?' she asked.

'Stop being such a baby,' he said, 'and do as you're told.'

A few minutes later, the pain eased, and Becky stood up alongside John.

'Ready?' he asked.

'I suppose so.'

'Okay, let's go.'

They started to walk around the edge of the building, hugging the walls to take advantage of the shadows. As they reached each window, they carefully peered inside, trying to see anything that may shed any light on the situation.

'Shit,' said John after they had passed another window blocked by curtains. 'This obviously wasn't one of my better ideas.'

'The curtains are open on this one,' said Becky, and John hurried along to join her.

She stood, peering through the window with her hands raised to either side of her eyes. The curtains were slightly ajar, but there were no lights on in the room.

'Can you see anything?' asked John.

'Not really, it's too dark.'

'Let me see,' he said and replaced her at the window. It took a few moments for his eyes to get accustomed to the darkness on the other side of the glass, but when they did, he started to make out familiar shapes. 'It looks like a bedroom,' he said, 'actually, more of a hotel room. There's a bed, a sideboard, a small table and a couple of chairs. It all looks very nice.'

'One of the rooms for residents, I suppose,' said Becky.

'Yeah,' said John, 'Hang on, what's that?'

'What can you see?'

'I'm not sure, I think…hang on. Oh, my god, I think it's an arm. It looks like someone is lying on the floor on the other side of the bed. I can't see them, but it certainly looks like an arm sticking out.'

'Let me see,' said Becky. As soon as her eyes became accustomed to the dark, she focussed on the bed area. Sure enough, she could make out the dark shape of an arm on the floor, sticking out past the bed frame.

'Oh, John, I think you're right. It looks like someone's collapsed. We have to help.'

'And how do you suppose we do that?' hissed John.

'We have to go tell someone,' she said. 'We can't just leave her there.'

'Or him?' said John.

'Whatever,' snapped Becky. 'Someone could be hurt and we have to help them.'

'But if we just go in there,' said John, 'then all this will be for nothing.'

'Look,' said Becky, 'you know how much I would love to find out something sinister about Samari or Montague, but this is the real world here. Somebody in there needs help and we may be the only people who know. We can't just ignore it, we have to go and tell someone right now. Whatever happens, none of this will bring my dad back, so I guess I am just going to have to live with that. What I won't be able to live with, is if we ignore the fact that somebody may have needed our help and we walked away.'

'You're right,' said John. 'Enough is enough, come on, let's go and find someone.'

'Where?'

'The main entrance,' said John, 'I guess there should be a reception of sorts. They'll probably want to know how we got in here, and especially, why we were peering through their windows, but we'll worry about that later.'

They left the protection of the wall and stepped out onto the tarmac roadway, heading toward the entrance. A few moments later, they were at the ornate oaken door.

'Here goes,' said John and rang the bell. When there was no answer, he tried a few more times before turning to Becky.

'Odd,' he said.

'Try the handle,' said Becky, 'we may not have much time.'

John turned the handle and was surprised to find it unlocked. The door swung inward and they nervously stepped inside.

'Hello,' called John. 'Anyone here?'

They both looked around the ornate hall. A reception desk lay along the left wall, but it was completely unmanned.

'So much for security,' mumbled John as he walked in.

The house was strangely silent and they walked up to the reception desk before calling again.

'Hello,' called Becky. 'Is anyone here?' But again there was silence.

'I don't like this,' said John. 'Something isn't right.'

'John, look at this,' said Becky, and leaned over the desk to rub her hand along the lower inner counter.

'What is it?' asked John.

'It looks like blood,' said Becky examining the smear on her fingers, 'I think we had better call the police.'

'Hang on,' said John, 'we may be getting a bit carried away. The receptionist could have cut her finger and has gone to get a plaster?'

'Okay,' said Becky, 'but I still don't like this.'

'Come on,' said John, 'let's see if we can find someone else.'

They continued through the quiet hallway and to a closed door that was set in the wall.

'What's that smell?' asked Becky.

'I don't know, but it's disgusting,' said John.

'No, not that one, there's something else, I think it's smoke.'

John opened the door to pull it toward him and as he did, Becky screamed out in terror as the body of an old man who had been sitting against the other side, fell to the floor before him.

'Aaarrgh!' shouted John, as he involuntarily stepped back.

'John, is he okay?' shouted Becky.

After a few seconds to calm his nerves, John came to his senses and crouched down to see if the old man was okay.

'Hello,' he said, 'can you hear me? Are you okay?'

He placed his hand to the side of the man's neck to check for a pulse, but quickly brought his hand away again, covered in blood. He turned the man's head, and then dropped it suddenly, when he saw the side of the man's throat was ripped to shreds.

'He's been murdered,' he said.

In the distance, they could hear people shouting for help. John got up and turned to Becky.

'Becky, phone the emergency services. Tell them we need the police, fire brigade and ambulance.'

'Where are you going?' asked Becky.

'I have to go in there,' he said, 'see if I can help anyone.'

'But the murderer may be in there,' whispered Becky.

'It's a risk that I have to take;' said John, 'if there is a fire, there may be people trapped.'

'But John…'

'Becky, the people here are old and they will need all the help they can get. You call the emergency services and set off the fire alarm. We need to alert anyone else in this building that there is a fire. Anyone that comes running, tell them to get out onto the lawn. Help them as much as you can, but do not come back in here, do you understand?'

'But John…'

'Becky,' shouted John, 'we are wasting time. I'll be fine. If I think it's getting out of hand, I'll get out, now move!'

She watched him turn and trot down the corridor. Wisps of smoke were creeping along the ceiling and the screams of people calling for help were getting louder. She turned and scanned the walls of the foyer, looking for a fire alarm break glass. A red box next to the fire exit caught her eye and she ran over before hitting it with the palm of her hand. She looked up in expectation, but the foyer stayed silent. Again, she pressed the button behind the broken glass, but the alarm didn't sound.

'Damn,' she thought, 'Of all the times to be a fault.' She knew there had to be a control panel close and ran into the office behind the reception desk. The fire panel was instantly visible on the back wall and she reached up to turn the switch from automatic to manual, but was horrified to find it locked in the 'silence alarms' position. Becky was getting frantic with frustration and knew she had to do something, but first, she needed to call the emergency services. She put her hand in her pocket for her mobile and stopped dead in her tracks when she realised it was missing. She checked all her pockets over and over again, but when she finally realised she must have lost it when she fell in the flower borders, she ran to the reception desk to use the landline. She picked up the phone and her anger finally erupted when she realised the line was dead.

'For God's sake,' she screamed, 'doesn't anything work around here?'

Becky looked around in panic. She knew that if she couldn't raise the alarm, then many more people could be at risk. There was no way of contacting the emergency services at the moment, so her focus had to be on the people still in the building. John was right, it was pointless going into the smoke filled corridor after him, and she had to concentrate on the others. She ran to the door opposite the one where John had disappeared and walked inside. 'At least the lights work,' she mumbled to herself and walked along the corridor.

'Hello,' she called, 'anyone here?'

When again, there was no answer, she tried some of the side rooms. All were more or less the same, and set out in the manner of an upmarket hotel suite. All were immaculately clean and every bed looked fresh, as if it had just been made.

She tried a few more rooms before focussing on the door at the end of the corridor. 'Day Room,' said the sign, and Becky sped up, hoping that there would be someone in there to help. By the time she got to the door, she was almost running, and throwing the door open, she virtually fell into the room.

Immediately, she straightened up and stared at the scene before her. Her head turned slowly, taking in every morbid, soul destroying detail and when she finally remembered to breathe, it was for one reason only; to scream!

John coughed as he ran along the corridor. The smoke was getting worse and seemed to be coming from a side stairwell leading down from the main corridor, but the screams were coming from the rooms to his front. He tried the door, but found it locked.

'Hello,' he shouted, 'who's in there?'

'Oh, thank god,' said a man's voice, 'There's someone here. Can you open the door? There are twelve of us in here and some are very sick.'

'Why are you locked in?' asked John.

'Matron brought us,' said the man. 'She seemed very scared and said it was for our own safety.'

'Scared of what?' asked John.

'She didn't say,' said the man. 'Please, you have to get us out. The room is filling with smoke.'

'I can't,' shouted John, and glanced back over his shoulder. The smoke was now billowing into the corridor and he could see the reflection of flames on the ceiling. 'Where's the key?'

'Matron has it, ask her.'

'I don't know where she is,' said John. 'Is there a spare anywhere?'

'I don't think so…oh, hang on. I have just been told there's one in her office. It's back up the corridor, third door on the right.'

John looked up at the old door in front of him. It was solid oak and he knew there was no way he could barge it down.

'Okay,' he shouted, 'I'm going to get the key. I'll be as quick as I can, try to stay calm.'

'Please hurry,' said the man.

John turned and, crouching low, ran back along the corridor, coughing violently as he did. He passed the burning stairwell, found the office marked 'Matron' and breathing a sigh of relief to find it open, hurriedly stepped inside, before stopping dead in his tracks, confused at the scene before him.

The office was smoke free and lying on the floor in the centre, was the body of a portly woman in a dark blue nurse's uniform. Kneeling beside her, with her back toward him, was the figure of a young woman dressed in what seemed to be a dirty white nightdress.

'What's going on?' stuttered John. 'Who are you?'

The woman's head lifted sharply and she got slowly to her feet without turning.

'What human dares to approach Nephthys unannounced?' she snarled in Egyptian.

'What?' gasped John, momentarily thrown by the change of language. He thought quickly before speaking again, this time in Egyptian. 'Who are you?' he asked, 'and what is happening here?'

Nephthys turned around to face him and as she did, his face fell as he took in the full horror before him.

The girl's hair was mostly burnt away and the flesh was hanging from her scull in charred sheets. Her face was burnt and one eye socket

181

completely empty, though the other was filled with a red-black depth he had never seen before. The lips had been burned away, revealing two rows of jagged teeth, still dripping with the blood of the nurse, now dead at her feet.

'You speak the language of the kings;' hissed Nephthys, 'yet you are dressed as the demons that make flames from air.'

'I don't understand,' said John. 'Who are you?'

'I am Nephthys, daughter of Sekhmet, nightwalker of Kemet and I have returned to take my rightful place amongst you mortals: to farm you, to enslave you and to feed on your blood.'

'Oh, my god,' said John, 'that can't be true. It is impossible'.

'I tell the truth, mortal,' said Nephthys. 'Let not these wounds fool you, for I will soon recover, and when I do, I will wreak my revenge across your lands like a desert storm. No one will be safe. I will create sisters in my form and men will lose their souls to provide servitude to my name.'

'I don't believe you,' said John. 'I am a man of knowledge and I know that this can't be. You are not of Egypt. You are a sick woman who needs help. I can provide that help, but first we must save the old people from the fire.'

'Your words are as empty as those of Ramesses and I will fall for them, no longer. I will let my blood run through your veins, and you will become the undead, with no thoughts and no memories. Such is the fate of man. I am Nephthys, daughter of Sekhmet and defiler of Amenemhat's corpse. Behold me, human, for I am eternal.'

'Amenemhat,' stuttered John, thinking furiously. 'I was in his tomb, but a few weeks ago. What would you know about his defiled corpse?'

'It was I who ripped him from his perceived security.' said Nephthys, 'and I, who tore his body apart in retribution for his false tongue.'

John was astonished. Apart from Samari's people, no one except him and Becky knew anything about the damaged remains of Amenemhat back in the hidden tomb in Itjawi.

'But you can't be,' said John. 'There was only the one body there, the corpse in the sarcophagus, unless of course…' He stopped talking and stared at her.

'You can't be,' he said, 'it's impossible.'

'His mortuary became my resting place for more years than I have numbers, mortal. For time untold, I waited, unnourished in the dark. At first, we fed on the one human Ramesses left us, but when he was gone, we fed on each other until we could go on no further. Finally, Sekhmet gave me the ultimate sacrifice and for an age, I fed on her while she withered away, and even as I chewed on her bones, I knew she was conscious and with me always. Since that time, I have waited for this day and while I do not know your magic, mortal, I will prevail. All who stand before me will fall to my hunger or serve as undead.'

'I don't believe it,' said John.

'That is your species' problem, human, you never believe. I am Nephthys and I am immortal. Soon your blood will feed my veins, and then you will know the truth.'

'Wait,' said John, delving into his pocket, 'If what you say is indeed true, answer me one question, so I will indeed know the truth of your words.'

Nephthys paused.

'Play your game, Mortal, but it will not save you.'

'If you are who you say you are, then tell me what this is.' He pulled out the chain and bejewelled Ankh he had stolen from the tomb of Amenemhat.

Nephthys was visually shaken and her gaze swept back and forth, from the Ankh to John's face several times, before she spoke again.

'It is the symbol of Amenemhat,' she said, 'and it was buried with him within the labyrinths of Itjawi. Give it to me, human. I will wear it in my new realm, so his spirit will always know our kind prevailed and his memory is only kept alive by the whim of the nightwalkers. It will be a fitting curse on his memory.'

John still wasn't convinced, but as she lifted her hand to take the necklace, he saw the final proof. The index finger on her left hand was missing, and he knew it was the one that had been removed by Becky's father. Somehow, despite all his training and everything he had ever believed in, he finally accepted that this creature was the corpse from Amenemhat's tomb.

'Oh my god,' he said, 'then it's true, you are a vampire.'

'I do not know this word. I am a nightwalker and I will feed on the blood of mankind as will the many sisters that I will create. Give me the necklace, human, and I will make your death quick.'

'You want it,' he said, 'you get it.' He threw the necklace across the room.

Though she was momentarily distracted, Nephthys didn't move from where she was standing, but John took the opportunity to run out into the smoke filled corridor. The fire was raging throughout the corridor now and totally blocked off the route to the room with the trapped people.

'Shit,' he shouted, and stumbled through the smoke toward the foyer, hardly able to breathe for the swirling black smoke.

The dayroom in front of Becky was a scene of carnage. Everywhere she looked, bodies had been torn apart, and lying in the grotesque poses that violent death often brought. Blood dripped from the ceiling and countless rivulets had congealed on the walls where they had run freely only half an hour earlier. Two severed heads stared up at her from the floor, their terrifying eyes accusing her, as if to say, 'Where were you?'

The carnage was unbelievable and the fact that every victim had been very old, and thus unable to defend themselves, made the whole scenario even more horrific. But the more she stared at the bodies, the more she realised that most, if not all, had had their throats ripped out. Fighting the need to be sick, she clamped her hand over her mouth and with tears running down her face, ran back to the foyer, and straight into the arms of Adrian Montague.

'Becky,' he gasped, 'what are you doing here? Are you okay?'

'Mr Montague,' she sobbed, 'something awful is happening, the building is on fire and there are dozens of people dead.'

'Dead,' he gasped, 'where?'

'Up that corridor,' she sobbed, and Montague turned to the man at his side.

'Go and check,' he said.

The second man ran up the corridor and checked the room. Within seconds she had returned.

'She's right,' he said. 'It looks like a lion has been let loose in there. What happened?'

'I don't know,' sobbed Becky, 'but you need to call the police.'

Montague nodded to the man, who pulled out his mobile to make the call.

'John,' shouted Becky suddenly, 'where's John?'

As if on cue, John came stumbling out of the smoke filled corridor opposite, coughing and spluttering as he gasped for breath.

'John,' shouted Becky, and ran across to grab him.

For a minute, he gasped for air before standing upright, the oxygen at last reaching his scorched lungs.

'John, there's a room full of murdered people along the corridor. I don't know what's going on.'

'I do,' gasped John, 'Nephthys is here; the mummy from Itjawi. It's all true, Becky. The blood tests, your father's concerns, it all fits. They have managed to bring back the dead. She is in there as we speak and she feeds on blood. Amy was right, Becky, she is a vampire.'

Becky's face fell.

'John, you don't know what you're saying,' she said. 'There are no such things as vampires. I know something awful has happened, but you have to pull yourself together.'

'Becky, I saw her with my own eyes, I spoke to her for heaven's sake. She told me herself, she has spent the last three thousand years in that tomb and now she wants vengeance.'

'Look,' interrupted Montague, 'I don't know what all this is about, but you are obviously mistaken. The first thing we have to do is fight this fire; we may be able to stop it in its tracks.'

184

'Why aren't you listening to me?' screamed John. 'The place is an inferno back there. We have to go around the outside and break the windows.'

'Why?' asked Becky.

'There are people still trapped,' he said. 'This whole house is going up, but we may be able to break the windows and get them out.'

They started toward the door, but before he reached it, it was slammed shut by the second man who turned around with a gun.

'Nobody's going anywhere,' he said.

'What are you doing?' asked John. 'Get out of my way.'

'Mr Leatherman is right,' said Montague. 'There are things at risk here that are far more important than the lives of a couple of people who will be dead in a few years anyway.'

'You can't just leave them to burn,' screamed Becky.

'It's too late,' said Leatherman. 'People have seen too much. It's better this way. Let the building burn.

Becky stared at Leatherman as realisation sunk in.

'Oh my god,' she said, 'it was you.'

'I have no idea what you are talking about,' said Leatherman.

'The fire alarms. You disabled them and disconnected the phones. It was deliberate so nobody could call the emergency services.'

'It's better this way,' said Leatherman, 'at least the fire will hide her handiwork.'

'Her handiwork?' asked Becky. 'Who are you on about?'

'Nephthys,' said Leatherman.

'You mean it's true?' gasped Becky.

'I saw it with my own eyes,' said John. 'Now we need to get those people out and then deal with her before she escapes.'

'I don't care if she escapes,' said Leatherman, 'I'll have her back by morning.'

'And how do you intend to do that?' asked John.

'Easy,' he said, 'we have her chipped. Just like a dog; but this chip can be picked up by satellite. We had it done on the way over from Egypt. She is a valuable commodity, and we wouldn't want to lose her, would we?'

'You are sick,' said John, 'look; we still have time to help those people. Please, let me go out and help them,'

'Too late,' said Leatherman, and his gaze went from John's face to focus on something on the other side of the foyer.

John turned around and was horrified to see Nephthys emerge from the smoke to stand just behind Becky. Her ragged nightdress was smouldering and her whole body was covered in blood. Everything seemed to move in slow motion for John, and as the vampire's clawed hands reached out to grab Becky, he launched himself forward, using his momentum to drive the creature back through the door into the burning corridor.

185

Becky turned around and screamed as she saw him disappear into the flames, and though she struggled to release herself, Montague held her tight.

'It's too late,' he shouted. 'He's gone. Now, we have to get out of here.'

'*Nooo*,' screamed Becky, and as Leatherman opened the door, she fainted into Montague's arms.

Two minutes later, the two men were out on the lawn, watching the flames spread from floor to floor.

'What now?' asked Leatherman.

'Have you called the emergency services?' asked Montague.

'Not yet.'

'Give it another ten minutes,' he said, 'and put the call in. By the time the fire brigade gets here, it will be an inferno.'

'What about Nephthys?' asked Montague.

'Best we can hope for is that she escaped. If not, hopefully we can salvage some fragment of her flesh and see what the scientists can do.'

'What about her?' asked Leatherman, nodding toward the unconscious form of Becky on the ground.

'Don't worry about her; I'll take her with me. We have some special medication that will help her forget. In a couple of months, all this will be yesterday's news, and when that happens, we start again. Now, you wait here for the police. I've made a few calls and the guy coming is one of us, so there won't be too many awkward questions. But if anyone does ask, I wasn't here.'

'Got it,' said Leatherman. 'It's a shame though, we were so close.'

'This isn't the end, Leatherman,' said Montague. 'Nephthys can't have been the only one out there, and now that I know they exist, I will make it my life's work to find another. Immortality is possible, Leatherman, and within my grasp. All we need is vampire blood.'

186

Epilogue

Amy opened her eyes and stared at the wall in front of her. She was lying on her side in a large ornate bed, the curtains were drawn and the room was in darkness. Behind her, she could hear the slow and heavy breathing of Lucas, obviously still fast asleep. Slowly, the memories of the last few days came back to her. It had been everything that she could have hoped for. A wonderful, handsome man had finally taken her to his bed and introduced her to the wonderful world of lovemaking. Lucas had been a patient and attentive teacher, and in her wildest dreams, Amy had never imagined that it could be so wonderful. In fact, they had been so besotted with each other, that Lucas had made some calls and secured the cottage for a whole week. Amy had called work to book some leave, and sent a text to her mother, telling her not to worry, she was safe and would be home in a couple of days. After that, the time was all theirs.

They had dined in local pubs, walked the forest paths, and even risked a freezing skinny dip in one of the secluded pools in the forest. All in all, it had been amazing, and even when a heavy storm had been forecast, they both got quite excited about being stranded for a few days in their secluded cottage. They had stocked up on provisions and added a few extra bottles of red wine to the shopping list.

Lucas had piled up the log basket alongside the fire, and by the time the first thunder clap came, they were cuddled up in front of a roaring, comforting fire, enjoying a bottle of deep red wine.

That had been last night, and Amy felt slightly uncomfortable at the way the night had unfolded.

At first, it had been wonderful. They had made love in front of the fire and the quality wine had flowed freely as they discussed the world in general and how they were going to spend the rest of their lives together. But as the storm increased, the conversation turned to darker things. Their shared interest in the occult came to the fore and they found themselves comparing stories of everything paranormal, supernatural or simply mysterious. Eventually, the subject had turned to vampires, and Amy had been surprised to find Lucas's passion about the undead matched hers for intensity. They talked for hours, getting steadily drunker as the night progressed, and with the storm now in full swing outside, the atmosphere was positively gothic. Suddenly, Lucas had jumped up and staggered out of the room.

Amy recalled the conversation.

'Where are you going?' she asked.

'Back in a second,' he said, 'I just remembered something.'

Within a minute, he was back and resumed his place alongside Amy. He grabbed the bottle of wine and filled their two glasses to the brim. The look on his face was intense, and when he had finished, he stared at her for a few seconds without speaking.

187

'Lucas, what's the matter?' giggled Amy.

'I've got a fantastic idea,' he said.

'What idea?'

'This,' said Lucas, and pulled out the vial of blood.

'I'd forgotten about that,' she said. 'What about it?'

Lucas undid the lid and after a moment's hesitation, poured several drops into either glass.

'Lucas, what are you doing?' she gasped.

'Come on,' he whispered hoarsely, 'let's do it. Let's toast the undead in wine, the colour of blood, containing the life force of a vampire.'

'Lucas, that's disgusting,' laughed Amy, 'I'm not drinking that.'

'Why not? You won't taste it, it's hardly anything.'

'I don't care; it may contain germs or something.'

'Human blood is a natural substance,' said Lucas, 'and anything contained therein will be destroyed by your stomach acids before they can do any harm.'

'You may be right,' said Amy. 'But still. What if it is from a vampire? We may become one.'

'Oh come on, Amy,' said Lucas, 'all that guff about vampires turning people into vampires is rubbish. Vampirism may exist, but it is a condition of the mind, not the body. I've left enough in the vial for testing, but this is a special occasion.'

He picked up both glasses and handed one to her.

'How many people on this planet can say that they actually drank vampire blood?'

She took the glass nervously.

'Are you sure?' she asked.

'Positive,' he said and raised his glass. 'Where's that fearless Goth, I first met only last week?'

As the glasses clinked, her eyes bore deep into his and after a second's pause she put her glass to her lips.

'To vampires,' she said.

'To vampires,' he repeated, and they both drained their glasses in one draught.

Today was their last day and Amy stood up to open the curtains. She threw them open to find the storm had stopped and the sun was streaming through the branches of the trees. She turned away as the light hurt her eyes, but left the curtains open.

'Bloody hangover,' she murmured.

She wandered into the kitchen and opened the fridge. She was surprisingly thirsty and drank almost a litre of milk straight from the carton, a habit that usually disgusted her.

'Lucas,' she called, 'do you want breakfast?' When there was no answer, she shrugged her shoulders and pulled out the pack of bacon. 'Nah, sod that;' she said to herself, 'I'm having steak.' She put the bacon back, and placed the thick piece of rump steak in the cold frying pan, before returning to the bedroom.

'Are you waking up today?' she asked as she walked to the window, but only received a moan as an answer. The light still hurt her eyes, so she closed the curtains before sitting at the dressing table and stared in the mirror.

'Oh, my god,' she said, 'I look awful.' Her head moved closer to the mirror as she focussed on her own eyes.

'Bloodshot eyes,' she said. 'Never had that before; must be too much red wine. Right, wake up sleepyhead. I'll make us some breakfast and then we need to make the most of our last day before you go back to Germany.'

Lucas groaned and swung his legs out of the bed.

'Hah, lightweight,' said Amy. 'Drink like a man and get up like a boy.' She walked out into the kitchen, still talking as she went. 'So, what are we going to do today, then? Do you fancy going for a walk, or shall we go down to the village?'

'I feel awful,' murmured Lucas.

'Sorry,' called Amy, 'I didn't hear that.'

'Amy, I'm sick,' he said, 'I need a doctor. Something's wrong.'

Amy walked back into the room with a concerned look on her face, still chewing on something she had placed into her mouth.

'Are you okay?' she mumbled. 'You look terrible.'

Lucas stared at the girl with a look of disgust.

'Amy, what are you doing?' he asked.

'Me? Making breakfast, why?'

'What are you eating?'

'Oh, this,' she said, holding up her hand. 'I found it in the fridge. Best quality rump steak.'

'I know what it is, Amy, but it's not cooked. *It's raw!*'

Amy looked down at the slab of bloody steak in her hand, before spitting out the chewed meat from her mouth. She looked up at him, her face confused.

'I didn't realise,' she said. 'Oh, my god; why did I do that?'

'I don't know,' said Lucas, 'and I don't care. I need a doctor. I think my head is going to explode.' He stood up and tried to walk, but as he did, he collapsed and lay shaking on the floor.

'Lucas,' screamed Amy, and knelt to help him. His body was convulsing violently, and as he did, he retched up a thick red fluid over the bedroom carpet.

'Don't worry, Lucas,' cried Amy, 'I'll get some help.'

She grabbed her coat and ran to the front door, but as she opened it, a more overpowering need tore at her senses. For an age, she stood at the open door, struggling with the two emotions, but as the stronger need triumphed, she slowly closed the door and returned to the bedroom.

'I will get you help, Lucas,' she said. 'I promise I will. Just as soon as I finish this.'

Amy picked up the steak that she had thrown across the room and with only a few seconds pause tore into the raw meat, relishing the way the blood ran down her throat.

Deep inside her veins, strange shaped blood cells were already absorbing her own natural cells, and though she didn't know it, their cannibalistic tendencies would soon demand more and more blood.

When that happened, then and only then, would Amy begin to realise the true meaning of hunger.

The End

More books by K M Ashman

The India Sommers Mysteries
The Dead Virgins
The Treasures of Suleiman
The Mummies of the Reich
The Tomb Builders

The Roman Chronicles
The Fall of Britannia
The Rise of Caratacus
The Wrath of Boudicca

The Medieval Sagas
Blood of the Cross
In Shadows of Kings
Sword of Liberty
Ring of Steel

The Blood of Kings
A Land Divided
A Wounded Realm

Novels
Savage Eden
The Last Citadel
Vampire

Audio Books
Blood of the Cross
The Last Citadel
A Land Divided
A Wounded Realm

WWW.KMAshman.com

Printed in Great Britain
by Amazon

39680759R00106